SILVER MOON

GREAT NOVELS
OF
EROTIC DOMINATION
AND SUBMISSION

NEW TITLES EVERY MONTH

www.silvermoonbooks.co.uk

TO FIND OUT MORE ABOUT OUR READERS' CLUB WRITE
TO;
SILVER MOON READER SERVICES;
Suite 7, Mayden House,
Long Bennington Business Park,
Newark NG23 5DJ
Tel; 01400 283488

YOU WILL RECEIVE A FREE MAGAZINE OF EXTRACTS
FROM OUR EXTENSIVE RANGE OF EROTIC FICTION
ABSOLUTELY FREE. YOU WILL ALSO HAVE THE CHANCE
TO PURCHASE BOOKS WHICH ARE EXCLUSIVE TO OUR
READERS' CLUB
***
NEW AUTHORS ARE WELCOME
Please send submissions to;
The Editor; Silver Moon books
Suite 7, Long Bennington Business Park
Newark NG23 5DJ

Tel: 01400 283 488

All characters and events depicted are entirely fictitious; any resemblance to anyone living or dead is entirely coincidental

Slaves Of The Bloodline

by

Falconer Bridges

PROLOGUE

Strung up in the gloom of the dank cellars beneath his country mansion, a striped, mercilessly punished Julian was suffering endless taunts from Mistress Madonna. Although he had never fucked her, that was most definitely not allowed, she was nevertheless scathing in her derision of his penile inadequacy in comparison to her favoured cock-wielder and his hated rival; The Colonel.

Unfortunately for Julian, The Colonel fucked like he had invented fucking and Mistress Madonna often invited him down into the cellars to treat her to an animated and noisy shagging in front of her bound, chained, miserable and sexually unfulfilled slave. Although he sprouted an almost permanent straining erection, especially in Mistress Madonna's presence, Julian had not only never fucked her but he had never actually had his priapic weapon up any woman's vagina.

He was a virgin.

In contrast The Colonel had fucked more women than he could count, as he was fond of telling Julian. Mistress Madonna did not mind one little bit, so long as he kept on shagging her, in fact he was as useful an implement in Julian's humiliation as any cane or whip. Torture does not need to be purely physical, the mental agonies that Julian endured watching the old codger mashing his mistress' twat were almost too great to bear. Mistress Madonna knew that his only consolation was his firm belief that The Colonel was just a silly old sod blessed with a big prick.

However The Colonel was not such a witless old codger as Julian would have liked to believe. He had not only the cock of a god and a well-practised expertise in the sexual arts that drove Mistress Madonna to the brink of insanity, but he also possessed other more esoteric qualities that even she did not suspect. And so it had come as quite a surprise when one day he had told her that although he was officially retired from the Armed Forces, he was still called upon every now and then by the United Nations to help investigate threats to the security of Europe, and in particular, England. In that connection he had been ordered out to the Middle East to join an international team probing a suspected terrorist plot, he was leaving immediately and had no idea when he would be back.

He had been away for several weeks now and another of his surprises was about to land on Julian's doorstep. An authoritative set of knuckles beat upon the heavy front door of the imposing country house. Even down in the cellar it was loud enough for Mistress Madonna to pick up, and as Julian dismissed all the servants from the house while she was treating him to a session of her very special disciplinary talents, it was up to her to take over the duties of the butler. So slicing Julian with one more cutting lash of her deftly administered buggy whip, with the stiletto heels of her outrageously skyscraper-heeled and buckled ankle boots clacking on its steps she climbed the cobweb-bedecked staircase leading up to the entrance hall.

Naked apart from a black ruched suspender belt, intricately embroidered lace-top stockings and the boots, she calmly opened the door. A uniformed army officer stood before her. A quickly flustered, unbelieving Captain who could not decide whether to feast his eyes on her amazing breasts with their staggeringly protuberant nipples or her inviting, succulent heavily-forested sex. Dumfounded, he said nothing, only thrusting into her hand an urgent military communication addressed to her, with the legend 'Top Secret' emblazoned across it. As he handed it over, whatever his rehearsed speech was going to say remained unsaid as his eyes continued to soak in her unexpected, cock-rousing appearance. Flushing with both embarrassment and lust, he turned on his heels and almost running, rushed back to his waiting staff car.

Mistress Madonna closed the front door and wandered into the drawing room, turning the letter over and over in her hands before finally opening it. It was from The Colonel and there was wonder in her eyes as she read it. When she had finished, she clattered back down into the gloom of the cellar. Her legs widely spread, her fabulous sex on clear display, she held the note up to Julian.

"Alright cretin, listen to this. The Colonel's investigation is finished and he's gone to the Continent with a French government official he's been working with. His name's Thierry and he and The Colonel have known each other casually for several years but during the past few weeks, they've got on famously and become firm friends. This Thierry is going to take The Colonel on a sea-fishing trip and they're staying with an acquaintance of his, a Baroness no less. He says she lives in a bit of an eerie place, a part derelict medieval castle buried in a pine forest in Brittany. Apparently it's really atmospheric and there are standing stones and prehistoric monuments everywhere, and what's more Thierry has told the Baroness about me and she's invited me over to join them."

Julian sulked wretchedly, misery written all over his face. His mistress was going to fuck off and fart about with The Colonel and some rotten Frenchman. The Colonel would have his cock up her day and night; he'd fuck the arse off her and if he asked her to, she'd probably let the Froggie swine fuck her as well.

But the situation was not quite as bad as he had dreaded.

"I can't think why, but he says that if I want to, I can take you as well!"

ONE
THE HUNTING LODGE

The Rapping On The door of the lodge was loud and insistent.

Mistress Madonna snorted in annoyance and stayed her actions for the moment, her right arm held motionless where it was, raised high above her head with her fingers wrapped tightly around the haft of a wickedly-plaited flexible riding crop. The displeasure she was feeling at the unceremonious interruption to the delivery of a well-deserved beating to her worthless, witless slave was written plainly on her face. Suddenly the commotion stopped and tipping her head to one side she listened intently for a few moments. Outside there was now nothing but silence and deciding that whoever it was had gone away she whipped the crop down with all her considerable strength.

Although Julian had been ordered to act like a real man and to steel himself against the pain and remain silent throughout his disciplining, nonetheless a deafening tortured shriek rent the air as the crop ripped into his naked, exposed buttocks. And that stroke was only the latest of many. Other countless scalding strokes had already fallen, but struggling to follow his mistress' orders he had utilised all his inner strength and striven to steel himself against their biting impact. But whatever inner strength he possessed it had not proved to be enough. From the beginning the agony had been unbearable, but this was fiery and sickening, worse than anything she had inflicted before.

"That should teach you to . . ."

What it should have taught him to do was never made plain as her words were interrupted by a renewed assault on the door.

"Ouvrez la porte. Maintenant!"

The voice was loud, female and adamant.

The reply was equally forceful.

"Allez faire foutre, whoever you are."

The response did not surprise Julian one little bit. Not withstanding the franglais mixture of French and English of her reply, his mistress was not going to open the door to a person unknown and telling the intruder to 'get stuffed' was nothing more than he would have expected. She was so strong and dominant that he could not have imagined her responding in any other fashion. The intruder however was not going anywhere.

"Ouvrez. Immediatement!"

Mistress Madonna was in no mood to open the door, right at that moment or later. And the worst mistake that anyone could make when dealing with her was to order her to do something. The door remained closed; she was not frightened of anyone and neither was she to be intimidated by unidentified voices in the night.

"Who the hell are you anyway?"

The answer was not really that unexpected. And this time it came in clear English.

"Police. Open up."

The door handle was tried and rattled impatiently.

Sighing audibly, Mistress Madonna instructed Julian to remain still and quiet before unlocking the door and inching it open just enough to enable her to peer around its edge at her unwelcome visitors. Unceremoniously she was bustled aside as two agents de police pushed their way into the room. One was male, heavily built and crop-haired; the other was female and even in her uniform, of striking impact. She was tall, with a well-honed athletic body and looks to match but her lack of make up and short dark hair added a touch of the sapphic to her appearance. Exuding strength of character and authority, the crowd-control baton she was swinging in one hand did nothing to diminish that image.

Two pairs of police eyes immediately took in both Mistress Madonna's fiendishly erotic and intimidatingly vampiric appearance and the hapless position of the slave, the woman's lighting up in instant recognition of the circumstances. Her original tense stance melted into easy relaxation and taking charge of the situation she directed the male officer to close the door.

"Things here are not as we thought. You just stand by the door while I sort things out."

Hesitant but unquestioning, he did as he was bidden, standing with his hands clasped behind his back and watching intently.

It was clear that Mistress Madonna held an instant fascination for the policewoman, the tongue that ran over her lips and the eyes that roamed over every inch of the magnificently statuesque, dark-eyed and sex-laden woman who stood before her betraying her inner feelings. Momentarily she seemed to lose control of her senses as her arm reached out as if she were about to fondle Mistress Madonna's jutting breasts but suddenly she checked herself and wrenching her eyes away turned her attention to the slave.

He was standing in the middle of the main room, bent over with his arms spread wide and pulled outwards towards the sides of the room by iron chains attached to Gothic-looking iron wristcuffs. Chains that were anchored to large iron hooks that had been not too expertly driven into its walls about three feet from the floor. Chains that were so taut that his arms and shoulders plainly showed every painful, strainingly-agonised stretched muscle. His legs were forced several feet apart by a metal spreader bar attached to anklecuffs of similar design and faded mottled matt-black colour to the cuffs clamped to his wrists. A broad spiked iron collar was fastened around his neck, again with an iron chain clipped into the ring attached to it, which was stretching his neck upwards towards the metal bracket to which it was fixed. A bracket that normally housed a heavy pike with a wickedly sharp 'fleur-de-lis' spearhead. The pike lay on the floor, discarded so that a better use could be made of its usual home.

And yet, despite his desperate circumstances he was sporting an unbelievably rigid, straining erection.

And that erection itself was subject to its own restraint. A circular metal clamp had been screwed tight just below his bell end, causing it to swell in a grotesquely obscene fashion. Fastened to the clamp was a much thinner iron chain that cruelly divided his bollocks as it passed between his legs and with difficulty dragged his cock downwards towards its anchoring point, another large hook that had been hammered into a crack between the stone paving of the floor between his widespread feet.

After silently digesting the scene, the policewoman crossed over to him and pointed the baton at his more than usefully-sized penis. She snorted in an exaggeratedly derisory fashion.

"That pathetic thing is what you Englishmen call a cock, is it? Here in France you'd be laughed out of any self-respecting woman's bedroom. Even a whore wouldn't do business with that."

After studying him closely for several seconds she suddenly whacked him smartly with the baton over the crimson weals striping his pale rump, following it up with a swingeing wide-armed strike to the chain anchoring his cock to the floor.

"Yeeoow!"

The strangled scream that tested his vocal cords to the limit was not in the least quieter than those that had summoned her in the first place.

"Shut up you wretch, how can you make so much fuss over a little discomfort such as you are suffering."

She paused to cast a glance at the policeman guarding the door, before continuing. "Men are all the same, wimps and whingeing poofs. A woman would never allow herself to crumble into such an outburst of gutless caterwauling just because she had been dealt a little pain. Women can take pain, soak it up and laugh at it . . . And maybe perhaps, love it. But men, they are nothing but worms, insects to be crushed under the feet of women."

She directed Mistress Madonna's attention to the policeman.

"Look at him. He is my superior officer but sexually he is a wimp. He will ignore orders, debase himself and do anything I ask just to be within sniffing distance of my vagina. Yet I have never allowed his nose, never mind his cock anywhere near it."

And then turning back to Mistress Madonna, she added, "And that is the same with your slave, is that not so Madame?"

Astounded by the turn of events and also by the policewoman's perception and perfect use of colloquial English, for once Mistress Madonna was at a loss for words, taking several seconds before she stuttered out an answer.

"Yes . . . yes, you couldn't be more right."

Even then, unsure of the policewoman's motives, her reply was hesitant, almost questioning. The policewoman seemed eager to enlighten her.

"Madame, I have some experience myself in these matters and this useless specimen seems more vocal than most, although I have to say that with a little forethought you could have avoided my having to call on you. The noise that he was making was so loud that it could be heard in the castle itself and the Baroness and her guests were convinced that someone was being attacked or murdered. They were mistaken, that much is obvious, but if you intend to continue take my advice and gag him."

Gag him? The slave's instant reaction showed that he did not like the idea of that at all.

"No Mistress. Please don't do that. I'll be good, I won't scream again I promise."

Promises from a turd such as he were worthless. At least that was the policewoman's opinion.

"I didn't gag him because I wanted to hear him scream, he's such a wimp and he squeals just like a stuck pig. I enjoy the shrieking, it tells me that I'm doing a good job on him."

The policewoman agreed that Mistress Madonna's explanation had great credibility but added that in the circumstances it was not really wise to allow his cries to echo resoundingly around the otherwise silent countryside.

"Here. If you have nothing suitable, use this."

And what she handed over to Mistress Madonna was very suitable indeed. From the depths of a jacket pocket she pulled out an instantly recognisable object - a leather strapped ball-gag. A question formed itself on Mistress Madonna's lips but quick on the uptake, the policewoman provided an answer before the words could be delivered.

"Ah yes, you're wondering about the gag. Let's just say that it comes in very handy sometimes if a suspect gets awkward and decides not to be co-operative."

To emphasise her point, she smacked the baton into the palm of her hand.

"Keeps them quiet while I work on them, if you get my meaning."

Mistress Madonna did get her meaning. And so did Julian. He also got the ball-gag. But he did not want it, clamping his jaws tight shut to prevent her getting it between his lips until the policewoman came to her assistance, digging her thumb and forefinger deeply and painfully into his cheeks until he was forced to open his mouth. She pinched even harder and as his jaws opened wide, Mistress Madonna pushed the hard rubber ball into his mouth and held it there with her flattened palm as the policewoman buckled the leather straps tightly at the back of his head.

"Voila. Now he will make no more trouble."

The ball was hard despite being formed of rubber and wedged between his teeth it stretched Julian's jaws to the limit and laying heavily on his tongue its bitter taste assailed his cultured taste buds. Almost ripping it from his scalp, the policewoman grabbed a handful of his thick professionally-styled hair and pulled his head towards her as much as the restricting chain would allow so that she could look him straight in the eyes. Her own eyes took on a menacing look, dark and piercing, they became suddenly hard and cruel and a shiver of dread shook his limbs as he withered under her stare.

Mistress Madonna punished him when he'd been naughty it was true and there was no denying that she often hurt him quite badly, but never more than he really enjoyed. And she did it for his own good, to keep him from straying too far from the straight and narrow and he understood that and made the best of the situation. This woman however was frightening, the sort who would no doubt delight in inflicting pain merely for the sake of it. Bad pain. His throat dried and his heart thumped into his ribs as a tide of panic surged over him. Was it possible that Mistress Madonna might let her loose on him? Surely not. But what if she did? He closed his eyes, shuddering at the prospect of such an action and so his obvious relief when she disentangled her fingers from his hair was overwhelming.

"Remember worm, no more noise."

He could no more make a sound at that moment than he could wank his tethered cock. And she obviously knew it, her words were merely intended to reinforce the sense of dread that she had instilled in him. And they worked. He was terrified, his terror increasing by the second as she held him in a prolonged contemptuous stare. Pausing for a moment she took a closer look at the Gothic iron hooks and chains that held him in bondage, paying particular attention to what appeared to be two blood-tinged puncture marks on his neck, partly hidden by the spiked collar. Looking up at Mistress Madonna with knowing eyes, she then inspected the marks once more before bidding her a 'bon soirée' and casting one last covetous glance over her magnificent black leather and satin-clad body, she added a somewhat mysterious final comment.

"It's a greater privilege than you realise to have been invited to stay here. You can see for yourself that the site itself is very ancient, there's a lot of mystery surrounding it, and the castle itself dates back to before the dark ages. The Baroness has gathered some very interesting people here, and judging by what I see before me I'm sure you'd fit in with them very well indeed. So if you intend staying it would be wise to try not to upset her, she does not like attention being drawn to this place.

It would be a very great pity if you had to be asked to leave like some other unwelcome guests."

"And who might they be?"

"Oh, the local fishermen had their quotas cut recently, and because now they can't put to sea every day they're finding other ways to make a living and making quite a nuisance of themselves in the process. The Baroness has been having trouble with them digging up the burial mounds trying to find prehistoric treasure, poaching the wildlife and things like that. We cleared them off but we come up here a couple of times a day to keep an eye on things. If you have any trouble with them, just let us know and we'll deal with it."

Then returning to deliver a couple of final gut-wrenching baton strikes to the back of Julian's legs, in a steely voice she addressed him once more.

"Adieu little man and remember, no more noise. I don't want to have to bother your charming mistress again, just because *you* can't keep your mouth shut."

Although her business with Mistress Madonna was finished, she seemed strangely reluctant to leave, her eyes once again dreamily eating up Mistress Madonna's fabulously enticing body. A discreet cough from the policeman broke her reverie and pulling herself together, she made for the door. Mistress Madonna followed her uncertainly, standing watching as the policeman, in a servile fashion opened it for her and she stepped out to be rapidly enveloped by the inky blackness of the night.

Very thoughtfully and deliberately Mistress Madonna swung the door shut and returned to her business with Julian. It was all his fault of course. That much she made clear before resuming his punishment with renewed vigour

"See what you've done now. Got us in trouble with the local police. For that, you're going to suffer."

Thwack!

The crop struck with vicious intent again and again, a strangled gasp forcing its way past the stifling ball-gag as the lashes landed. In between each blow Mistress Madonna posed a question.

"And apart from anything else, I want you to tell me what it was you did that forced me to have to punish you in the first place?"

How could he answer?

He tried to but all he could manage was a muffled snuffle.

Crack!

"Could it be because of the filthy way you behaved earlier on?"

Of course it could.

Smack!

"And after the last time, didn't we agree that you wouldn't try and do naughty things like that again?"

It was true, they had agreed on that point. With very bad grace on his part it must be added.

"So why did you?"

Straining in his bonds he attempted a shrug to try to imply that he did not know the answer to the question. It did him no good, this time several wicked, cutting strikes fell in succession before she rephrased the question in a fashion that even a cretin like him could not misinterpret.

"Why did you put your animal's paws on my thigh?"

An incoherent mumble was all he was able to muster.

"And don't think that I didn't see that disgusting bulge in your trousers. You had a hard-on, didn't you?"

He had.

"And you know very well that I didn't give you permission to get yourself all worked up, don't you?"

He did.

"So why did you get that filthy erection when you knew that it wasn't allowed? Especially as anyone passing by could have looked into the car and seen you behaving like the perverted sex-crazed beast that you are."

What else could he have done? Earlier in the small village bar she had deliberately and outrageously flaunted her body before him in a manner that could not have failed

to set his pulses racing and his cock twitching. Not to mention the local Gallic sardine fishermen, who to a man were puffing the hell out of Gitanes or choking on their minute glasses of vin rosé, their eyes glued to her firm, bullet-nippled and partly-exposed breasts and her fabulously enticing, undulating backside. With their cocks already iron-hard and leaking sperm, after her display there would be many a surprised and sorely-fucked fanny when the lusting men got back home to their wives and girlfriends.

Following that, sat in the passenger seat of the Ferrari, she had pulled her black leather micro-skirt right up over her thighs, exposing not only a succulent expanse of creamy flesh between them and her stocking tops but also a glorious and luxuriantly thatched mons. And as if that were not enough she had then stretched herself out and with her eyes closed was murmuring in aroused delight as one hand slipped between her open thighs to caress her sex, while at the same time her other hand roamed sensuously over the breasts that were straining her clinging, deeply scoop-necked satin top to the limit. Then the fingers that had slipped up and down the moist lubricated slit between her musky, open sex lips were passed under his nostrils, the heady aroma of her vagina flooding his senses, turning his brain into jelly and his cock into steel. Actions all purposely designed to drive him into a delirium of lust.

And she had succeeded. Even though he knew full well that she was toying with him, stoking up passions that had no possibility of being sated. But he did not dare to make matters worse by being disobedient and telling her that she was a teasing, heartless bitch. So he made no answer to her question. Not that he could speak in any case, the ball-gag saw to that.

"Right, don't answer. Why should I care? If you don't want to speak to me that's your affair."

The sense of injustice overwhelmed him. Of course he wanted to answer her. To tell her once again that his life was lived only for her. That she could have anything money could buy. That she was the most wonderful woman in the entire universe.

Tears of frustration trickled from his eyes; his body ached, his mind was in turmoil and his cock hurt. He was in no doubt that she knew that, after all her plan was always to humiliate him, to stimulate him into sexual arousal and then deny him fulfilment. And on his part he was always more than happy to let her do so. That was one of the main reasons that he loved her so much; she understood a contradiction in his personality that no woman he had encountered before had. And that was that to be really happy he had to be wretchedly miserable, preferably suffering the tortures of Hell.

Now held immobile in his chains; desperately, pleadingly, his eyes sought hers, trying to make her understand what had happened. He'd got a fucking great hard-on in the car because she had made him do it. It was not his fault. But without words no communication was possible.

She tapped the crop impatiently against her creamy, suspender-adorned thigh.

"You're only making things worse for yourself. You either tell me why you tried to touch me up or I kick your arse from here to England and back. Make up your mind, it's up to you."

But it was not up to him. He was helpless. Mute. She held all the strings, he was just a puppet, dancing to her every whim. And her whim at that moment seemed to be to make him suffer interminably. And suffering he was, but despite the murderous lashes that continued to stripe every inch of his battered body, he could still only think of one thing - sinking his throbbing cock into his mistress' wondrous, hot juicy steaming vagina.

That was what had got him into trouble in the first place. He *was* man of sorts after all and subject to the same desires that beset all men. He couldn't help it if his balls were full to bursting with sperm through lack of sexual relief. That was her fault in any case, she kept him frustrated on purpose and he was fed up with being a right-hand lover. He had told her again and again before they left England that he wanted a fuck. He had wanted one then and he wanted one now. He always wanted a fuck. Nothing that she could do to him would alter that.

But she could play with his mind and wreak havoc with his emotions.

"Your associates, your business friends or whoever it is who you drink with at your stuffy Establishment clubs; they all tell you about how their wives, girl friends, high-priced hookers or whatever let them shag themselves silly, don't they? They all get their cocks sucked and their bollocks licked and perhaps they get to shag an arse now and then.

"And you're always sulking because Mistress Madonna doesn't allow that sort of thing; but you and I know that you get something better. You're forever begging me to let you fuck me, but if I did, what would you have to look forward to? Nothing! What you get is something that satisfies you far more than having your infantile cock waving about in the channel tunnel, because believe me I know that most of those bloody high society tarts have *fucked* their way into those men's bank accounts. They've got cunts as wide as the Grand Canyon, so what good would they do a tiny-pricked prat like you?

"And not only that, how many of those toffee-nosed, snooty upper class women would even dream of giving their men the special attention that I do you? If you only stopped to think for a minute, you'd realise that you are the luckiest little boy on the planet. You public schoolboys all want the same thing. Your housemasters caned your naked arses because they enjoyed it, and even though it was agony you enjoyed it as well. And you wanted more, didn't you? because every time you were beaten you got a hard on. And then you went to your study and had a good wank.

"That's why you still like to be caned. And so do most of your other cissy boy ex schoolmates. Only they don't get it because their hoity toity tarts are above that sort of thing. Or so they say. But the truth is that they're only interested in their men's money and not their well-being. How many of them care enough about their men to discipline them, to thrash them into submission and beat them into orgasm? Can you name one who would give any of them the treatment that I'm giving you right here and now?"

There was no answer to that question, but Mistress Madonna's remarks were made even more hurtful for Julian because he knew that in her private life she was the equal, and more, of any of those supposedly socially superior women. Educated, sophisticated and cultured, the dirty talk was only for his benefit. He loved it. Cunt, Fuck and all the other filthy words that rolled from her tongue never failed to send a tingle up his spine and served to greatly inflame his passions. There were two other words however that also never failed to upset him greatly. And those words were: The Colonel!

The mere mention of The Colonel was guaranteed to drive Julian to distraction and so it was inevitable that Mistress Madonna would turn her comments in his direction. With the crop dangling from one wrist and the fingers of her free hand stroking and delving between her sex lips, her skirt again hitched high, she stood wide-legged in front of Julian and with her lecture over, she altered tack and began taunting him mercilessly. Everything about him was wrong, his every action was incompetent, his cock belonged on a little boy and wasn't big enough to satisfy a rat. The Colonel on the other hand was magnificent, perfect in every way and his cock was the biggest and best she'd ever seen. The insults went on and on, driving Julian into an almost insane bout of agitation, his limbs helplessly fighting the restrictive chains and muffled grunts pouring from his gagged mouth.

Suddenly, interrupting her diatribe, a more restrained hand than earlier rapped on the cottage door.

"Hello. Anyone in there?"

The voice was instantly recognisable, a pleased smile lighting up Mistress Madonna's features as she crossed to open the door.

"Ah Colonel. I've been expecting you."

"Yes. Sorry it's so late m'dear, got held up at the castle, don't you know. Didn't think I was ever going to get away."

"Well you're here now and that's enough for me."

Entering the room, The Colonel eyed Julian's chained, bruised and striped body.

"The blighter been up to his old tricks, has he?"

"Yes Colonel, he's been a very naughty boy and Mistress Madonna's had to teach him a lesson."

"Don't know how you put up with the bounder m'self. In the old days I'd have had him neutered and shipped off to be stabled with the eunuchs in some sultan or other's harem."

Walking around Julian, he leant his foot on the taut chain anchoring his cock to the floor and then pressed heavily downwards several times. Agonising bolts of intense, sickening pain radiated from Julian's cock to his every nerve end and despite the gag his squeals of agony ricocheted around walls of the hunting lodge as his already tortured bell-end was almost wrenched away from the shaft of his penis.

"Nothing more than you deserve, you cad. If it were left to me I'd thrash you to within an inch of your life."

"Don't be too hard on him Colonel. You know what silly little boys like him are like, they can't help themselves. They've got cocks like yo-yos, up and down at the slightest hint of female flesh. And I have given him a pretty thorough going over."

Although Julian's haunches and back were glowing crimson and the blood-tinged stripes that covered his body showed only too clearly the extent of the savage treatment that had been dealt out to him by Mistress Madonna, The Colonel bent closer and inspected him thoroughly, before straightening up once more.

"Um. If you say so, old thing. Personally, I'd give him another hundred."

"Oh, I think he's had enough of the crop for the moment," Mistress Madonna said, and then pointedly staring straight at The Colonel's crotch, she added, "but with a little help from you, I can make him suffer a great deal more than if I just carry on beating him."

The instantaneous bulge that erupted inside his trousers signalled that The Colonel was in full agreement and Mistress Madonna wasted no time in sliding her palm over it before tugging down his zip and slipping her hand inside.

"Oh, Julian! The Colonel's cock feels wonderful. It's all hot and hard and throbbing. Mistress Madonna wants it up her cunt right now. This instant!"

Sighing with expectancy at the pleasure that lay ahead, she freed The Colonel's rampant ramrod and slid her clenched hand up and down its length.

"Oh God Colonel, you're bigger than ever, your cock's so fat I can't get my hand round it."

But she could get her lips round it.

And she did.

Just inches away from Julian's face, Mistress Madonna bent herself over, legs wide apart and her sex fully available to both his eyes and his nose. With the musky sex-laden aroma of her arousal flooding his nostrils, unbelievably Julian's erection hardened even further. The pain in his cock was incredible but the pain in his heart was insufferable. And it got worse.

Mistress Madonna's lips slid backwards and forwards over The Colonel's bulbous glans, her tongue dipping into the eye of his penis and lapping the rigid shaft like a hungry cat. Then slipping several inches of its throbbing length fully into her mouth, one on top of the other she clamped both hands around its base and began wanking him upwards to meet every downward plunge of her mouth. The Colonel sucked air between his clenched teeth, his face screwing up in agonising ecstasy as more and more of his cock disappeared into her warm, saliva-filled mouth as she drove him towards ejaculation. Up and down, faster and faster, her head bobbed as her mouth plunged over his steely erection, his bell-end now battering her throat. Suddenly The Colonel grabbed her head and held it rigid, bucking his hips as he fucked her mouth and exploded in a shuddering orgasm, spurting torrents of hot salty sperm over her welcoming taste buds and down her swallowing, gulping throat.

And he was not alone in emptying his bollocks. Although the pain was beyond belief, with his eyes glued to Mistress Madonna's widening sex lips, a crazily thrashing, demented Julian had tugged his chained and steel-clamped cock until it too had spurted gushers of spunk. But his ejaculate had not shot into the appreciative mouth of his mistress, spattering instead over the stone flags of the floor. He was in for it now, that was for sure, Mistress Madonna always punished him severely when he did disgusting things like that. But he did not care. She had sucked The Colonel off and swallowed his spunk right in front of his eyes. He hated her. And The Colonel. She could do to him what she liked. And if she ordered him to lick it up, he would not!

But amazingly, she did nothing.

Not to Julian anyway. She was in a frenzy of need herself. The need for a good stiff cock to be stuck nine inches into her red-hot twat. Hungrily swallowing the last traces of The Colonel's seed, she straightened up, turned around and once more bent herself over, this time with her fabulous backside pointed straight at The Colonel's still erect weapon.

"Colonel I've got to have you now. Don't bother with the preliminaries, I'm all juiced up at the thought of that wonderful dick stuck up me. So just do it. Fuck me."

Reaching between her legs with one hand, she grasped his penis and guided it to her dribbling vagina, wriggling herself backwards and skewering it deeper and deeper into her until she was plugged solid and totally impaled on its solid length.

"Now Colonel, fuck me! Fuck me like you've never fucked me before."

And that is exactly what he did. From behind, with her fingertips touching her toes, he battered against her buttocks, ramming into her with such energy that she rocked on her feet. Grunts, 'oohs' and finally full-blooded screams of satisfaction poured from her lips as she reached a body-racking climax.

Julian screamed too. In anger and frustration, although his screams were strangled, muffled animal-like whines and snuffles. And he screamed even louder when The Colonel suddenly pulled out of Mistress Madonna and finishing himself off with his hand, squirted fountains of sperm all over him. Julian's face, hair and body ran with The Colonel's spunk, driving him even further into the realms of dementia.

"Oh, well done Colonel. I can always count on you, can't I?"

Mistress Madonna's words of praise were gasped out, her breath still short and her breasts heaving in the aftermath of her shattering orgasm.

"Hmm . . Nice of you to say so m'dear."

The Colonel's understated reaction was absolutely true to his nature, calm and collected, he never got too excited over anything although for him to screw Mistress Madonna in front of Julian was always a rewarding experience. The sex was great, that went without saying, but Julian's insanely demented reaction was a sight to behold.

Mistress Madonna slowly pulled herself together in time to lay a restraining palm on The Colonel's wrist as he began to tuck his penis back into his trousers.

"We haven't finished yet, have we Colonel? I needed that quick shag, I was desperate but it doesn't have to be so fast and furious from now on; I want you to stay here and fuck me long and slow all night long."

The Colonel was hesitant, now quite unlike his normal self.

"Ah, there's a slight problem there m'dear. I've got to be getting along; things to do, letters to write, that sort of thing."

Mistress Madonna's eyebrows raised questioningly. This was not The Colonel she knew.

"Come on Colonel, this is Mistress Madonna you're talking to. You've never turned down the chance of a few hours fucking before. What's going on?"

"Can't pull the wool over your eyes, can I gel? The truth is that things up at the castle aren't quite what I expected, a bit queer if you know what I mean. But you'll love it, it's right up your street; in fact I think it's you that the invitation was really for. They won't miss me."

"All right Colonel I'll take your word for that. But that's no reason for you to leave me with a hot, juicy vagina that's crying out for your lovely cock and go out in the middle of the night."

A very uncomfortable silence followed.

"Come on Colonel. Out with it."

"Um . . er . . It's like this. Thierry's a member of this club and he's fixed it up for me to spend a few days there as his guest. He's waiting for me now and I'm dashed late already."

"And just what club is this, Colonel?"

"Er . . It's called Le Manoir. It's nothing special, it's just to get me away from the castle you understand."

Mistress Madonna did not understand.

In fact she had never been less understanding. She knew all about Le Manoir, in her line of business you had to. It was a very exclusive Gentleman's club, a sister establishment to The Lodge, itself an especially venerated institution back in England. Both clubs were dedicated to the pursuit of sexual pleasure, especially of the BDSM variety, their members being restricted to the rich and powerful; clubs that boasted as their stock, the prettiest girls in Europe.

So, as a sop to her anger, although she knew that it was far from the truth, she told herself that The Colonel was turning her down to go off and fuck some French tarts in a common whorehouse.

"All right then Colonel, if that's the way it is you'd better go. Right now."

Her voice was iced with controlled anger.

"I don't suppose I'll be seeing you again, will I?"

It was not a question at all. She said it in a way that implied that if The Colonel knew what was good for him, he would keep out of her way. She indicated the door.

"Close it after you."

Red-faced and sheepish, The Colonel hurried to the door. He paused and turned as if he were about to try and offer some further explanation, but the frosty look on her face obviously changed his mind. Shrugging his shoulders he left without another word. Mistress Madonna stared after him, her eyes flashing with fury.

Somebody was going to suffer for this.

And that someone was Julian. He was in for a long, hard night.

TWO
THE PIKE

Absolutely furious with The Colonel, Mistress Madonna vented her spleen on Julian, verbally and physically abusing him until very late in the night, finally leaving him still chained and convulsing in agony she retired to her room. But sleep proved an elusive quarry and so for a while, with her pillows fluffed up behind her, she sat up reading. Three books were lying on her dressing table; Bram Stoker's Dracula, Notre-Dame de Paris by Victor Hugo - the story of the hunchback Quasimodo, and a biography of the sixteenth century plunderer of virgins, the Hungarian Baroness Erzebet Bathori. She chose the biography and even though the gory, bizarre and blood-laden tale whetted her vivid imagination, she found it difficult to concentrate; her demanding vagina still crying out for The Colonel's uniquely satisfying cock. Eventually, driven to desperation, she decided that *any* cock would do to relieve her intense frustration.

But there was no cock, was there? Only Julian's, and that was unthinkable. So there was only one solution, she would have to find something else to sink into her sex. Something big and fat. And the only thing in the lodge that came anywhere near that description was the pike. The diameter of its shaft would plug her very comfortably, but the bloody thing was six feet long. But there was no alternative and so she would just have to find some way to make it suit her purpose.

Sliding out from beneath the covers, she stepped down naked from the raised four-poster and padded out of the bedroom and into Julian's presence. Immediately his eyes fell on her, his sniffling and moaning stopped, his eyes widened and his cock stiffened. Mistress Madonna could not help noticing it throbbing back into full erection.

"Stop that this instant. Haven't you ever seen a naked woman before?"

As the words slipped from her mouth she realised that he had very rarely, if ever, seen her absolutely naked. And as she knew that her body was flawless and enticingly proportioned it was only natural that her slave should react in that way. He loved to see her in basques and stockings and now he had shown that he was equally thrilled to see her in the raw. Cupping her breasts, rolling her nipples and stroking herself between her legs, she paraded provocatively before him. She smiled in satisfaction as her display prompted his cock to harden and lengthen even further and so caused the iron chain attached to the ring clamped around his glans to tighten. His face screwed up in agony as his cock strained upwards against the restricting chain. He was going to have one hell of a sore weapon when she finally took the clamp off.

But that would not be for a long time yet. He had a lot more suffering to endure before that was going to happen. In the meantime another question and answer session commenced.

"Mistress Madonna's come back in here because she wants something. Would you like to know what it is?"

When she had left him to go to bed she had not eased his misery in any way and so he was still chained in an agonisingly contorted position, it was not only his cock that was going to hurt when he was released, his back probably would not allow him to straighten up for hours. But more importantly he was still gagged and so he was unable to speak coherently. But that hardly mattered now because he had not been allowed to drink anything for many hours and his throat was so cracked and dry that he would not be able to utter any more than a hoarse croak.

Mistress Madonna knew that perfectly well and that only helped her to add to his torment.

"Still sulking are we? All right be like that, it makes no difference to me, I'm going to tell you anyway. Mistress Madonna's here because she wants a cock rammed up her. A big fat cock, plunging up and down her lovely, soaking vagina. Any cock would do, but there isn't one anywhere, is there?"

That had the desired effect. Julian went completely bananas; silently bananas because he could not make a sound. Mistress Madonna did not have to hear the words that he was trying to blurt out, she could imagine them with ease.

'I've got a big cock. A fucking great big fat cock. Let me do it. Let *me* fuck you.'

They would be something very close to that and if the truth be known, he did in fact have a very usefully big and fat penis that if it belonged to anyone else would have suited her purposes admirably. But it did not and so it was out of the question. If she allowed him to fuck her, that would be the end of everything. Her vagina was a 'no go' area, something that he could fantasise about but which in reality remained completely out of bounds to him. Besides it was the misery and anguish he felt at constantly being denied a shag that kept up his interest in her; it allowed him to wallow in the mire of his own self pity.

Ignoring him completely she continued her musings.

"If I can't get a cock, what *can* I do. At home I've got dildos. Big dildos. Just the right size, but they're not here, are they? But I've got to have something up me or I'll go crazy. What do think I could use?"

Her eyes slowly swept the room until they alighted on the pike.

"Ooh Julian, just look at that. That's fat alright, it's perfect. But it's too long. What can I do?"

It was a purely rhetorical question, she already knew exactly what she was going to do. Broad oak stanchions, several feet apart and running from floor to ceiling, were set into each of the walls. Equally broad beams ran from the tops of the pillars across the ceiling, joining those opposite each together. The timber was ancient, obviously part of the original structure of the building and was cracked with age.

Picking up the pike and holding it at shoulder height, with her hands wide apart grasping its shaft and pointing it downwards, Mistress Madonna measured her distance and ran full tilt at one of the stanchions. She struck lucky at her first attempt, the 'fleur-de-lis' spearhead driving deep into one of the cracks at just the right height and angle. Tugging on the shaft with all her strength she found it so firmly embedded that it proved impossible to pull out, exactly how she wanted it.

"Thank God for that crack," she murmured to herself; the timber was still so hard that without it she would not have been able to bury the spearhead so deeply into it. Projecting immovably upwards from low down on the stanchion at a shallow angle, at the end of its six foot length the pike was six inches or so higher than Mistress Madonna's crotch. Perfect.

Bending down she clasped both hands around it as if she were caressing a giant penis, slowly and appreciatively running her fingers upwards over the smooth, polished wood. Positioning herself behind it she closed in and measured it for height, finding that the end dug into her belly just above her pubic mound. Raising herself onto her toes, she widened her legs and stepped over it, lodging the end between her open labia and into the entrance to her vagina. It was fat. Really fat, more so than she had realised.

Although she was wet and ready, it was obvious that she could use a little more lubrication to aid its penetration of her sex. And that was when she hit upon a devilishly brilliant idea. Something that would help her to achieve carnal satisfaction and at the same time would drive Julian berserk. Easing off the stave, she flattened her feet to the floor and walked over to stand before Julian once again.

His eyes were wild and excited, sweat dripped from his brow and he was snorting air. And his cock was leaking. Mistress Madonna's antics had stoked his lust into an inferno. Her voice was soft and seductive, not the usual schoolmistress' tone she adopted with him.

"Julian."

She half whispered his name in a husky, prick-rousing voice.

"Julian, you've always wanted your spunk up Mistress Madonna's hole, I know you have. Well, I've changed my mind, I've decided that that's what I want as well. Lots and lots of it. But I've got to get you in the mood first."

Julian's face reddened, his prick jerked and it did not take much imagination for her to interpret his muffled gabblings as affirmations that he was already in the mood, that he did not need any help and that he could fuck her rotten right then if she would only let him loose. Ignoring him, she carried on with her plan. Bending over backwards into a 'crab', with her palms and the soles of her feet flat on the floor she presented him with a heart-stopping view of her glorious sex. The wavy lips were widening and the entrance to her vagina was clearly visible.

"Look Julian, can you see? Can you see my lovely hairy beaver? It's just waiting for your sperm. See, there's love juice running down my thighs. I can feel it, so I know that you can see it. It's all sticky and slidy and it'll be even slippier when your spunk's all mixed up with it."

Shuffling closer to his struggling, bound form she supported herself on one palm and ran her other hand over her belly, down her mons and using two fingers widened her sex lips and then dipped them into her vagina. Julian's grunts, groans and snorts grew more and more frantic and just in time Mistress Madonna pushed herself to her feet and raced to him as he erupted in a cock-torturing ejaculation. Fountains of sperm gushed from his chained cock and diving under his legs, her palms cupped together, she captured most of it as it pumped and spewed out in a series of seemingly unending spurts.

When he finally stopped convulsing and she was certain that every last drop had been milked from his now empty bollocks, she got to her feet, being very careful not to allow any of his warm emissions to slip through her fingers. Her voice returned to its normal severe tone.

"Thank you very much Julian. That will do very nicely indeed."

Hurrying back to the pike shaft she palmed Julian's sperm all over its top five or six inches and then legs splayed, she again lifted herself on tiptoes and leaning backwards she eased the wood into her vaginal entrance. This time, just as she had hoped, the mixture of sperm and vaginal juices helped it to slip in more easily. But only for an inch or so before it stuck solid. It certainly was fat, even fatter than The Colonel's magnificent weapon and she knew immediately that it was going to be the perfect substitute for that magical instrument. She lifted her bottom, pulling backwards off the shaft until only its very tip lodged into her hole and then thrust her hips forwards, using the full meaty weight of her fabulous backside to press herself forwards and downwards onto it.

In it went, just another couple of inches, making her gasp as it widened her tunnel. Again she pulled back, rolling a projectile nipple with the fingers of one hand and rubbing her clitoris between the fingers and thumb of the other, in an effort to increase the flow of juices into her vagina. Despite being plugged solid by the shaft, juice trickled from her stretched sex lips and down her thighs and with another sharp gasp she lowered herself again and the shaft sank further into her belly. Two more times she raised and lowered herself before the pike was sunk into her right up to her cervix and she could feel it stretching her to the limit. Julian's sperm combined with her own juices had served its purpose, easing the shaft's entry as it bored into her until she was completely impaled on it. In fact it was buried so far into her tunnel that her feet were now flat on the floor.

She had never felt so well and truly stuffed before and just stood there enjoying the feeling for a minute or so before raising her bottom and experimentally pulling back and thrusting forwards on the shaft. And the sensation was glorious. Unbelievably arousing and exciting. Purring with undisguised pleasure she rolled and bucked her hips, fucking herself with the pike and stirring up a volcano of lust. Groans of ecstasy fell from her lips as her hips bucked faster and faster and her fingers worked on her nipples and her fully-unhooded clitoris. Beads of perspiration formed on her brow, stinging her eyes and planting their salty taste on her tongue as they rolled down her face. Her breath began to come in ragged gasps until suddenly she flung her arms forward and grasped the shaft firmly in both hands, holding it rock-steady as she writhed on its end until she exploded in a shaking, convulsing orgasm that saw starbursts of multi-coloured light flashing before her now tightly-closed eyelids and wave after wave of raging pulsing currents storming through her love-box to render her into a state of near paralysis.

Slowly her eyes opened and the tremors in her limbs calmed down.

"Oh God Julian, that was good. The best fuck I've ever had; and I did it to myself."

Gingerly, almost regretfully she eased herself off the pike and ruefully massaged herself between her legs. She had treated herself to quite a battering, her sex petals and her inner soft vaginal flesh still tingling, but bruised to hell.

"Mistress Madonna's really sore now. I'm almost tempted to let you suck my twat and kiss it better. But I'm not going to because too many treats can spoil a silly boy, and you've already had the biggest treat I could ever think of giving you."

Grunts and snivels were Julian's anguished reply. As ever she interpreted them with uncanny accuracy.

"What do you mean, you haven't had a treat? Of course you have. You got what you've always wanted more than anything else - your spunk squishing deep inside my cunt."

But he had not put it there himself. It had not squirted from his cock as it reamed her into orgasm as she knew that he had always dreamed of doing. And it never would. Once again she had crumbled his dreams into dust. Apart from The Colonel, matters had turned out quite satisfactorily indeed.

"I'm going back to bed now. You're staying where you are. You're a bad, ungrateful boy. Perhaps I might release you in the morning - and then again I might not."

Vigorously tugging on his cock chain several times, she gave him one last taste of agony before heading off to bed and hopefully a good revitalising sleep for what remained of the night.

But even after her cataclysmic body-weakening orgasm Mistress Madonna still found sleep difficult to attain. She had not drawn the heavy curtains because although the pitch darkness outside was impenetrable to the eye and she could see nothing of the lodge's surroundings, in the heavens above all the glories of the night sky sparkled and shone with a wondrous intensity. Enveloped by the covers, she lay marvelling at a cosmic display that she could never have enjoyed back home in London where the ever-present street lights, neon signs and brightly-lit store windows blotted out the distant twinkling of the stars.

Eventually, rather than just lying there waiting for sleep to decide whether to visit her or not, she turned back to the grisly book. Erzebet Bartholi had indeed been a particularly gruesome person, but she found herself constantly looking up from the pages; for some unknown reason she felt uneasy and unsettled. She could not put her finger on it exactly, perhaps it was the influence of the sinister evil of the book but it seemed to her as if some malevolent presence lurked in the gloomy recesses of the hunting lodge, watching her. As finally she felt herself at last sinking into sleep, although she knew that it was impossible, she imagined that she could hear the howling of wolves out in the pine forest and when at last she managed to drop off completely she was plagued by nightmares in which among other strange fantasies she saw a giant bat with viciously sharp teeth fluttering outside her window.

THREE
THE MIRROR

Up at the castle, The Baroness stood facing a full-length mirror. Of great age and size, the mirror was set into an ornately carved frame, its surface reflecting everything it saw with undistorted clarity. It was her practice to regularly stand gazing into the glass for hour upon hour, examining her flawless complexion for the slightest sign of ageing. But if she so wished it, her reflection would fade, to be replaced in the glass by either darkly mysterious images or remote scenes that she wished to view. Scenes such as the interior of the hunting lodge, which she had now been watching for several hours.

When Mistress Madonna had climbed back into the bed, the Baroness had not stopped studying her until she fell into a fitful sleep. Now reluctantly deciding that she would witness no further action from her guest that night, the Baroness turned away from the mirror and concentrated her attention on the mixed pair of very nervous and frightened slaves she had summoned to her presence in anticipation of requiring their services for sexual duty. Ordering the young male to the back of the room, the Baroness sank into the depths of an all-enveloping armchair and fixed her eyes on the slim young waif of a girl, savouring her total dominance over her.

Stolen from her parents several years earlier the girl had been sold to the Baroness' slave gatherer by a band of wandering Romanian gypsies who from time to time provided extra stock to replenish her continually decreasing herd of virgins. The unfortunate girl was now fast approaching her eighteenth birthday and as had the boy, she had performed her duties as a body slave to the Baroness' absolute carnal satisfaction. She would have liked to have continued to enjoy them both for longer, but circumstances made that impossible; to be eighteen and a virgin were the two requirements for the participants in her revivification ritual and that was now very close at hand. Feeling some regret that after midnight the girl would have reached the necessary age to be sacrificed in the Ceremony, the boy having attained that age several days earlier, she rued the fact that she would very soon lose the services of two very competent and satisfying sex slaves. But there was one thing she needed far more than their lust-sating ministrations: their blood!

Being the epitome of cruelty that she was, there was no trace of pity or concern for the slaves in the Baroness' thoughts; she just did not like to lose a good thing. And in any case, when she thought about it, it was of not really of any great matter, after all there were plenty more where they came from.

Beckoning the girl over, in a cold emotionless voice the Baroness ordered her to pour her a glass of wine.

"And be very careful, it is of a singularly unique vintage. Spill a single drop and I will flay the skin from your back."

Watching with eagle eyes, the Baroness sat in growing impatience as the girl picked up a crystal decanter, hesitantly filled a glass and handed it to her. Waving the girl back into the shadows to join her companion, the Baroness swirled the crimson elixir around the glass and took a deep draught. Then closing her eyes she began to re-run the events of the evening through her mind, soon losing herself in a reverie of diamond-sharp, swirling lascivious recollections, the scenes unfolding in her mind just as if they were happening at that very moment.

But recollections were not enough to satisfy her, she needed more and gathering all her concentration, she peered deeply into depths of the mirror. A heavy swirling mist clouded its surface and just as if she were re-winding a modern day video, the Baroness willed time to fly back, the fog eventually clearing to commence displaying a clear playback of the succession of lurid and arousingly inspirational events that she had witnessed during the evening.

In vivid clarity, the mirror showed a scene that had been played out in reality several hours earlier. The Baroness' iron-willed English guest was disciplining her slave and as she watched, just as she had when she had seen the scene unrolling in actuality, the Baroness felt herself becoming increasingly impressed by the way Mistress Madonna handled him. Hard as iron, showing no mercy and with a steely determination to inflict the greatest level of pain, both mental and physical, that he could endure without permanent damage, the woman was everything that The Colonel had led her to believe.

As the scenes rolled on, one after another, she saw the arrival of the two agents de police, whom, being greatly desirous of a more first-hand assessment of Mistress Madonna, she had dispatched to conduct a close-up inspection of her activities.

Their explanation that the slave's tortured screams were the reason for their visit was not questioned by Mistress Madonna and if the marks on her slave's neck turned out to be what the policewoman obviously thought they were, then that meant that Mistress Madonna was one of the Baroness' own kind. She was also darkly beautiful, a distinctly welcome added bonus. Everything was going perfectly.

As the two police officers duly took their leave, the Baroness silently praised them for their more than efficient handling of the situation, seemingly having aroused no doubts or suspicions in the mind of her guest. Carrying on with her surveillance of the hunting lodge, she nodded in grim appreciation as the slave's punishment grew in painful severity.

She had not been altogether surprised when she had first witnessed The Colonel's arrival on the scene and now, once again her excitement notched up several levels when the action reached the point where it became obvious that Mistress Madonna was going to let him fuck her. As he fed his weapon into her dripping, eager vagina, the Baroness felt her own need rising and when he began to cannon into Mistress Madonna's sex she marvelled at his magnificent cock and his masterly shagging technique, rolling her nipples through the material of her long black dress and throwing open the slit that ran down its front to delve between her legs

The flame of Mistress Madonna's passion roared higher and brighter as The Colonel stoked her towards her climax. And so did the Baroness', her fingers working on the hard nub of her clitoris and sinking between her sex lips and into her juiced-up minge. As Mistress Madonna's orgasm neared, the Baroness' own ministrations to her sex grew more frantic until at the very moment The Colonel drove Mistress Madonna over the edge, the Baroness screamed and shook in the throes of her own fulfilment.

Although she much preferred sex with younger persons of her own persuasion, The Colonel's performance prompted the Baroness to toy momentarily with the idea of seducing him herself. Married at the age of fourteen, sex with her husband the Baron had been less than memorable and since his mysterious death so very many years before, although she had led a full and inventive sex life, she had only rarely taken a male lover. And only with one exception never one with a cock like The Colonel's! She soon dismissed the idea however, a dalliance with him would only complicate matters and that had to be avoided at all costs. It was all to the good that he and Thierry had left the castle for a few days of carousal and fornication at Le Manoir. It would keep them well out of the way during the Ceremony; and it was not as if she had not sold a few spare female virgins to that establishment in the past. Although none of those girls had known it, they were the lucky ones.

What really drove her over the edge however, was when the display in the mirror reached Mistress Madonna's episode with the pike. Inventive in the extreme, it was also deeply arousing. The Baroness' lips curled up over her lips as she drank in the supremely erotic images, revealing her unusually pointed eyeteeth. Her tongue ran over her deeply-red-tinted-lips, lips that contrasted markedly with her otherwise pale complexion.

Standing to her rear, motionless, quiet and wide-eyed, in opposite shadowed corners of the candle-lit room, the pair of sex slaves drank in every moment of her self-administered arousal and fulfilment. One the dark-haired girl and the other a blond boy, they both possessed a natural unembellished beauty, smooth-skinned and with unusually wan features. As she trembled and shook in the frenzy of her orgasm, they showed no emotion themselves. They knew better. The Baroness was an exceedingly strict disciplinarian, her punishments for disobedience or slackness in obeying orders being brutally harsh. And upon being summoned, their orders had been to watch in silence and to say or do nothing unless she so directed.

Not only was the Baroness' power over them absolute but the two slaves held her in great awe because of the use she made of mirror. Standing where they were, they could both see into the mirror, but all they could see were the reflections of themselves, the room and its contents. They could see neither their mistress nor whatever it was that she was obviously able to perceive in its depths. And watching the spectacle unfolding before her of Mistress Madonna attempting to pleasure herself with the shaft of the pike was stirring the Baroness greatly, re-lighting the kindling of her passions.

"Over here! Both of you."

The command was not been exactly barked, the Baroness was far too feminine for that, but it was urgent and emphatic.

"You! On your knees."

The boy immediately did as he was bidden, positioning himself in front of his mistress, with his back to the mirror and his head on a level with her crotch. She once again swept aside the split skirt of her long dress, revealing her juicy, lusting sex.

"What are you waiting for? Get on with it."

Inching forwards on his knees, the boy shuffled between her widespread legs and she stiffened in eager anticipation of what was to come as she felt his strong fingers separate and widen the protective petals of her sex lips. His breath wafting hot on the insides of her thighs he did as she had ordered and burying his face into her crotch he sought out the erect nub of her clitoris with his tongue. Shivers of delight ran through her as he licked and sucked her aroused and unhooded love bud and she could sense his own rapture as her juices began to flow over his taste buds. Then as her labia engorged even further, his rasping tongue notched up into overdrive, wringing a gasp of joy from her lips as it speared deep into her open vagina. And just as if he had thrown open a switch to her emotions, a continuous circuit of electrifying sensation connected her clitoris to her nipples. Murmuring in aroused delight she watched avidly as Mistress Madonna tried to ease the fat shaft of the pike into her eager sex.

"And you girl! Here."

Shrugging the top of her dress from her shoulders, she let it fall to her waist. Lifting her full, heavy breasts in her palms, she offered them to the young girl. Her nipples were as solid as bullets and a shiver ran down her spine as taking one of them between her teeth, the girl nuzzled and teased it with her tongue before plunging her cool wet mouth over it and sucking avidly. Without any further prompting, the girl took the other nipple between her thumb and forefinger, pinching and rolling with the expertise born of constant practice.

But watching Mistress Madonna, The Baroness was overcome with the need for something to be stuck up her own lusting tunnel and looking down she saw, just as she had expected, that the boy had sprouted a straining erection. Not only that, it was wonderfully big and fat and would have been ideal if it were not for the fact that just as with Mistress Madonna and Julian, although for a very different reason, she was not able to take advantage of its eminent suitability. In her case it was because the boy was a virgin. And that was the way he had to remain. It was great pity, but just like her guest she would have to find some other stiff implement with which to fuck herself. Sighing inwardly she cast her eyes around searching for something equally as appropriate for the task.

And there it was.

On her dressing table lay an ornate and exceptionally long and thick-handled hair brush; something that she never used for its intended purpose but frequently employed in the disciplining of her slaves. Smacked onto the more fleshily padded parts of their anatomy, particularly the haunches, it dealt out a sickening blow even when wielded by a delicate hand, leaving an expansive and darkly-coloured bruise in its wake.

Now, she saw another much more pleasurable use for it.

In the mirror she saw Mistress Madonna give up on her struggle to impale herself on the pike. Earlier, when the incident had actually taken place, she had watched questioningly as Mistress Madonna disported herself in front of Julian's chained and straining figure. As his erection had grown ever more steely and throbbing, the Baroness had suddenly guessed the reason for Mistress Madonna's erotic performance. What a wonderful solution to her problem. She could have used baby oil or some other lubricant but this had been much more inventive; Mistress Madonna had certainly lived up to what the Baroness had at first thought to be a very overstated opinion of her powers and originality that had been given to her by The Colonel.

For some unfathomable reason the Baroness was consumed by the notion that she had to feel and experience as closely as possible, everything that Mistress Madonna had savoured at that earlier moment. And to that end the boy's erection was very fortuitous indeed; it would provide her with just what she needed.

Sperm!

The same lubrication that Mistress Madonna had used.

The Baroness' boy and girl slaves were all medically examined and certified virgins when they were delivered into her service and once there they were not allowed to fuck each other. The horrific punishments she threatened, and indeed sometimes carried out as an example of what would happen to them if they disobeyed her edict, saw to it that they never crossed that particular line. But they were not completely forbidden all sexual activity; as a matter of fact she greatly enjoyed watching them. Sometimes she spied on them surreptitiously in the mirror, while at other times she would make her way down to the pens beneath the castle and order her entire herd to perform for her entertainment.

So the girls, or other boys if they so wished, would suck a rigid cock into spurting orgasm. Girls played with each other, sucking or fingering each other to a climax. Boys sometimes buggered each other, although she did not really approve of that, but what they most definitely never did was to have full sexual intercourse. No cocks were allowed inside female orifices. The girls therefore, with un-penetrated maidenheads remained virgins and as for the boys, no matter what other sexual experiences they indulged in, to the Baroness the fact that they had never soaked their throbbing meat in a dripping, juicy vagina meant that technically they too were all virgins. Although they might not be the purest form of innocence, in her eyes every single one of her slaves was still untainted and fully qualified for the special use for which she had purchased them.

So she was not breaking her own code when she suddenly issued an instruction to the girl.

"Spunk!"

The girl jerked her lips from the Baroness' nipple, a question written plainly on her face.

"Spunk, I need spunk. Now! I know you suck him off when you think that I can't see. Well do it now, and when he comes catch every single drop in your hands. Swallow any and you'll wish that you were dead; something that I can easily arrange."

Beckoning the boy to his feet, the Baroness pushed the girl down on to her knees and firmly holding her head, guided her mouth over his throbbing penis. It was plain to the Baroness that he was already extremely excited and very close to orgasm.

"If he comes before I get back, you're both in for the thrashing of a lifetime."

With that she made her way over to the dressing table, picked up the hairbrush and returned to stand over the girl.

"Now, get that mouth working."

Looking into the mirror she saw that events had already reached the point where Mistress Madonna had milked Julian of his creamy elixir and was smearing it over the pike shaft. If she were to keep pace with her guest, the girl would have to bring the boy to ejaculation in double quick time.

"Don't make a meal of it. Bring him off now!"

The boy had been on the brink of orgasm as it was, the relief springing to his features as he was finally able to let go. The girl did not really have to do any more than tighten her lips around his shaft and pull her mouth back over the sensitive underside of his bell-end to catapult him into a convulsing orgasm. Cupping her hands over his jerking glans she caught spurt after spurt of his hot ejaculate, desperately fighting to contain every drop in her palms. As his cock ceased its twitching and nothing but bubbles puffed out from his meatus, the Baroness held out the brush with the handle pointing down towards the girl.

"The sperm. Spread it over the handle."

Raising her arms upwards, the girl tilted her palms sideways and ran them over the proffered handle, transferring the thick sticky load of come to its hard wooden surface. Parting her inner sex lips with the fingers of one hand, the Baroness inverted the brush and with her legs splayed apart pushed the brush handle between her grasping inner sex lips and up into her ravenous, sopping hole. She had not really needed the extra lubrication of the spunk as Mistress Madonna had done but she welcomed it nonetheless, she wanted to feel exactly the same sensations as her guest in the hunting lodge had felt.

As Mistress Madonna slid on and off the pike shaft, driving it deeper and deeper into her sex, the Baroness pushed the handle of the brush in and out of her own love tunnel. They were both questing for same fulfilment, but the Baroness was able to call on a little more help than had been available to Mistress Madonna.

"You girl, stay down there and help me. Use your fingers on my clitoris; stroke it, massage it, do anything. But don't get in the way of the hairbrush, more than anything I need to feel that pumping inside me."

Grunting and gasping both with the effort and with the increasing eddies of arousal that were coursing through her, she turned her attention to the boy.

"Up on your feet! My nipples; suck them."

The boy leapt to obey her command, his lips fastening around one of her almost bullet-sized nipples. His wet lips and purposeful tongue felt marvellously cool on her hot, heaving breast, his greedy mouth hungry for the taste of her flesh. But she wanted more.

"The other nipple. Work on that too, come on boy, use your imagination."

Laying a flat palm over her other breast, he squeezed and massaged the firm mound for a few moments before taking the nipple between his thumb and forefinger, rolling, pulling and nipping it with a grip that rang the bells of pain as much as those of pleasure. And she loved it. A hairbrush handle firmly stuck up her clinging, sucking vagina; fingers manipulating her clitoris and one of her nipples and an excited mouth biting and sucking on the other, she writhed and bucked in an ever-growing tide of ecstasy.

It could not last much longer and it did not. Even though she tried to delay her moment of fulfilment, an unstoppable raging ocean of electrifying physical fireworks swept over her as in the mirror she saw Mistress Madonna reach her own peak. Tearing her eyes away from the glass, as the flames of her emotions burned at their white-hot peak, in the throes of a gigantic body-racking orgasm she let out a hideous, soul-destroying scream and jerking the boy's head upwards from her breast, rolled back her lips and sank her teeth deeply into his neck.

FOUR
THE ARMOIRE

Mistress Madonna having finally sunk into a deep, exhausted sleep; it was with the warming rays of the mid-morning sun already streaming into the bedroom that she awoke. The unfamiliarity of her surroundings confused her for a moment until she shook herself into full awareness and the memories of the previous night came flooding into her mind. Remembering the ghastly punishment that she had dealt out to Julian and the awful, contorted and strained position she had left him in, it crossed her mind that he must be in a dreadful state by now and she should do something about it. But then again, why should she? Julian revelled in torture and misery, so he was probably enjoying himself. And if he was not; too bad. He could stay how he was until she got things straight in her mind.

It had been a strange night for her after all. The Colonel's behaviour was incomprehensible and although she knew full well that back in England his cock was not reserved solely for her and was in constant demand by the ladies of the County Set, she still could not believe that over here he had abandoned her to go off fucking and carousing with a bunch of tarts; even if they were the most highly prized and glamorous female flesh in Europe.

Although she had never doubted herself before, she began to wonder if her appeal to him was fading. Was she losing her looks? She did not think so but all the same she wandered over to the full-length-dressing mirror that stood in a corner of the room and inspected herself closely. In that dim location the light was really quite poor and so the mirror being on castors she wheeled it over to where she was able to see more clearly.

Lifting the hair from her forehead she examined it closely for the slightest sign of a wrinkle. Of course there was none. She peered into her dark liquid eyes and found them still bright and sparkling. Pressing hard she dragged her fingertips down from her cheekbones and over her chin, smiling in a sort of grim satisfaction at the firmness of her flesh. Running her palms down the length of her neck and over her breasts and their proud nipples, she satisfied herself that nothing was awry. Twisting this way and that she checked every part of her anatomy for any indication, no matter how slight, for signs of sagging or cellulite. There were none. Her buttocks were still perfectly rounded and solid, her legs long and unblemished and her sex just as it had always been; fully thatched and inviting.

Mistress Madonna's eyes lingered for a while on her sex before she ran a palm down over her pubic mound and sighing heavily, slipped a forefinger into the crease between her labia. Her sigh was born of the knowledge that the sexual adventures that she had expected to enjoy with The Colonel on this visit were not to be. The fantasies that she had played out in her mind once again filled her thoughts, blotting out what her eyes actually saw in the mirror.

She imagined herself being pleasured by The Colonel in the midst of the dense pines, laid out on one of the fallen standing stones that were strewn everywhere on the forest floor. His beautiful cock plunged into her powerfully muscular vagina, the walls of her love tunnel contracting, squeezing and pulling his mighty weapon deeper into her until his pleasure dome was smashing up against her womb. Again and again he cannoned into her with hugely deep thrusts as he drove her to heights of ecstasy that she had never known before. Her orgasm was the stuff of dreams, hitting her vagina with seemingly endless waves of body-numbing tremors as she gasped and groaned in a paradise of rapture, digging her long black-painted fingernails into his back as her limbs thrashed helplessly under the delicious torment of his onslaught. It was sex at its most thrilling, satisfying, debilitating pinnacle.

Only minutes later, even though she had milked his bollocks dry, surrounded by giant ferns, she bent over with her legs wide and took him into her most private of places, the tight hole into which he so loved to sink his iron rod. The Colonel could go on forever and once more he stoked her into oblivion, both of them jerking frenziedly as their orgasms hit, gasping and screaming in unison with the intensity of their climaxes.

Then kneeling before him, she slipped her impatient lips over his bulbous purple bell-end, licking and sucking before grasping his buttocks and pulling him so close that her nose sank into his pubic hairs and the full length of his mighty weapon buried itself down her throat. The taste of his thick salty sperm delighted her taste buds and in return The Colonel greedily guzzled on her fragrant vagina, drinking every magical drop of her copious juices of love. Gently opening her love petals with his fingers he sank his tongue deep inside her, his nose rubbing and stimulating her clitoris as he treated her to an expert and deeply arousing tongue-fuck. The muscular walls of her vagina clasped his tongue, showering it with oceans of ambrosial nectar and almost drowning him in her secretions as he ceaselessly pleasured her into orgasm. An orgasm so tremendous that it left her whole body drained and weak.

The Colonel deserved something special for that and guiding his cock into the deep valley between her magnificent breasts, she pressed them tightly around the hot throbbing shaft. Encouraging him to thrust as strongly as he could, she gave him the tit-wank of a lifetime and by bending her chin downwards she was able to take his helmet into her mouth on each upward stroke, so taking him to greater levels of gratification, once again tasting his gourmet spunk as it spattered up onto her lips and face.

And her fevered orgasms were not only in her mind. As her imagination had notched into overdrive, driven by her thoughts, her sex became a sopping river of lust and her nipples, swollen terminals of pulsing excitement. As The Colonel fucked her in her daydream, she frantically fucked herself in reality; firstly with just her index and forefingers and then as her need increased and her orgasm neared, with her all her fingers and her thumb crammed into her sucking vagina. With two fingers of her other hand working on the hard nub of her clitoris she drove herself to several very real and electrifying climaxes, timing them to hit at the very moments that The Colonel performed the same feats in her fantasy.

As the tremors within her subsided and her vagina revelled in the warm, satisfied wetness that comes with sexual fulfilment, Mistress Madonna's thoughts reluctantly returned to Julian. She really ought to check on him, it would not be to her benefit if anything untoward were to have happened to him.

He was just as she had left him, but now visibly wilting in his bondage, the chains supporting his exhausted body. He looked absolutely awful; grimy and sweat-soaked he must have spent the entire night fighting his restraints but his eyes still sparked into worshipful devotion as she stood before him, arms folded and with a look of utter scorn upon her face. After everything that she had put him through he was still overjoyed to see her.

And as usual, so was his cock!

"Still not learnt your lesson, I see. When are you going to learn that good little boys don't spend their entire lives shagging and playing with themselves?"

She was as cruel as they come. In his desperate predicament Julian of course was completely unable to do anything with his sorely abused but still rock hard weapon. He could not fuck because it was not allowed in any case, but neither could he wank, and with his penis so tautly and excruciatingly erect he was also completely unable to piss. With his shoulder and arm muscles almost wrenched from their sockets, his back breaking, his bladder at bursting point and his foreskin rubbed to an angry reddened, shredded and bloody mess by the iron cock clamp, he was suffering as he had never suffered before.

Which meant that he was having the time of his life.

Mistress Madonna congratulated herself, smiling inwardly. Everything was as it should be; when this little trip was over she would no doubt be collecting a sizeable bonus from her pathetically besotted slave. Outwardly showing no obvious regard for his well being, she checked him over closely, reaching the conclusion that he had come to no harm and she could carry on where she had left off the previous evening.

"I really don't know how you've got the gall to present yourself to me in this despicable condition. You're filthy, you smell worse than donkey diarrhoea and I don't know how you did it but you appear to be covered in spunk. You are altogether one revolting little person. Well, Mistress Madonna will soon put that right."

Although she had not noticed one the previous day, somehow she knew that if she went outside she would find a well close to the lodge. And so it proved. It was very deep too judging by the length of time it took for the pebble she tossed into it to reach the bottom. The water in a well of that depth would be absolutely freezing she concluded, just the thing to get Julian's day off to a memorable start. Lowering the heavy wooden bucket down into the water she filled it full to brimming, hauled it back up and untied it from the thick rope wound around the winch.

Staggering a little under its unexpected weight, she carefully transported it and its ice-cold contents back into the lodge.

"Right turd. This is what cock-happy vulgar little guttersnipes get when they look as if they've spent the night stuck up Mary Poppins' chimney."

And that was it. Julian got it. The entire freezing bucketful hit him like a solid sheet of ice as with all the force that she could muster, Mistress Madonna flung the water over his straining form. He shivered uncontrollably as the gelid river plastered his hair, ran down over his face, his arms and legs and dripped from the end of his nose. It did not however drip from his cock. That was still practically on fire and although any drops of water that found their way onto that burning rod of flesh did not actually flash into steam, they all evaporated before they could run down to his bell end. All that dripped from that were droplets of the seminal fluid that constantly leaked from his priapic weapon.

Julian's jaws had now been prized apart by the ball gag for well over twelve hours and it was time she did something about it if he was not going to finish up with a permanently gaping mouth. As his mistress she could not show any sign that could be interpreted by

Julian as tenderness or compassion, not that she felt any, Julian only got exactly what he deserved but she did not want him permanently damaged and so the gag had to be removed. However there was a way that she could do it without seeming to have weakened.

"I'd better take this off, no doubt that nosy bitch of a policewoman will turn up sooner or later wanting it back."

So off it came.

"Thank you, thank you Mistress."

In a dry, cracked-mouth rasp his obeisance was nauseating.

"Thank you for what, cretin?"

His reply surprised even her.

"Last night. It was wonderful. It still is wonderful. You're wonderful."

Not a word about the gag, which is what she had been expecting. It just went to show that nothing about Julian could be taken for granted.

But it did not really matter, because she was still burning with resentment at her treatment at the hands of The Colonel; she found it impossible to stop thinking about it and Julian was destined to continue suffering until she had worked that resentment out of her system. She had still not broken him. Although she had subjected him to punishments that transcended the awful, he was proving to be incredibly resilient. He was enjoying it altogether too much and that only made her even more determined to smash him into a grovelling, totally insignificant piece of offal.

Staring into her much more elaborate mirror, the Baroness had once again been watching as her guest engaged herself in what was almost a perfect duplication of her own daily ritual; the search for the telltale signs of encroaching age on her flawless body, followed by sexual gratification and the disciplining of her slaves. Mistress Madonna could not know it but the Baroness was becoming more and more certain that the two of them were kindred spirits and alike in more ways than one.

Standing by her side sharing the view, the policewoman remained silent until the Baroness turned aside for moment. Seizing her chance, the policewoman posed a question.

"Mistress, now that you've had the opportunity to watch her in action, what do you think? Is she for us?"

There was no doubt on the Baroness' part.

"Oh yes Anna. She's perfect. And her slave could prove to be useful too, if he is still a virgin as The Colonel told me he was. And speaking of virgins, it's time you got down to the creek to check on the last batch that those gypsies and their fishermen friends should be unloading about now. And on your way there call in on Madonna and invite her to the castle this evening. Say that I'm throwing a little dinner party or something like that. Just make sure that we get her up here in time for the Ceremony."

Having taken a welcome respite and a few refreshing sips of Dom Perignon, Mistress Madonna stood looking around, searching for inspiration as to what punishment Julian could be subjected to next. Suddenly she noticed for the first time that set into the oak beam running across the ceiling above his head was a large iron hook. And hanging from the hook was a pulley. A thick rope, tied off to a hoop in the wall ran over the pulley and attached to it was a T-bar with studded wrist cuffs affixed to each end of the ball-jointed horizontal section. Things just kept on getting better, it could not have been more ideal if she had put it there herself.

As her eyes lingered on the bar, Julian's own eyes followed her gaze. Instant panic. "No Mistress. Not that. Please. Don't string me up, I've think I've had enough now."

That settled it. Enough was never enough where he was concerned. Pulling over a

chair, she climbed onto it and unhooked his neck chain from the bracket that had held the pike. Julian swivelled his head and stretched his neck in instant appreciation of their newfound freedom of movement. Getting down from the chair she next concentrated her attention on his wrist cuffs, releasing them both before doing the same with his ankle cuffs and removing the spreader bar from between his widespread feet.

Now that all his limbs were free, he would be able to stand upright; that is if his strained back would let him. But if he had thought, even for a moment that because she had released his bonds that she was softening, he was in for a rude shock. She addressed him as would a sergeant major admonishing a raw recruit.

"What are you waiting for? Stand up straight, feet together, arms by your side, head up."

"But Mistress . . ."

"But Mistress what?"

"My cock. It's still chained and it hurts. And I need a piss. Badly."

"Of what interest is that to me? I'm glad your cock hurts and your bladder can burst for all I care. Just do as your Mistress tells you. Understood?"

"Yes Mistress."

His response was a feeble, small-voiced testimony of his acquiescence to her command. Her response to his totally inadequate reaction was a lightning flurry of slaps to his face that left him reeling.

"You can do better than that."

So he could. This time the answer was loud and clear.

"YES MISTRESS."

"Right. Let's get on with it, shall we? Or have you got any more pathetic whinges before we start?"

He had not.

Untying the rope fastening the pulley, Mistress Madonna lowered the T-bar.

"Now. Hands above your head."

After spinning the bar around to make sure that it moved freely, she fastened Julian's wrists to the cuffs on the bar and began hauling it back up to the ceiling. Julian was balancing right on the tips of his toes, his arms stretched tautly above him before she was satisfied and finally tied the rope off on the wall hoop. His savagely abused love gun was drawn out to double its normal length and half its circumference by the taut iron chain. He certainly had something to whinge about now.

And he did.

And not quietly either. His screams, pleas and whines would have sent a decibel meter into meltdown, his squeals rising so high in pitch they were reaching the point where they could only be heard by dogs. But then, he was an animal himself Mistress Madonna told him and animals of whatever kind had to be trained to obey their owners, that was the nature of things.

"And Mistress Madonna owns *you*, doesn't she? All of you. From your feeble brain to your tiny excuse for a willy. You're mine, body and soul, and don't you forget it. But you're not like other animals, they need discipline just like you but all other wild things from dogs to donkeys can be taught to behave through patience and consideration. But not you. You don't understand kindness, the only thing you understand is pain. And more pain. So you're going to get it."

"But Mistress, please . . . my cock . . ."

"Yes, I've seen it and I wouldn't fuss about it if I were you. Any self respecting man would try to keep a winkle like that out of sight, he wouldn't go around flashing it to all and sundry like you do."

"I didn't flash it. It was you. You put that rotten iron ring on it and it's killing me. Take the fucking thing off right now or you'll be sorry."

"I'll be WHAT?"

Her voice was steel, her tone measured and her contempt unequivocal. Julian had gone too far and the haunted look that suddenly glazed his eyes showed that he knew it.

"I'm sorry Mistress, I didn't mean it. I'll be good, I promise I will."

"You're not sorry at all. But you will be; in fact Mistress Madonna is going to make you sorry that you were ever born."

When she was travelling, Mistress Madonna carried with her in a specially constructed flightcase a veritable armoury of instruments of discipline and it was to this that she was about to turn for inspiration when suddenly her gaze was caught by a huge medieval armoire standing close to one of the walls. Where had that come from? She could not recall seeing it the previous night and it was certainly of a size that commanded attention. Very strange! However she immediately dismissed her doubts, telling herself that she had just been too intent on disciplining Julian to take proper notice of her surroundings.

The flightcase was driven from her thoughts as she was overcome by an incontestable compulsion to explore the interior of the armoire and pulling open its single carved door she was astounded by what she saw. It was unbelievable, an Aladdin's cave filled with very weird and wonderful ancient devices of correction that presented far more possibilities for inventive fiendish torment than did her own equipment. She knew without question that it was all there for her benefit. And Julian's, of course. She did not need to be told that someone, the Baroness possibly, had provided her with a storehouse of the most perfect devices of discipline. There was basically nothing there that was not in her own armoury back in England, but it was just all so old and wonderfully crafted.

Whips and canes of all thicknesses and sizes were there in abundance. There were ancient leather-strapped ball gags, with the balls being of solid tooth-shattering iron, much akin to small canon balls. There were iron handcuffs; wrist and elbow clamps of the same metal; spreader bars, thumbscrews, cock and ball clamps, iron-spiked leather paddles and cod-pieces. Multi-thonged martinets, scourges and genuine cat–o–nine tails lined the back and sides of the giant cabinet along with pincers, rasps and sharpened pokers.

Mistress Madonna had suffered enough of Julian's inane, childish and pathetic behaviour and now was the time for a reckoning. A painful reckoning. And here were the perfect instruments with which to subject him to a lesson he would long remember. It was a great pity that The Colonel would not be present to witness the event; he enjoyed the sight of Julian getting his come-uppance. As that thought flashed into her mind, Mistress Madonna felt a twinge of resentment. The bastard. Why did he mean so much to her? when many much younger suitors constantly assailed her with protestations of love, obedience and offers of untraceable offshore bank accounts.

The answer was easy. It was because he was The Colonel. The man who possessed the biggest, fattest, most satisfying cock in the universe. And he had buggered off and left her to go waltzing with shit. How could he? The wound would never heal, she would never forgive him.

But she had other things to think about besides him. Julian was her bread and butter and she had to concentrate on him. Her attention reverted to the task in hand. She had a job to do, a function to perform. Julian was rich beyond belief, if need be he would throw away his entire fortune on her, she knew that but that was not what she wanted. It was true that she revelled in the lavish lifestyle that his wealth afforded her but she relished even more the power that she wielded over him; the physical pain to which she subjected him and the mental pain she made him suffer. She held complete dominion over him and with the ease that she tore it apart, his heart might just as well have been made of paper.

His heart might have possessed some similarity to paper but his prick most certainly had not. Despite all she knew about Julian and his permanently active dick, she still found herself marvelling at its pulsing, twitching refusal to admit defeat. His iron-hard poker having been tortured beyond belief was mangled, shredded, bloody and without doubt was agonising him as if it had been thrust into the heart of a fiery brazier. But still it was as hard and solidly erect as a column of granite.

Once again she found herself regretting the fact that she could not turn such an impressive and useful appendage to her own advantage. Alright. If she could not benefit from it, then neither would anyone else. Not for the immediate future anyway. A diabolical thought had formed itself in her mind.

He was strung up and primed and so it was unthinkable that she would not take advantage of the opportunities that that offered. But now that she had thought of it, she was anxious to put her new plan into operation and so in the event she treated him to what was for her a somewhat perfunctory thrashing. A particularly whippy cane cut and striped his buttocks. A plaited, knotted whip bit into his thighs and the backs of his calves. Pushing on one of his shoulders, she set him turning slowly on the end of the pulley and lashed his back, his chest, his arms and shoulders as they presented themselves to her in turn. In truth when she threw down the whip, he did somewhat resemble a skinned carcass. He probably felt like one as well, but he showed genuine surprise when she lowered him to the floor, released his wrists and allowed him to stand upright with no restricting shackles of any kind. Even the chain stretching his cock was released.

But like the floor, her heart was made of stone. The iron chain had been unclipped, but the clamp screwed tight around his cock just below his bell end was left in place. The second that the chain had relinquished its restraining influence, his cock had sprung upwards in an attempt to reach for the sky. And so there he stood; naked, feet wide apart, arms by his side, and a jerking rock solid and metal-clamped severely ravaged cock rearing up in front of his belly. He looked down at it with gleaming eyes.

Mistress Madonna looked down at it with malevolent eyes.

Rolling her palms over her magnificent breasts, she smoothed them down her body over her hips and between her legs. Deliberately widening her stance, she slipped a palm over the top of each thigh, and delved the fingers of both hands into her succulent, juicy sex. Julian's burning cock swelled to even greater proportions, the agony plainly showing on his face.

"Mistress Madonna is going to show you now exactly how caring and kind she can be. She knows that you want to fuck her brains out, but she's told you time and again that that is never going to happen. But that doesn't mean that she doesn't care about her little cuddly-wuddly baby because she does; very much. So she's going to let you wank yourself off while she watches, she knows you like that, but because your little tiddly-widdly looks so sore she going to give you something to put on your hands while you do it. So you just be a good little boy and wait there while she fetches it."

Julian perked up considerably at that and looked even happier when she returned from the bedroom with a jar of expensive cooling skin cream. Screwing off the cap, she dipped her fingers into the jar and scooped out a fair sized globule of the thick white cream. Transferring it to both her palms, she massaged it into her breasts and shoulders with rolling circular motions.

"Uhmmm . . that feels really good. Cool and smooth, and look at my skin, not a sign of a wrinkle anywhere. Not like your cock, that's all horrid and disgusting. In fact now that I think about it, this cream is far too expensive to waste on that stinky thing."

Julian's face dropped as she screwed the top back on the jar.

"But never mind, Mistress Madonna knows something else that's far better than cream anyway."

This was it, Point Doom for Julian. Something bad was coming his way.

Mistress Madonna dipped again into the mysterious armoire and once more her exact requirements fell immediately to hand: a pair of metal gauntlets of the type that the Knights of old wore as part of their combat armour. Pulling them out, she handed them to Julian.

"Put them on."

He made no move to obey her, standing turning them over in his hands."

"Come on, get on with it. What are you waiting for?"

He was hesitant, obviously not wanting to raise her ire any further. He held them out and presented them to her, palms upwards. There was a marked difference between this pair and the ones used for fighting; it was not uncommon for the gauntlets to be spiked, but the spikes were usually on the back of the hand, this pair had the spikes on the palms and underneath the fingers.

"So, what's the problem?"

"The spikes Mistress, they'll rip my cock to shreds."

"Don't be silly, they'll just make it feel more wonderful. That's why I'm letting you wear them, even though you *have* been bad and don't really deserve a treat. Now be a good little boy and put the gloves on."

He still made no move to obey.

"Now look worm, I want to see you wanking yourself good and hard. And I want to see you doing it now! PUT THE GLOVES ON."

Very, very reluctantly, Julian pulled on the gauntlets.

"Now, get going."

This really was something new. Forced masturbation. She had never needed to order him to wank before, given the slightest opportunity he could not keep his hands off his cock. And they were not really on it now, his thumbs and fingers were circling his rigid erection very loosely indeed, something that she did not fail to notice.

"Mess me about and you'll be even sorrier than you're already going to be. Clench those fingers tight and start tugging."

Fighting back the tears, Julian did as he was told. One spiked hand gingerly stroked upwards over his tormented babymaker, the spikes digging into his turgid cockflesh and rasping over the iron ring that was still clamped tightly just beneath his bulbous pleasure dome.

"Yeeooooww!"

Julian's tortured scream was glorious music to Mistress Madonna's ears. His hand flew away from his dreadfully abused manhood.

"I can't do it Mistress. Look, it's leaving bloody great grooves in my dick."

And so it was.

Good.

"You do want to please your Mistress, don't you?"

"'Course I do."

"Well, in that case put your hand back where it was and this time use the other one as well. And put some effort into it, you weren't trying before."

And just as they would have done if he really were a naughty schoolboy, the tears rolled down over Julian's grimacing cheeks as he scraped, pulled and punctured his rigid cock, for despite everything it still reared skywards, straining and granite hard. The pain must have been horrific, Mistress Madonna knew that, his manhood had been well and truly shredded and battered before but now it was rapidly beginning to take on the appearance of something that would usually be thrown into the offal bin in an abattoir. Perfect! He deserved nothing less. And when it was all over, she knew that he would be thanking her for her inventiveness. He liked something new and different every now and again, and for him this was certainly new.

It was also new for her. She had toyed with the idea of palm-studded gloves for some time but had never found any and suddenly there they were. In fact she found it more than puzzling that everything she thought of using seemed to be on hand, whether she had noticed them before or not; the ceiling pulley for instance, and even the armoire full of goodies itself. It was all very odd. Odd but extremely fortuitous, so why worry about it? Taking her own advice, she dismissed any such thoughts from her mind and concentrated on her demented slave.

And demented he most certainly was, growing more so as every second passed and the spikes inflicted ever greater mutilation to his poor, abused cock. It was a masochist's dream. He was submitting himself to self-torture and enduring unbearable agonies on the orders of his mistress. He was suffering to please her. There was no greater sacrifice that he could make to prove his devotion to her. Mistress Madonna knew that these were the kind of thoughts that would be running through his mind, in fact he probably thought that he was in Heaven.

But it could not last and Mistress Madonna was not at all surprised when suddenly, with an anguished scream he threw his hands from his bleeding, wretched penis.

"I can't go on. It hurts like hell and I can't stand it any more. Please Mistress; you've got to let me stop."

She had actually been becoming quite concerned about the damage he was causing to his weapon and so was relieved that he had stopped of his own volition. She could not show it of course.

"Well, things are coming to a pretty pass, aren't they? You won't do as your mistress wishes when she's being kind and generous and wants to watch you wank. You like wanking, she knows that, so what's the matter? Are being disobedient just for the sake of it?"

"No Mistress. My cock hurts too much. Have mercy, please."

"Mercy? For a wretch like you? A insubordinate little oik who deserves a good spanking. Well, you're not going to get away with it, no matter what you might think."

She had him exactly where she wanted him now. Physically and mentally wrecked. And more was to come.

"Give me the gauntlets."

Julian tugged off the gloves and handed them to Mistress Madonna, who with a derisory snort threw them contemptuously into the armoire

"Now, arms up above your head."

"Oh no Mistress, not again. Please."

"Oh yes. Again. I told you that I wouldn't let you get away with it. Disobedience has to be punished."

"But I can't take any more."

"So now you're a wimp as well as everything else, are you?"

"No Mistress."

"Right. Do as I say and get those arms up."

Julian had no spirit left in him and very quickly Mistress Madonna had him strung up to the ceiling once more, a thin, whippy cane clasped in her hand.

"OK, let's get on with it!"

When the Policewoman and her male sidekick arrived at the hunting lodge, Julian was still chained in agony, receiving the thrashing of a lifetime. Mistress Madonna did not pause in her assault for a moment when the heavy knocking came upon the door, merely calling on whomever it was to come in.

"Ah, I thought it might you two. What can I do for you this time?"

But if *she* did not pause, the policewoman expressing false surprise, did.

"Mon Dieu Madame. You have not been beating him all through the night, have you?"

"No, he's had a nice long rest and now it's time for him to receive some more punishment. Naughty boys have to be taught to behave you know. Especially this one, *he* never learns."

"Madame, I'm impressed. You have stamina, of that there is no doubt, but him, he is made of tougher material than I would have thought from his pathetic exhibition last evening."

"Don't go flattering him. It'll go to his head and then I'll be forced to discipline him even more harshly. Anyway, like I said, what can I do for you this morning? And more to the point, when do I get to meet the Baroness?"

"That's why I'm here now. To deliver an invitation from The Baroness to a little gathering at the castle tonight. She's really looking forward to meeting you."

"In that case, perhaps I could wander up there and introduce myself to her this morning."

"Ah. That won't be possible I'm afraid. The Baroness is strictly a night person; she keeps to her own rooms during the daylight hours and she only comes alive when the sun goes down. But when it does, the castle comes alive with her and whatever guests and friends are present are guaranteed an extremely enjoyable night in her presence. There's always plenty of good food and wine but more often than not her guests are only interested in the entertainment she provides and quite often, the partying goes on until dawn. She usually retires herself before the sun comes up, sunlight's bad for the complexion you know; or it is at least if you have a delicate pale skin like hers. But everyone else is welcome to carry on until they drop, and believe me some of them do."

Mistress Madonna was intrigued.

"So exactly what kind of entertainment does she put on?"

"The Baroness doesn't exactly *put on* anything. She normally starts it off and the guests gradually take over and she lets them get on with it in their own way. Everybody always has a good time and I'm sure that you will too, there's always a good supply of willing flesh."

"Hang on a minute. What are we talking about here? Orgies? Is that it?"

"Well, that's putting it a bit crudely, but yes I suppose you could say that's what I mean. You'll love it, I know you will."

Mistress Madonna was not so sure. Being shagged by The Colonel was one thing but she most definitely was not about to participate in group sex with a bunch of garlic-breathed foreigners she had never met.

"I'm sorry, but I'm not letting all and sundry fuck me. If that's what I was invited here for, then she can forget it, I'm off back to London."

The policewoman hurried to re-assure her.

"No, no, you've got it all wrong. What we do is much more in your line. People do get fucked, I have to admit that, but only if they want to. Please accept the invitation and come to the castle tonight. You won't regret it, once you see for yourself you'll love every minute."

Despite her reservations, after thinking it over for a few moments Mistress Madonna agreed and told the policewoman to inform the Baroness that she would be only too pleased to attend her soireé.

"Good. Oh and by the way, bring your slave along as well."

The policewoman flashed an enigmatic smile and with the policeman trotting dutifully behind her, walked off along a path that led though the pine forest and down to the calm waters of the bay.

"A bientôt," Mistress Madonna murmured as the policewoman was enveloped by the deep shadows of the trees.

There was no doubt in her mind now, she certainly *would* be seeing the policewoman later. The sudden inclusion of Julian in the invitation had been most unexpected. If she had been intrigued before, now she was doubly so.

"So, it seems that you've sparked a little bit of interest somewhere."

Mistress Madonna's tone was disparaging as she turned back to Julian, but deep inside she was consumed by the need to have her questions answered. She had already pondered over the reason that she had been asked to come to this strange castle in Brittany, but now it seemed that Julian was also the centre of some attention.

Very strange.

And it was vital that he did not suddenly become filled with ideas of his own self–importance.

"Listen to me, you slug. Nothing's changed. We may be in exalted company but you're used to that in any case, so maybe you'll just get to be thrashed with a somewhat more aristocratic audience than you're used to. You never know, it could be that the Baroness wants to give it to you herself. Well, if that's what she wants she's welcome, I don't know what the attraction is but to me you're still the disgusting little shit you've always been."

Mistress Madonna put down the cane and stood thinking for a few moments.

"I'd like to know what those two are up to though. Something doesn't ring true here, two police agents spending all their time wandering around a derelict castle, it's very odd. As soon as I can dress myself in something suitable, I'm going to follow their tracks – and you're coming with me."

FIVE
THE TUMULUS

With her thighs stretched wide over his back and her moist, generously proportioned sex flaps sucking maddeningly at his flesh, Julian crawled on his hands and knees towards the edge of the pine forest. He was stark naked and not having been allowed the luxury of clothing, the loose silver-speckled granite chips dug into his arms and legs as he progressed painfully in her chosen direction. His only accessories were an iron collar around his neck and a small but exceptionally heavy iron canon ball attached by a chain to the ring that still constricted his mercilessly mutilated cock. The chain passed between his legs and dragged the rust-pitted ball along the murderously uneven ground several feet behind his lacerated buttocks.

Even though his wrists and ankles had been freed from their restraints, his penis had not similarly been spared suffering. Every ridge, grass clump or protruding tree root momentarily halted the ball's progress, tugging along the length of the chain to inflict mind-shattering shards of agony on a prick that had never learnt the lesson of pragmatism. If Julian's ivory shaft had adjusted to its current circumstance and slackened off, as would almost any other man's in the same situation, then his suffering would not have continued to be as ghastly as it was now proving to be. As it was, the weighted chain continually pulled back, released and then pulled back his cock again and again as if it were the heavily-muscled arm of a barman coaxing ale from a barrel in a faraway cellar.

On the other hand if what Mistress Madonna was wearing was really her idea of a suitable outfit in which to traverse the depths of a dense bramble-strewn forest, then she was losing her senses. But, of course she was not. Spectacularly erotic, she was looking her tempestuous best in an outfit of matt black leather. A micro skirt was hitched high over her crotch, with no knickers of course, revealing long silky thighs; every time she moved exposing a flash of her enticingly flattened and naked sex.

Although Jean-Paul Gaultier's biker's jackets had long been her favourite, she had recently become enamoured with the designs of Roberto Cavalli, whose showroom was to be found only a few minutes away from her Belgravia mews hideaway. Never really intended to adorn the figure of a genuine Hell's Angel, one of his creations, open and lavishly decorated, now fought to contain the mounds of her breasts; thimble-sized nipples pushing against its smooth inner lining. Loosely fitting folded down, thigh high, stiletto-heeled and wonderfully decorated boots, Cavalli again, and a studded black leather collar around her neck added to the sombrely threatening image she presented. Her hands were slipped into fingerless leather gloves and an expertly cut ruby glowed in her navel, her long fingernails and lips now painted in a matching shade of red. The rounded contours of her hips and haunches added the finishing touches to a perfectly-proportioned body and from the wide belt that was threaded through the top of her skirt hung a coiled, wicked-looking bullwhip.

The 'pièce de résistance' however was a pair of staggeringly-spiked medieval steel spurs that were buckled around the ankles of her boots. Spurs that no doubt had been used in ages past by a Crusader or a Knight of the Court to spur his lumbering carthorse of a charger forwards into action. Mistress Madonna knew full well that modern day images of fully-kitted knights on the backs of handsome thoroughbred stallions thundering into battle with the Moslem heretics was a complete travesty of the actual fact; the spines of those delicate interbred mounts would have fractured under the combined weight of the warrior and his armour. Julian however, by no means fell into the same class as the Arab steeds; although he was a weak pathetic wimp where she was concerned, in reality there was nothing of the delicate about him His body was magnificent, honed to perfection and possessing more than enough strength and stamina to carry her wherever her quest might lead.

But the spurs were an absolute joy and she was not one to let opportunities pass, Julian howling in agony as she jabbed both of them simultaneously into each of his thighs. Wallowing in the sound of his ringing squeals, once more she reflected on how strange it was that any and every instrument of torture she thought of using suddenly seemed to become available, the spurs appearing as if by magic in the now-fabled armoire.

Mistress Madonna's feet widened on either side of Julian's thighs and then clamped together, the spikes driving into his flesh with even more vigour.

"Come on, you useless slacking tosspot. Mistress Madonna hasn't got all year, get a move on!"

With Mistress Madonna swaying on his back, his cock a raging, tormented rod of mutilated throbbing gristle, Julian scuttled on at as fast a pace as he could manage without dislodging her. That would be fatal. The retribution would be catastrophic and he knew it.

Once into the forest, after only a short distance the track between the tall pines narrowed and became overgrown with giant ferns and criss-crossed with murderously thorned brambles that tore at Julian's naked form. What remained of the ancient path was covered with a thick layer of pine needles that at first blessedly cushioned his elbows and knees; but torment soon returned as fallen pine cones, viciously-thorned brambles and loosely scattered twigs stabbed deep into his flesh and flayed his dreadfully-burdened cock. The leather of Mistress Madonna's outfit protected her from the most damaging attacks of Mother Nature's army and although Julian made every possible effort to ensure that she suffered not a single scratch, it was inevitable that she would eventually suffer some sort of injury.

And she did.

Pushing through the brambles, one particularly recalcitrant branch sprang back, scouring a bloody line over one of her exposed thighs. The previously immaculate, unblemished thigh of an angel.

"You clodhopping imbecile! You did that on purpose, I know you did."

Mistress Madonna never minced words, especially when true or not, they were to her advantage.

Julian spluttered in agonised denial.

"Mistress, you know that I'd never do that. I'd rather cut my throat than hurt you."

"That's easy for you to say and I'll remember it. But I could say that I'll never kick you in the balls again and we both know that would be a load of shit. If I can lie, so can you."

And as if to attest to her statement, she leapt from his back and taking deliberate aim, drew back her leg and then throwing her foot forwards, landed a disabling, mind- numbing blow to the bloated bramble-scoured bollocks hanging between his thighs. A screaming, strangulated howl sent the forest's floor dwellers scurrying away through the undergrowth in search of safety. Seconds later as that same scream died on his lips, the monstrously pleasurable pain of its body-racking aftermath sent Julian catapulting at light speed towards Heaven.

Standing back, Mistress Madonna gave time for the writhing, wretched wreck before her to pull himself together. No matter how long it took, he would still be her slave, of that there was no question; but the whining, moaning and sobbing seemed as if they were set to go on forever. Enough was enough.

"Stop blubbering you retarded fart. Get up this instant, they must be miles in front by now. And from now on you can carry me piggy-back."

Staggering to his feet, Julian straightened up. Mistress Madonna knew that without any doubt he was totally unable to believe his luck as he grasped her thighs and hoisted her legs over his waist. This was the very first time that she had ever allowed him to actually touch her flesh and as his fingertips dug into the fabulous firm meat of her thighs, she imagined the spicy, tingling and electrifying currents of sexual energy that would now be surging through his being and ravaging his pulsing, wrecked cock. Pulling the two front panels of the jacket to either side to allow her magnificent tits to press against the back of his shoulders, she threw her arms around his chest, clasped her hands together and clung to him tightly. Yves St. Laurent had painted the lips that brushed his flushed neck and scented the breath that whispered in maddeningly erotic undertones into his ears. As always, even in difficult circumstances, there was a method to her actions.

Her rigid bullet nipples dug deep into his well-exercised flesh and even though he was now standing virtually upright, with her legs clamped vice-like around his waist, her succulent twat still sucked clamlike onto his lower back.

"This is what you've always wanted, isn't it? Mistress Madonna's flesh pressing on your flesh. They feel wonderful, don't they? my tits. Big and hot . . . and my nipples, they're on fire, like red-hot pokers. And you can feel them as well, squashing against your back, rubbing up and down and throbbing and tingling and getting bigger and harder all the time, can't you?

"Ooh Julian, I can't stand it; my nipples are driving me crazy and because they're getting me all worked up, they're making my cunt dribble. It's all wet and gooey and sticking to your back. My clit's poking out and love juice is running down my thighs. You never thought you'd ever have Mistress Madonna's cunt juice flowing all over your miserable body, did you? But it is . . and the scent . . it's heaven, all musky and steamy, just like my twat. You *can* smell it, can't you?"

Whether he had deluded himself into believing that he could detect the purely imaginary vaginal lubricator or not was purely academic. It was all too much for Julian and just as Mistress Madonna had expected, in an obscenely erotic reaction her pitifully joyous slave was propelled into juddering orgasm. Stumbling and fighting valiantly to keep his feet, Julian was racked by tremor after tremor as his cock spurted gushers of hot spunk; spraying the ferns, the brambles, the pine cones and the innocent but multitudinous bugs, spiders and slugs that crawled beneath the densely-carpeted forest floor.

Mistress Madonna had no interest in the creepy-crawlies. The spunk was a different matter. Not only had he coated arachnids and polypodiaceae with his beastly bollock juice, but great lumpy globules of the sickening stuff stuck to her boots. Her mission accomplished, it was back to business; with a vengeance.

"You filthy, slimy slug. Look what you've done to Mistress Madonna's lovely new boots. Do you know how much they cost?"

It was a purely rhetorical question. She knew that he did; as usual it had been he who had settled the enormous account.

"Now look at them. They're ruined. And all because you can't control your horrid little boy's cock. Well, you're going to pay for what you've done, believe me and it's going to hurt; your pocket as well as your cock because when we get back to England you're going to buy me some more. Not just boots but everything Roberto Cavalli's got in his showroom that appeals to me. And almost everything in there does.

"And then we'll go round the corner to Agent Provocateur and you can set me up with a whole new collection of lovely, sexy underwear. We'll start with see-through camisoles, all silky and smooth; you know, the ones that let my nipples stick right through and get you all excited. And then we'll buy half a dozen basques; basques that show my tits and are nice and short so that you can see my curly twat hairs. And just in case I should ever want to wear any, lots of matching French knickers, with wide legs and loose gussets so a big prick can get inside them without me having to take them off. And tight waspies. And embroidered suspender belts. And lace-topped stockings. . . and . ."

She did not need to go any further. As her tongue reeled off the shopping list of seductive garments from one of fashion's most erotically creative designers, his cock reared like a startled stallion, unbelievably and agonisingly dragging the iron ball forwards and once more showered the flora and fauna with thick sticky white effluvium.

"You filthy pervert. Put me down this instant!"

Very reluctantly, Julian lowered her to the ground, Mistress Madonna shaking herself free of his grip and making an exaggerated show of avoiding the thick spunk clinging to the ferns and brambles.

"You've been a bad boy. A very bad boy and Mistress Madonna can't let it go. What do you think she should do about it?"

No reply.

Only silence. She waited but no words were forthcoming. The interior of the forest was silent, shadowy and somewhat forbidding in any event; the canopy of branches high overhead permitting only a smattering of light to permeate through to the ground below; but now the hushed stillness began to trouble her. No birds sang, there was no breeze to rustle the ferns; of the buzzing of bees, there was none. The only discernible sound of nature was the rasping chirping of crickets; and suddenly it stopped.

The silence was complete, overpoweringly oppressive; the gloom seemed to intensify and she felt a strange foreboding, as if the trees were crowding in on her. Julian's own silence somehow added to the eerie, menacing atmosphere that enveloped her and although it was not even chilly, she shivered and crossed her arms tightly across her breasts. Mistress Madonna was not of a nervous disposition, nothing frightened her in the normal scheme of things, but now she could not deny that she was becoming increasingly unsettled. Julian had to be disciplined, but not there, not now; she had to get out of the forest.

To her comfort, some distance ahead the trees appeared to thin out and rays of golden sunshine pierced the timber barrier. Of course none of her unease could be communicated to her slave, so steeling herself into her most formidable persona, she rounded on him.

"Right! If you want to play dumb, it's up to you. You're still going to get everything you deserve, but you'll get it where I can see properly. Now, get going!"

A full-blooded kick to his arse got Julian started on his way and suffering hideous scratches to his naked flesh, he pushed his way through the thorny barrier in the direction that his mistress had indicated. Following close in his wake, Mistress Madonna sighed inwardly in relief as they stumbled from the edge of the forest into what was obviously an ancient man-made clearing; in the centre of which was an impressive tumulus. A well-worn path led between the two giant standing stones guarding the granite-pillared entrance of the huge fern-covered prehistoric mound and although she could see nothing of its dark interior, she was certain that rough stone steps led deep down into its dank underground chambers.

Mistress Madonna was fascinated by the thousands of megaliths and dolmens crowding Brittany and was sorely tempted to investigate this one, having to give herself a serious reminder that she was there for business not pleasure. Looking around for inspiration, she found it almost immediately. The mound was surrounded by a circle of smaller standing stones, some connected together across their tops by lintels, making it look somewhat like a small version of Stonehenge. It would do very nicely indeed.

"Pick that up."

She pointed to the cannonball.

Julian shuffled backwards over the iron chain that hung between his legs and using both hands lifted the heavy ball from the ground.

"Now, over there."

He was too slow, his reward being a punishing backhander to the balls; his resulting dance of agony looking quite comical as he struggled to hang on to the ball as he hopped from foot to foot, trying to quell the pain.

"I'm fed up with you. I can't be doing with a slave who doesn't give a toss for his mistress."

"But Mistress, I do. You know I do. I worship you."

"Then why do you take so long to do what I tell you? I've seen a slug move faster; but then again, you are a slug yourself, aren't you?"

"Yes."

In a very quiet voice.

"Speak up. What did you say? I can't hear you."

"I'm a slug Mistress."

"That's better. You're a slimy, filthy, squashy turd of a leech aren't you?"

"Yes Mistress."

"Come on, say it then. I want to hear you say it loud and clear."

Julian's lips quivered and he seemed as though he were about to cry.

"I'm a slimy, filthy, squashy turd of a leech, Mistress."

"Alright. Now we've got that sorted out, let's get on with it."

With her palm firmly planted into his back, she guided him to the stone circle, finally positioning him before two of the lintel-connected megaliths. That they did not match the size of the two giants guarding the entrance to the monument was a fact that could not be doubted, but even so they stood nine or ten feet high.

"Right. Throw the cannonball over that lintel."

"No, Mistress. Please don't make me do that. What'll happen to my cock?"

"It'll probably get torn from your body. But that's of no consequence, and what do I care anyway? Just do it."

She had deliberately presented Julian with a real dilemma. He had two choices. If he obeyed and thrust the ball over the lintel, when the chain reached the limit of its length, his already mutilated manhood would halt its fall; and in doing so would be tugged with undeniable force by the chain. Exactly what damage that would cause she did not know, but one thing was certain: it would be horrendously painful. He could possibly even be rendered cockless. On the other hand, he could refuse to do as she ordered and suffer the consequences. Either choice could prove to be equally painful. That he understood that fact fully, she was in no doubt.

The wait seemed interminable but eventually he appeared to have reached a decision. At Eton and later Oxford, he had excelled in field sports; Mistress Madonna knew that, because he had proudly showed her his cups and trophies on countless occasions, so it came as no surprise when he transferred the ball from two hands into the backwardly-bent upturned palm of his left hand. Then, just as if he were 'putting the shot' he brought back his arm, concentrated intently for a few moments and in a swift movement, suddenly pushed his palm skywards. Propelled with inordinate strength, the ball cleared the lintel before falling earthwards.

The resulting ear-shattering scream of agony even startled Mistress Madonna. No matter what punishment she inflicted on him, his wails had never bothered her before; even though back in the hunting lodge they had been loud enough to summon the police persons. But now they were threatening grave damage to her ears and seriously concerned she rushed around to inspect his ravaged cock. It was with a great exhalation of relief that she greeted the sight of his mangled but still intact manhood. The cannonball had come to a halt a couple of feet above the earth, the iron chain stretched taut over the lintel. With both arms raised high above his head and his hands clasped around the chain, with absolutely no chance of succeeding, Julian was fighting to haul the ball upwards to create some slack in the chain and so ease the strain on his cock. The chain steadfastly refused to slide back over the lintel and remained cruelly wrenching his prick upwards and tugging him up on to his tiptoes. But although his wails, screams and curses rang through the clearing, thankfully he still remained a whole person.

Her dark eyes pierced his.

"Oh, come on. That didn't really hurt; you're just playing to the gallery. But I'm the only gallery you've got and I'm not impressed. If I were you, I'd think about that before you land yourself in even more trouble."

The caterwauling only seemed to increase in intensity, although Mistress Madonna was quite wrong in her assertion that she was the only audience to his histrionics. Up at the castle in the murky gloom of the chamber in which she passed the daylight hours; the Baroness stood peering into the depths of her magic mirror, avidly drinking in the scene in the clearing as it unfolded before her eagle eyes.

Mistress Madonna paused momentarily, overcome with a strange feeling that someone or something was secretly observing her. She turned a full circle, searching the forest for any sign of spying eyes; but there was none and only a few more moments passed before she shrugged off the notion, putting it down to the discomforting effect of her spookish surroundings.

She had work to do and time was wasting. She turned her full attention back to Julian.

"Alright, if that's the way it's going to be, see if I care. Don't you bother about me, you just hang around enjoying yourself like you always do. I'm sure I can find something to occupy my time while you play the fool."

Just like the floor of the forest, the tumulus was thickly covered in nettles and ferns. Strolling over, with her palms protected by the leather gloves, Mistress Madonna pulled a couple of bunches of well-leafed nettles from its earthen covering. Wafting them slowly back and forth, staring purposefully at his genitals, she positioned herself in front of Julian until at last he opened his tightly screwed-up eyes for long enough to catch sight of the nettles. The wailing stopped abruptly. As abruptly as if his vocal cords had been severed by Madame Guillotine.

"Oh no. Mistress, you wouldn't."

"Oh but I would. And I am. Right now . . "

But she did not. The stinging torture could wait for a few minutes until she had him in a more accessible position. A much more suitable option had just presented itself. Why she had not noticed them before she did not know, but just above head height, fastened into the sides of the two upright stones by metal rivets, were iron wrist manacles.

Ideal.

Julian had by now relinquished his grasp on the chain and with his hands cupped around his bollocks was desperately attempting to shield them from the threatened onslaught.

"Get those hands off your cock this instant!"

"No. Shan't."

Mistress Madonna reached for the bullwhip at her hip.

"Would you care to reconsider that statement?"

He would. His hands dropped and laying the bunches of nettles down on the ground, Mistress Madonna clamped first one wrist and then the other into the restraints. His outstretched arms only just reached to the manacles so that when she was finished, the muscles of his shoulder and upper arms were clearly delineated, showing the intense strain she had put them under.

She stood back and inspected her handiwork. Not bad; it was a pity though that she could not shackle his feet off the ground and have him strung up in perfect X.

But she could!

There at the base of both stones were ankle cuffs, about a foot from the ground. Absolutely perfect. Julian was still perched on his tip toes, so pulling his legs apart, she lifted his left foot and clamped the ankle into one of the iron cuffs, leaving just the toes of his right foot scrabbling for contact with the ground. But not for long. The dancing foot was unceremoniously pulled over to the other iron cuff and clamped as solidly as the first had been, so that just as she wished, he was tautly suspended in mid air between the two stones; his tortured cock drawn out and lengthened to its limit by the unholy partnership of the chain and cannonball.

And what a cock!

Given the horrendous circumstances, Mistress Madonna fully expected that for once Julian's overly-active joystick would give up the struggle and detumesce into a slacker state. But Julian would be forever Julian and it was not an obligingly stretched thin, flaccid rod of gristle that was suffering the torment of Hades but a rampant, solid shaft of steel that still refused to surrender, no matter what mutilating persecution it was subjected to. At least he remained constant in his reaction to punishment; the rougher the treatment, the greater the agony, then the more intense his joy. The very obvious thrill and the incredible gratification that he derived from the most extremes of cock torture were almost beyond belief, sometimes even confounding Mistress Madonna hcrsclf.

He was a martyr to his cock. And she knew it. And for the time being at least, she was thoroughly sick of martyrs. Stooping, she picked up the nettles, one bunch in each hand and once again stood facing him.

"Take that smile off your face!"

The fact that Julian most definitely had no smile on his face was beside the point.

"You think this is funny, don't you?"

As a matter of fact, he did not.

"Just because Mistress Madonna's been so nice to you, you think I've gone soft. Well, I haven't and you've got five seconds to stop that sniggering."

As there was no sniggering to stop, five seconds later his suffering began anew.

Being ambidextrous has great advantages, which Mistress Madonna utilised to the full. Thrusting one bunch of nettles between his wide-stretched thighs, she brushed the leaves over his heavy, bulging ball-sac, at the same time wafting the other bunch up and down the length of his savaged shaft. His bollocks and cock reddened up and blistered at the first touch, his stricken squeals once again ringing satisfyingly in Mistress Madonna's ears.

Widening the scope of her assault, she turned her attention to the rest of his body. Using both hands simultaneously, she lightly floated the stinging leaves up over his stomach and chest and down the fronts and backs of his thighs. His buttocks, back, shoulder blades and arms came next until only the soles of his feet had escaped the blistering onslaught.

But not for long.

Crouching on bended knee, Mistress Madonna pushed the nettles under both of his feet. Julian convulsed, dementedly alternating hysterical shrieks of agony with screaming oaths and foul-mouthed abuse.

"My my, we are getting tetchy, aren't we? I'm getting tired of this, I thought you liked me to show you a good time. I'll just have to try harder, wont I?"

"No, no, no! Leave me alone. Fuck off!"

"If that's the way you feel, I will. Mistress Madonna's been really pissed off since we've been here. You're an ungrateful, selfish little prick and I don't need you or your dirty mouth. Goodbye!"

Turning on her heel, she stomped off towards the forest. Julian's change of attitude was as swift as she had expected.

"No! Mistress, don't go. I didn't mean it. You know I didn't. Come back, please."

She did not have far to return. As she actually had no intention of deserting her treasure chest; once she was several feet behind Julian, when she was certain that he could not turn his head far enough around to see her, she had stopped, awaiting the plea that she knew would come. Steely-eyed, she confronted him, idly wafting the nettles over his genitals and cock.

"Give me one good reason why I should stay."

"You're my moon and stars. The Queen of my heart. I worship at the altar of your feet. I . . . ."

"Oh, for Christ's sake, spare me the crap; it just sounds silly. You've been reading those bloody stupid romantic advice columns again, haven't you? Well, it's done you no good; I don't care how flowery you get, it means nothing to me."

He changed tack.

"I'll buy you a new car. A Porsche."

"I've got two already."

"A Ferrari then."

"Alright, that's a start. What else?"

"I'll double your money."

"Oh, you'll do that anyway if I decide to stay. Carry on."

"That house you live in, in Belgravia; I'll buy it for you."

"It's mine anyway. Think of something else."

Seconds ticked by.

"I can't. You've got everything. Tell me what you want."

Mistress Madonna made a pretence of giving the matter some thought, although she had actually been waiting for a situation like this to present itself. Even knowing Julian's utter dependence on her, it was a big risk to take but she was fully prepared to chance it.

"I suppose I wouldn't mind another house. You didn't know that I've got three, did you? The other two are investments, in Chelsea, but compared to yours they're all small. A house like yours, the country house, would be wonderful."

"You can have one. As soon as we get back, I'll find one."

"That's not quite what I meant. When I said I'd like a house like yours, I meant exactly like yours. If you promise to sign your house over to me, then I'll stay."

Julian's country house was not just a house, it was practically an estate; a huge, rambling building with any number of outhouses and acres of rolling lawns. Mistress Madonna had purchased the SW1 properties with the proceeds of her liaisons with Julian and several other vastly rich clients, each one of whom mistakenly believed that he was her one and only slave and knew nothing of the others' existence. Rapidly escalating house prices had elevated the value of each of those properties to upwards of two million pounds, but Julian's country house was worth several times their combined value; so the seconds that passed as he hesitated over his reply were the longest that she had ever experienced.

"Alright, I'll do it. It's yours. Now, promise you won't leave me. Ever!"

Mistress Madonna's exultation was such that her self-control was tested to the limit as she fought to reply in cool, severe tones.

"I don't know about for ever, but I'll stay for now."

Inwardly she marvelled at how, given his horrendously painful circumstances, Julian had managed to carry on a conversation at all; even if his words had been somewhat strangled and blurted out with great effort. It all went to confirm that he was unique, a definite 'one off'. A true slave with absolutely no bounds to his submissive obeisance. And she knew that however much he might come to rue his foolhardy acquiescence to her demands that he would never renege on his promise to her. In the cutthroat world of business, he could lie and cheat with the best of them; but where she was concerned, his word was his bond, just as it had been in the days when stockbrokers could still be relied on to be trustworthy: the house would be hers.

"Right. Back to business. But because of all the fuss you've caused and the time you've wasted, you've gone off the boil. Look at yourself, you're as white as that albino blues player you like; Johnnie Winter, is that his name? At least he's good-looking, not an ugly runt like you. There's nothing for it, I'll just have to start all over again."

In truth, Julian's flesh was already fully prepared for what she had in mind next. From head to toe, cock and bollocks included, his skin glowed a livid red; but he got a full repeat of the nettle treatment anyway until despite his renewed resolve to take his punishment in silence, once again his wails rivalled those of a police siren.

"I've had enough of this. If you can't keep your mouth shut, I'll shut it for you."

Although his screams were very satisfying, the racket was getting out of hand and as they could not be too far away, she was somewhat surprised that the two agents de police had not turned back to investigate. And that was something that she did not want. The solution was simple, he had to be gagged and the scarf she had stuffed into one of the pockets of her jacket, if not ideal, would at least do the job.

However, digging into the pocket, her fingers encountered not the smooth feel of a silk scarf but something round, rough-surfaced and hard as iron. In fact it *was* iron. Pulling it out, it proved to be one of the leather-strapped ball gags she had discovered in the armoire; she must have absent-mindedly slipped it into the pocket, ready for use if it were needed. Congratulating herself on the fact that she was so well-ordered that without consciously thinking about it, she had equipped herself with what was now proving to be a vital disciplinary item, she silenced his screams by stuffing the iron ball between his teeth and buckling the straps tightly behind his head.

Now she was ready for the next stage. Before that however, just to give him something to think about, she took a hold high up on the chain and planting both feet on the cannonball, with her riding on it, set it swinging to and fro. It was only a few seconds before she jumped off, but with all her weight having been taken by his cock, he was absolutely demented; the iron gag, stifling as it was, failing to prevent the hideous shrieking escaping from his stretched jaws.

She unclipped the bullwhip from her hip, shaking it out to its full length.

"I'm glad you liked that . . . but you'll like this much better."

Standing well back, with a practised arm and a quick flick of the wrist, she delivered a well-aimed lash across his buttocks. The first of many; each one producing an audible 'crack' as the plaited leather snapped through the air before its tip bit into his muscular flesh. Expert tuition from an acknowledged master in the art of wielding a bullwhip had equipped her with an enviable skill; in the hands of an inexperienced flogger such a whip could cause untold and very bloody damage, but judging every lash to perfection, Mistress Madonna ensured that every one struck its intended target with most of its force expended; so leaving a gratifying welt but never actually cutting the flesh.

She did not count the lashes as they were delivered, but when Julian was striped to her satisfaction, from his shoulder blades down to the backs of his thighs; she supposed that he had taken somewhere around fifty. Fifty lashes, fifty perfectly aligned stripes and no blood. A very pleasing outcome, it was just a pity that he could not see the results for himself, he would have liked that. She could practically read his mind and knew full well that at that moment he was most probably wishing that he possessed some means of visually inspecting himself. Added to the pain he was experiencing, a vision of his welted, abused body would enormously heighten his appreciation of his well-deserved and admirably delivered punishment.

Deciding that he had had enough for the time being, she let the whip fall to the ground and pulled off the leather jacket; freeing her magnificent breasts. Breasts sheened with perspiration, the result of the physical effort of delivering Julian's whipping. Her nipples stood proud in the midst of their surrounding circles of nut-brown areola, commanding the anguished slave's attention as if by royal decree. She cupped her breasts with her palms, squeezing and massaging them, cooing with pleasure as she did so.

"This is all your fault. All this whipping, it's making Mistress Madonna feel all tingly inside again."

She dropped her hands.

"My nipples, look at them. They're all stiff and excited. They're like pokers. I need to feel a wet mouth around them, licking and tonguing. I'm so desperate; I'll even let you suck them if you want."

She looked up at Julian's tightly-restrained form. Incapable of any movement, all he could do was watch with angst-ridden eyes. She gave it a few seconds. She was once again making Julian an offer that he patently was unable to take advantage of and as always it was guaranteed to drive him into a fit of apoplexy.

Her hands returned to her breasts, this time rolling both nipples between her thumbs and forefingers.

"Are you sure *you* don't want to do this? I can keep on doing it for myself but it would be so much better if it were you."

Julian's eyes rolled into the back of his head as he was consumed with maddening frustration.

"And I don't just want you to suck my tits, I want you to fuck me. I'll go mad if I don't get a great big prick stuck up me soon."

Hitching her skirt up over her hips, she widened her legs and slid two of her fingers down the slit of her vulva, then dipped them into her vagina before holding them up before Julian's face.

"Look! They're all wet. Covered in love juice. My cunt's like a river, flowing with lovely musky juice. Here, smell them."

Julian's wretched countenance as she passed her fingers under his nose was pitiful to behold.

"These fingers could be your cock. I can't think why you don't get down here and fuck me silly. It's what you've always wanted. Still, if you'd rather fool around up there, that's up to you. You've had your chance, I'm not waiting any longer; I'll just fuck myself."

And that is exactly what she did.

Using two fingers of one hand, with her thighs wide apart, she widened her sex flaps and reversing her grip on the bullwhip, using the other hand she pushed the haft an inch or so into her love tunnel.

"MMmmm. It feels wonderful. And it could have been you. I think you're turning gay; why else would a man keep turning down a good fuck?"

Snorts of fury and muffled, despairing groans were all that Julian was capable of in response.

Using the two fingers, she massaged her clitoris into full erection and worked on it with increasing intent as the haft of the whip plunged deeper into her love tunnel. Slowly at first and then faster and faster, the leather staff bludgeoned up and down, accompanied by gasps of arousal until in a frenzy of flying fingers, she brought herself off in a shuddering, highly vocal orgasm.

Julian shuddered too. Or at least the only part of his anatomy capable of a shudder did so. Not only did it shudder and jerk but his unbelievable prick siphoned a fountain of hot spunk from the undrainable reservoir in his bollocks, powered it up through his urethra and shot the sticky mess a foot or more into the air.

Making sure that her outwardly miserable but inwardly elated slave was watching her every move, leaving the whip stuck immobile into her hole, Mistress Madonna carried on slowly and appreciatively massaging her clitoris, savouring every last tingle and twitch of her satiated vagina; until with a plaintive sigh, as if she were reluctant to release it, she slowly pulled the whip from her still-grasping sex.

Mistress Madonna felt more than pleased with herself. Wasted and wounded as he was, Julian had received full value for his money. There was just one thing still bothering her. Julian's appreciation of her efforts would be fully complete if he were to have some tangible memento of his ordeal to look back on; photographs of him hanging suspended between the stones for instance, with close-ups of his mangled, clamped cock and whip-striped body.

There was no chance of that however, and as they really had to get on and try to catch up with the police persons, she tugged her skirt back down over her hairy bush, picked up her jacket and slipped her arms into it. This time she decided to zip it up; Julian had had his treat, so for the time being it was not necessary to keep her breasts on constant view and she was not going to expose them to the possibility of being again attacked by brambles when they pressed on into the forest. As the silk-lined leather closed over her firm mounds, something hard pressed into her breast meat.

Instantly it hit her. Of course that was the answer; her mobile phone. No larger than a cigarette packet, it was one of the newer models and besides its obvious use it also possessed the capability to take pictures and transmit them to any device equipped to receive electronic transmissions; such as Julian's home computer. She had only purchased the phone a few days earlier and although she had tested it to familiarise herself with its workings, she had not actually used the image transmission feature, which was why she had not thought of it immediately. Well, now she would and Julian could have all the memories he wanted; visual images that he could print out or view in perfect detail on his computer screen anytime he wanted.

Doing a very credible David Bailey; from every angle, sometimes crouching, sometimes standing, she recorded the evidence of his beating by loading a string of images into the phone's digital memory and then sent them to his computer. That done, thinking the matter over, she decided to give him an extra-special treat; after all, when they got back to England he was going to give *her* an extra-special treat: his house! Once more easing her skirt back up over her hips, she opened her legs and widening her wavy sex lips to show the open hole of her vagina, took a close shot of her minge; an unexpected bonus that he would no doubt wank over time and again in the future.

With her clothing back in order and the phone safely stashed back into her pocket, Mistress Madonna set about freeing Julian. Firstly his feet and then his wrists were unclamped; Julian immediately falling to his knees, cupping the cannonball in his hands and raising it higher, attempting to ease the intolerable strain on his cock.

"Drop that this instant!"

In a conditioned response, without thought of refusal, he obeyed the order. The iron ball still stuffing his mouth muffled the hideous shriek that ripped up from the very depths of his being; tears streaming from his eyes as the ball dropped and his wretched cock transmitted searing agony to his every nerve end. As he sobbed and shook, Mistress Madonna ran his current situation through her mind. If they were going to stand any chance of catching up with their quarry, they would have to move as quickly as possible. With the iron ball still dragging between his legs, their progress would continue to be slow; so it had to come off. But he would have to release the cock clamp himself; she was not about to soil her fingers on him, not even if she had the surgical gloves that she wore when she had originally tightened it under his bell end.

Removing the clamp proved somewhat of a struggle, but eventually Julian eased it over his bell end and with a great, but muffled sigh of relief, allowed the iron ball to drop to the ground. Giving him no time to recover or rub the use back into his numbed wrists and ankles, nor even to comfort his wretched cock, she ordered him to move out.

"That stays where it is."

She indicated the iron ball lying on the ground.

"And so does that for the time being."

This time it was the iron ball stuffing his mouth.

"We've got to get a move on if we're going to catch up with those police persons and your piffling little dick's too puny to drag the cannonball at any more than a snail's pace. And the gag's staying because I don't want you giving the game away if we get near them and you decide that want to have a little tantrum."

Re-coiling the bullwhip, she clipped it back onto her belt and with Julian stumbling in her wake, still cradling his diabolically mashed manhood, set off at a brisk pace, circling the tumulus and heading for the far edge of the clearing. The path they took back into the forest appeared to be far more well-used than the one that had led them from the hunting lodge to the tumulus and although brambles and ferns still flourished in great abundance on either side of it, the track itself was relatively clear of obstacles to their progress. After a couple of hundred yards the path took a steep descent, the trees thinning out to reveal low, ancient lichen-covered stone walls and beyond them, the first glimpse of the bay.

The sun was bright and high in the sky, the tide was on the ebb and the shallow water alive; ripples, swirls and small whirlpools of silver dappling the cobalt blue of its surface as it flowed out towards the sea; the reflected images of tall pines for a moment falsely giving Mistress Madonna the impression that the water was as deep as the trees were high. A sardine trawler was keeled over in the middle of the bay, stuck there until the sea once more returned to re-float it at high tide; unidentifiable figures jumping from its deck into the water. The figures lined up and began wading through the water towards the shingly patch of beach that lay at the end of the path. A series of distinctly audible and instantly recognisable 'cracks' rang through the air; someone else apart from Mistress Madonna had obviously found a use for a bullwhip.

As the party neared the shore the figures became recognisable as a group of young women; accompanied, or rather being shepherded by what at first glance she took to be three olive-skinned men, one of whom every now and then lashed at them with what Mistress Madonna had correctly identified as a whip similar to the one she was carrying on her hip. Suddenly the two agents de police came into view, drawing their batons as they hurried across the strip of beach towards the incoming straggle of girls.

"Well, well. What do you make of this Julian? . . . Oh, you can't answer, can you? Never mind, I wouldn't have been interested in any case."

Mistress Madonna had forgotten herself, and the ball gag, for a moment. In normal circumstances she would never have sought Julian's opinion about anything, it was just that the situation intrigued her. And that intrigue heightened considerably, when, as the girls reached the beach, she realised that their guards, whom she had initially taken to be men were actually women. As the captives were lined up in single file, it was with a start that she saw that they were all linked together by chains fixed to collars they wore around their necks. The girls were all dressed in simple east European peasant clothing and counting under her breath, Mistress Madonna made them ten in number. Then, even more fascinatingly, with the three women standing guard, the policewoman and her partner began securing the girls' hands behind their backs with handcuffs that she pulled from a satchel hanging from her shoulder.

When all the girls had been cuffed, the woman with the whip exchanged a few unheard words with her two accomplices, who duly waded back into the water and headed for the boat. Urging the girls into motion with stinging lashes of her whip, with her bringing up the rear and now guarded by the two agents de police, the coffle shuffled across the sand towards the path.

"Quick Julian, into the forest. We don't want them to see us."

Clambering over a pile of tumbled stone blocks, Mistress Madonna and her slave crouched behind what remained of an ancient wall.

"Keep down and don't make a sound."

She had no idea what was going on. If it were not for the presence of the police officers she would have suspected that it was something decidedly untoward, probably criminal; slave trafficking or something of that nature. But with the law on hand that could not be the case. So who were these girls? The most likely explanation seemed to be that they were illegal immigrants trying to slip into France by a back route and that they had been caught and were now headed for jail. Whatever it was, she determined to get to the bottom of it.

Almost afraid to breathe lest she should be heard, Mistress Madonna waited in confused anticipation for the approach of the girls and their guards up the steeply sloping path. The suspense seemed to last an eternity although in reality it was only five minutes or so before they came into sight and then to Mistress Madonna's consternation, shuffled to a sniffling, miserable halt only yards from her hiding place. Immediately she recognised the whip wielder as the striking but somewhat daunting-looking gypsy girl that she had seen in the village bar a couple of days previously. Seemingly drawn to her like bees to honey, she had been in the midst of a bustle of gesticulating, fawning Gallic admirers; the focus of almost every man present, the exception being Julian. He had eyes for no one but Mistress Madonna.

Around thirty years old, she was strongly built for a woman and her dark, prematurely silver-streaked hair hung in waves down to her shoulders. Eyes that were black and penetrating searched the forest, causing Mistress Madonna to crouch even lower behind the wall; the fear of discovery generating a flurry of missed heartbeats. She looked every inch the classic Romany of fable, but there was something uncomfortably sinister about her and Mistress Madonna could not help but feel that her outwardly romantic appearance veiled a cruel, heartless personality; it was hard to believe that a woman such as she would have any legitimate dealings with the police.

Turning her attention from the forest to the path along which they had come, the gypsy woman appeared to be looking for someone, or some *thing*, and when it ambled into sight, Mistress Madonna could not have been more taken aback. The girl's voice rang out, commanding and impatient.

"Djali, there you are! Come here this instant."

Things were getting ever weirder by the second.

First a gypsy girl and now a goat name Djali. Before the policewoman even uttered the girl's name, Mistress Madonna knew without doubt what it would be. She cocked her head, half expecting the sound of tolling bells to come ringing into her ears and the sight of a shambling, red-headed one-eyed hunchback to fill her vision. However although in ancient elder days the interior of the dense forest had undoubtedly served as a cathedral for some now long abandoned religion, it was no Notre Dame and it was not the pealing of bells but the policewoman's voice that drifted over to Mistress Madonna's ears.

"All right Esmeralda, Donatien and myself will take it from here."

"If you say so. I'll get the men and bring up the other baggage."

The gypsy turned to leave but was halted by the policewoman.

"Yes you do that. But before I deliver *these* baggages, you're sure that they're all virgins?"

"Of course I'm sure. They're all still intact, I tested every single one of them myself. As I always do!"

"OK, OK. There's no need to get prickly. You know as well as I do that this is the final batch and the Baroness needs every one of them. She usually has a few in reserve, but this time there aren't any spare and these new ones will just make up the exact number she needs for the Ceremony. God help us if you're wrong."

"Well I'm not! You look after your business and I'll look after mine. I'll be up later to collect my reward. Make sure it's waiting for me."

"I will. And you can leave the whip with me. You can have it back later, but in the meantime it'll come in useful for keeping this lot in order. And watch your tongue; remember I'm not just a lackey like you, a few words in the Baroness' ear and you'll be back in chains where you belong."

Handing over the whip with a derogatory snort and the goat trotting behind her, the barefoot gypsy flounced back down the path. As she disappeared from view, Mistress Madonna's last thought before she lost sight of her completely was that tangling with her was definitely something that she would not relish.

Seemingly resigned to whatever fate awaited them, the string of miserable, downcast girls was urged into motion once again. With the occasional crack of the whip continuing to ring out, after giving them time to build up a fair lead, Mistress Madonna ordered Julian back out on to the path and stealthily followed in their wake. As Mistress Madonna and Julian neared the edge of the forest, she abandoned the path and keeping well out of sight, they both took cover behind a couple of the broader-trunked pines. The coffle was being marched across the clearing towards the entrance to the tumulus and with the encouragement of Anna's whip and Donatien's police baton was herded between the two giant standing stones; the girls finally disappearing down into its forbidding depths.

Mistress Madonna's already intense curiosity notched up several levels, she just had to know what was happening, finding the temptation to follow them below the earth almost impossible to resist. But resist it she did, very soon thanking her lucky stars that she had done so as the murmur of approaching voices presaged the arrival of Esmeralda, her two female compatriots and half a dozen unkempt, but somewhat picturesque, rough-looking men. With long black hair and heavy moustaches, their baggy trousers tucked into high boots, by the look of them, the men too were gypsies.

But if her curiosity and disbelief had been aroused before, now her amazement was elevated to feverish levels. Unbelievable as it was, between them, they were lugging three most unusual burdens through the forest: coffins! Except for Esmeralda that is. With the goat skipping and leaping beside her, she was striding impatiently ahead, trailed by the other two women and two of the men, who, one to each corner were struggling to carry an exceedingly ornate, brass-bedecked casket; while behind them two pairs of men toted on their shoulders two simple rough-hewn timber funerary crates. Esmeralda's exasperation obviously getting the better of her, she turned to deliver a sharp rebuke to the others.

"Put some effort into will you, time's running out. Those coffins have got to be down in the temple and everything readied before the sun starts to set. So, get a move on!"

Hurrying across the clearing and attempting carry out her bidding, one of the bearers stumbled; the coffin slipped from his shoulders and hit the ground with an almighty thump, its lid flying off and its contents spilling out. Mistress Madonna was in for another mighty surprise.

"Soil."

The word slipped from her lips unchecked. And luckily unheard.

"Earth. What on earth are they doing with coffins full of dirt?"

This time the words were whispered. Not to Julian, but to herself. Absolutely unable to believe what was happening before her eyes, she watched as the soil was scooped up, dropped back into the box and the lid fixed back down. Hoisting the rough crate back on to their shoulders, the two men joined the others and tracing the footsteps of the pitiable coffle were lost from view as they descended into the mysterious prehistoric mound.

Once again the strange feeling that distant eyes were studying her every movement swept over Mistress Madonna, causing her to look around nervously. Apart from that she had no idea how long the gypsies or the agents de police would remain inside the tumulus and with the fear of discovery now uppermost in her mind, she determined to get clear before they regurgitated themselves from what she imagined were foul under regions and spewed out from the stone entrance into the open space of the clearing. Signalling Julian to follow, this time keeping to the forest she crept stealthily around the perimeter of the clearing and set off back along the track to the hunting lodge. She had a lot of thinking to do.

And so did the Baroness.
Her eyes fixed to the mirror, she watched as Mistress Madonna led Julian to safety. She was not quite

so sure of her guest as she had been originally and that troubled her. Mistress Madonna was proving to be something of an enigma and the Baroness found herself unable to read her in any depth, which was a most unusual occurrence. Her actions certainly marked her out as a powerful and dominating woman and her darkly threatening appearance seemed to confirm that she was a fellow traveller, but were the marks on Julian's neck what Anna had taken them for? She had seen no evidence herself and if Mistress Madonna were a creature such as she, then she would fully have expected her to sense what was happening and to have stridden into the tumulus, dragging her slave with her to join the others. But she had not and as the Baroness now had more pressing matters to deal with, there was nothing she could do but wait until they met in person.

SIX
THE TEMPLE

Trailing behind her companions, Esmeralda trod the rough-hewn granite steps with much greater care than her sure-footed pet. Above her head the great roots of ancient trees threaded the earthen roof of the passageway with gnarled vein-like intricacy. Reeking with the decay of millennia, the steep tunnel descended in a straight line down into the bowels of the tumulus until the claustrophobic darkness of its confines suddenly opened up into a vast underground cavern. This was another world. Originally the underground temple of the ancient megalith builders, it shimmered with the diffused light of a thousand flaming torches and now housed the straw-strewn pens that held the Baroness' herd of sacrificial virgins.

Watched over by their eagle-eyed female guards, for a couple of hours in the evening the virgin slaves were usually allowed free reign to roam the temple but now that the time of the Ceremony was almost at hand, every one of them had been stripped naked, returned to their pens and chained to pitted iron hoops set into the rock walls; even the Baroness' two favourites. With the two agents de police close at hand, Esmeralda ladled out a jug of water and allowed the ten new arrivals to drink before they too were stripped and chained into the pens that awaited them.

Still toting their grisly cargos the gypsies faded into the pitch darkness of an unlit Hellish black chapel at the far end of the cavern. Although they ventured no further, beyond that chapel lay a further two chambers and a long underground passage that led up into the bowels of the castle. Returning empty handed shortly afterwards, obviously having deposited the coffins in their designated resting place, the men paused briefly and with much nudging and winking exchanged a few words with Esmeralda.

"The trawlermen are waiting for us so we've got to get back to the boat now, but don't fret, we'll be back tomorrow to collect our dues."

And those dues would not be only money. Esmeralda and her two companions would be fucking, sucking and drinking sperm until all six men felt that they had been fully compensated for their assistance in delivering the virgins. But that was a price that Esmeralda was only too delighted to pay because without their help she would have been in dire trouble with the Baroness.

"All right, you can have as much shagging, cock sucking and arse fucking as you want tomorrow for free, but then you go back to paying."

Smirking and telling each other exactly what they were going to do to Esmeralda and her companions, the men took their leave and headed for the surface. With a wry look on her face, Esmeralda watched them go before turning her attention to the two women.

"Is everything in order in the chapel?"

"Yes, the earth has been scattered and the Count's casket laid onto it just as you ordered."

"Good. It won't be long now; he's been asleep a long time."

Casting her eye around, she became aware that the virgins were becoming increasingly restless and muttering amongst themselves. It was hardly surprising that they had gathered that something important was to take place that night and their unexpected chaining seemed to confirm that it had something to do with them. Even though they were restrained, a vigilant eye had to be kept on them.

"You two, go and help Anna and Donatien keep those bitches quiet."

Esmeralda's use of 'bitches' included the boy virgins as well as the girls and whether they deserved it or not, the two women took great delight in landing slashing strokes of the cane to their unprotected bodies.

Unable to sense the tense atmosphere, Esmeralda's pet goat trotted up and down in front of the pens, stopping occasionally to 'sit up and beg', 'to play dead' or perform other tricks from his repertoire of stunts. She watched him with an affectionate eye; he was her only real friend and in return for his devotion demanded nothing from her but food and a little love. He was also a source of income too; the tricks that she had taught him bringing in a torrent of loose change when she had him perform at the street markets at Auray and Vannes and in front of the cathedral at Quimper.

With the coffle of weeping peasant girls, their guards, and the coffins now safely below ground, Esmeralda permitted herself a sigh of relief. The late procurement of the final ten virgins had been a great worry, cursing her with many sleepless nights, but with barely a second to spare she had delivered as ordered. She had no doubt however that she would be severely disciplined, cutting things this fine was something the Baroness would not let to go unpunished. Esmeralda was well rewarded to provide the Baroness with fresh virgins but although she was virtually free to behave as she wished, her mistress never allowed her to forget that she too was still a slave.

Her eyes flashed with hatred as she glanced over at Anna, the moment of their first encounter several years earlier indelibly burned into her brain. Although Esmeralda did not know what it was, Anna's current guise as a policewoman obviously served some purpose of the Baroness'; but back then, as the Baroness' trusted ally and responsible for keeping the virgin herd up to strength, Anna had persuaded Esmeralda's parents to sell her, ostensibly to be taken to the castle as a serving girl. Weird, lurid tales regarding the Baroness' family had been passed down through the centuries and knowing them, Esmeralda could not believe that her parents, desperately poor as they were, would dispose of her like a piece of worthless trash.

But sell her they had, although she still comforted herself with the thought that her mother and father did not understand what her final destiny was intended to be. In the event, it had proved her great good fortune that when she was subsequently delivered to the castle as part of a consignment of virgins specifically selected to take part in the Ceremony, that the Baroness had been on hand to inspect the new additions to her herd and had seen a strength in her that set her apart from the usual pitiful wretches that fell into her clutches. So she had been spared the fate that befell the others and had taken over Anna's role as the Baroness' procurer of slaves, returning to the old country every few months to either buy or kidnap virgins to ensure that her mistress' herd was kept to its full complement. Her two cohorts were in fact her older sisters, whom she had recruited on her first trip back to Carpathia to help in her slave-gathering, and who due to their well-fucked status had been ignored when she herself had been sold to Anna by their parents.

After the coming night's conclusion and the current herd of virgins was gone, she would immediately have to begin harvesting innocent girls and boys in readiness for the next Ceremony, which would take place in exactly one year. But the fruits of her entire previous year's scavenging lay before her, available and unable to resist any demand she might lay upon them. The temptation was irresistible, but first she had to get rid of Anna and Donatien.

"I know you've got a lot to do before the Ceremony and these frisky bitches seem to have calmed down now, so you can leave us to take care of things and get off if you want to."

Anna did want to.

There were sufficient guards to help keep the herd in check and by now the Baroness would be expecting her to be setting the scene for the night's events at the castle. She gave the virgin herd one last lookover, seemingly satisfied that they had indeed quietened somewhat.

"Alright, just make sure nothing goes wrong. I wouldn't like to be in your shoes if you fuck this up."

"I won't. And anyway I've got plenty of help. My sisters and the guards can take care of anything."

"Alright. You just better hope that I won't be seeing you later because that would mean only one thing for you: trouble!"

Esmeralda waited for the Anna and Donatien to take their leave and then turned her attention to her sisters, who to the accompaniment of agonised screams and howls, were still enthusiastically laying into the virgins.

"You two! Is that all your imaginations run to? You've got a hundred slaves laid out in front of you. Short of fucking them in the wrong hole, you can do anything you want. The Baroness doesn't give a toss so long as the girls remain intact and the boys don't actually get to fuck a cunt. That way they remain virgins in her eyes and it gives you lots of leeway. So, what are you waiting for? After tonight there'll be nothing left to play with in any case, so if you don't want to wait months for another chance, stop arseing about and get on with it."

Needing no further bidding, Esmeralda's two sisters delved into the herd and drew out six protesting unfortunates. Wicked, cutting slashes of the canes quelled any sign of rebellion, the slaves meekly accepting what was required of them. In a deliberately provocative motion one of the sisters stood upright with her legs spread wide, and under further threat of the cane, one of her selected slaves lost no time in tweaking and sucking her nipples while two others dropped to their knees, sticking their tongues and fingers up into her vagina and anus.

The other sister sank to the ground and laid herself out flat with her knees bent and legs wide open. Two girl slaves were ordered to suckle and fondle both breasts at the same time and judging by her facial grimaces and the way she sucked in air, she found their attention nothing less than exhilarating. A boy slave prostrated himself between her thighs and peeling her sex lips apart nuzzled her clitoris before burying his tongue deep into her dripping love tunnel. With three slaves working on each woman, there was not an inch of their bodies from which an arousing reaction could be wrung that escaped their attention. Writhing and squirming they both looked to be set on the road to climactic orgasms and Esmeralda felt she could safely leave them to their own devices.

As for herself, it was true that she was and would probably forever remain a slave. But she was in a favoured position in the distinct hierarchy that operated within the castle walls. The Baroness was of course her mistress and she or any member of her strange coterie could call upon her for any service they required, but in turn although ranking far below Anna, like her, Esmeralda held dominion over the slaves of the herd and could use them in any way she desired. Or at least, she thought that she could.

And at that moment her desire was to numb her anxiety by sating herself with sexual pleasure before the summons came. The summons to appear before the Baroness and explain herself. The summons that she knew would have only one outcome; punishment, excruciating pain and sexual abuse. And should the Baroness prove to be in no mood to accept her explanation, then something far worse would befall her, consigning her to a wretched half-existence with the pitiable zombies who inhabited the fetid horrors of the vile dungeons of doom in the catacombs deep below the castle. Zombies who had once been full-blooded, young and vibrant girls and boys until the Baroness had drained them of their vital life-sustaining forces.

Shuddering at the thought, Esmeralda took herself in rein. If that same monstrous and unthinkably satanic fate were to be the outcome of that summons, then before it was decreed she would gain some satisfaction for herself by using and abusing the Baroness' two favourites.

Slapping the coiled bullwhip against her thigh, she stalked the chained masses of the herd, now once more agitated and unsettled after seeing the unfeeling, brutal manner in which six of their number were being treated by Esmeralda's sister slave gatherers. Up and down, she strutted before the line of trembling, ululating virgins. The Baroness *was* her mistress, that was a fact, but she was not present; she was not there to enforce her authority and so if Esmeralda wished to use the Baroness' favourites for her own purposes, then so be it.

Rebelliousness flared up within her.

Fuck the Baroness!

If she was going to end up sharing eternity with a bunch of gormless brain-dead non-people, then she was going to shag them into eternity herself. The Baroness could go fuck herself and nothing she could do would make any difference. Striding the line of shackled penned-up virgins, she searched for the Baroness' two favoured slaves. And after a while, she found them.

Columbine and Arlecchino.

"Her, and him!"

The order was issued. Two of the guards detached themselves from the gaggle of female custodians and somewhat hesitantly, pulled the Baroness' favourites out from the herd. To them, Esmeralda's word was law; but these two particular slaves? That was another matter altogether. Usually the guards would have turned to Anna for guidance, but she was gone, and so the slaves found themselves thrust before the lustful, avenging philistine who had reaped them from their homeland in the first place.

The guards turned to one side. What was to be, was to be, and it was no concern of theirs. If Esmeralda wished to risk the wrath of the Baroness then the consequences were her lookout. First Arlecchino was delivered to her side, and then Columbine.

"Alright my pretty, come here."

She was addressing Arlecchino.

He sidled up to her, remaining motionless at her side.

"And you, over here on this side."

Columbine obeyed just as quickly as Arlecchino had done.

"You miserable pair of useless yokels have a task to perform. A special task. If you don't complete it to my satisfaction, I'll make you suffer; suffer more than you've ever suffered before. I know that you're the Baroness Elizabeth's little pets and that you're always down in that black chamber of hers, feeling her up, playing with her tits, licking her fanny and doing whatever else you do to her. Well, she's never tired of you so you must be doing something right. And now you're going to do it for me! And Arlecchino, we'll start with you."

Deathly pale and apprehensively rubbing his neck where the Baroness had sunk her fangs the previous evening, Arlecchino seemed to shrivel before her. Esmeralda savoured his nervousness; his fright was palpable, so intense that the feeling of absolute power over him generated a surge of excitement and anticipation deep within her. From the very moment of his arrival at the castle, he had been the Baroness' favourite boy slave and he had never been subjected to punishment or sexual attention from anyone else. He was absolutely terrified and that terror somehow thrilled and enlivened her. A sudden shard of electric tension speared her vagina and unbelievably she felt her sex lips peeling apart and her clitoris harden beneath its hood. She had disciplined countless slaves before but never with this outcome; and she had not even started. Now at last she understood that power and dominion over another was sexually arousing in itself and she would milk it to the full.

Grabbing both their arms, she pulled them over to an empty pen.

"Right, you girl. You're going to help me. Fetch me a pair of cuffs, a collar and those chains."

She pointed to the array of torturer's equipment hanging from the rough carved-out stone wall. Columbine was too slow in obeying. Her sluggishness was immediately rewarded with a series of very forceful and deliberate slaps to her breasts before Esmeralda pinched one of her nipples between a thumb and forefinger and squeezing tightly, pulled her close. Esmeralda's grip was vice-like, the agony showing on Columbine's bruised and reddened face.

"When I order you to do something, you jump to it like Jack Flash. Understand?"

"Yes."

Columbine's answer was hesitant and mumbled. The crushing pressure on her tormented nipple doubled, a frantic squeal ripping from her lips.

"When the Baroness asks you a question, is that how you answer?"

"N . .no."

Pushing her away, Esmeralda rained a flurry of clenched-fist punches to Columbine's heavy tits, almost knocking her to the ground. Begging for mercy, with tears streaming from her eyes, Columbine wrapped her arms around herself, seeking protection from any renewed attack. Esmeralda grabbed Columbine's wrists and pulling her arms down, clamped the fingers of both hands firmly into her breast meat, wrenching the supple flesh and digging her fingernails deep.

"Don't you ever learn? Try again; what do you call the Baroness?"

"Mistress."

"Yes, that's right. And that's what you'll call me. Understand?"

"Y . .yes."

This time, Esmeralda's attack was so vicious that Columbine did indeed stagger backwards and fall to the ground in a wailing heap.

"What!!"

"Yes mistress. I'm sorry mistress."

"You will be if you forget again. Now, get up and bring those chains and things over here."

Staggering to her feet, Columbine obeyed the order.

"Right, the cuffs first. And because I think there's something going on between you two, it will be all the better if *you* do it. Pull both arms behind his back and cuff his wrists. And make sure they're tight."

Whispering to Arlecchino that she was sorry, Columbine locked his hands behind him. Esmeralda tested their tightness, grudgingly affirming that it was to her satisfaction.

"Now, his ankles. Clamp them as tight as his wrists."

Columbine fitted an iron cuff around each of Arlecchino's ankles and ratcheted them tight.

"Good, now we're getting somewhere. Alright pretty boy, kneel down."

Arlecchino struggled to obey but with his feet clamped tightly together and his wrists cuffed behind his back, he had great difficulty in keeping his balance, almost falling over at one stage until finally he dropped very heavily onto his knees.

"This is taking too long, I'll do it myself."

Pushing Columbine to one side, Esmeralda took over and selecting a short length of iron chain looped it around the wrist cuffs, dropped it down and passed it under the ankle cuffs, pulling it as tight as she possibly could before locking it in position with a rust-pocked iron padlock. With his hands and feet bound together, Arlecchino's spine was arched backwards at an alarming angle; the pain must have been excruciating, exactly what Esmeralda intended.

Next, the studded iron collar was fastened around his neck, chain was clipped into the ring on its back and again locked tight to the ankle cuffs, forcing his head back and facing upwards. Esmeralda stood back and admired her handiwork.

"There, doesn't he look nice. But there's something missing."

She made a show of pondering for a moment.

"I know. A gag, that's what we need. There, that iron ball gag, fetch it!"

Columbine ran to the wall, she was not going to risk further punishment. Taking the gag from its hook, she handed it to Esmeralda.

"Open wide pretty boy, let's see how you look with this stuck in your measly cock-sucking mouth."

It was the work of moments to shove the ball between his teeth and fasten the straps behind his neck.

"That's it, we're all ready now; it's time to find out just how good you really are."

Lifting the skirt of her gypsy dress, she tucked the hem into its waistband, revealing long olive-skinned legs, smooth downy thighs and a prominent mons tightly enveloped by a miniscule thong. Slipping a finger between her legs, she hooked the gusset of the thong and tugged it down past her knees, letting it drop to the floor before she kicked it away.

Widening her thighs, she straddled Arlecchino's upturned head.

"Now, lick me out. Stick your tongue up my cunt and make me come like you do the Baroness."

With her vulva squashed against his nose and the ball gag stuffing his mouth, his tongue was trapped behind his lips. He could no more do as she ordered than he could wank his suddenly erect cock; despite the awfulness of his situation the juicy muskiness of Esmeralda's vagina had propelled his virgin weapon from inertia to full action stations in the blink of an eye.

Esmeralda gave it several seconds, then lifted herself from his face.

"I see. You don't want to get your teeth into my pubes and your nose stuck into my twat. I'm not good enough for you, is that it? You only want your stuck-up Baroness, don't you?"

Arlecchino's rock-hard cock told her that her accusation was far from the truth, but she pressed on. She was in absolute control of one of the Baroness' favourites and the feeling was delicious. A hesitant, stuttering protest from Columbine halted her momentarily.

"But . . But mistress, he's gagged; he can't do it."

In a rush of anger, Esmeralda leapt onto Columbine, and pushing her to the floor landed several hefty kicks to her stomach and breasts, feeling her toes dig into her flesh as she did so.

"Who asked for your opinion slut? Keep your mouth shut until I want you to use it."

Of course it was true. Gagged, bound and chained, there was no way whatsoever that he could obey her order, which was of course exactly as she had intended. She turned to Columbine, who was still squatting on the floor nursing her injuries.

"What punishment does the Baroness hand out if you disobey her?"

"We never do that. We always do as we're ordered. We've heard awful, horrible tales of slaves and servants being found dead in the woods and the cellars with their bodies all slashed and cut and drained of blood after they've upset her; we're frightened of her and we don't want that to happen to us so we do everything she says."

Esmeralda had heard those stories too and although she had never seen any bodies herself, she was fairly certain of what happened during the Ceremony and so she was well inclined to believe them.

"Alright. What does she do to you if you're too slow to do something she orders you to do."

"Sometimes she whips us, and sometimes she beats us with the cane."

"How many strokes?"

"Twenty five."

"Umm. . Twenty five eh? Well, for disobeying me, he's going to get fifty. From both of us! Get over there and fetch me that bundle of canes."

Columbine scrambled to her feet and scurrying over to the rear of the pen to collect the canes, handed them to Esmeralda. Pulling one cane after another from the bunch, Esmeralda bent them between her hands before slashing them through the air to test their pliability and resilience. Finally she settled on two canes that satisfied her, handing one to Columbine and keeping one for herself.

"You take his back and shoulders, and make sure you strike his flesh and not the chains. Now, go!"

Obviously fearful of damaging Arlecchino, Columbine drew back her arm and landed a strike to his shoulder that lacked any real measure of force. In a flash Esmeralda lashed out with her own cane and delivered a devastating, cutting slash across both of Columbine's heaving breasts, the white-edged groove turning almost instantly into an angry red tramline. Columbine's screams were of such intensity that momentarily a hush descended over the muttering herd. Esmeralda glared in their direction.

"That's right. Any of you upset me and you'll get the same treatment. Now you're quiet, keep it that way."

Then she turned to deal with Columbine.

"I said beat him, not stroke him gently like my beautiful Djali. He's not a pet goat, so hit him again and this time put some muscle into it."

Undoubtedly fearing further punishment, Columbine needed no second bidding and flailed into Arlecchino with all the force of which she was capable. The boy's flesh marked up just as her own had done, angry weals striping his back and shoulders.

"Stop, stop. That's better but this has got to be done right; slowly so that he can fully appreciate the pain. I'll beat him, then you beat him; one after another. I'll start and you count the strokes out loud so we know where we are."

Esmeralda landed the first devilish stroke, followed by Columbine; Arlecchino's firmly-muscled flesh rippling under the savagery of each blow. Slowly and very deliberately the beating progressed with Columbine counting the strokes as she had been ordered. Over his shoulders, up and down his back the crippling strokes fell until his torso was a bloody criss-crossed mess. And still only fifty of the one hundred strokes had been delivered.

"You're doing well, keep it up and maybe I won't punish you as severely."

If Esmeralda's words were intended as some kind of sop to lessen Columbine's fears, they certainly did not work. The poor girl still looked terrified.

"Now we'll go for his arse, his legs and his cock. I'll go first this time."

And so the beating carried on until Columbine counted the hundred. Arlecchino's backside, his thighs, the backs of his legs, the soles of his feet and his sorry mashed cock were all glowing crimson and rivers of tears flowed from his bloodshot eyes.

"He looked nice before but he looks even better now. That blood and those stripes and bruises suit him very well. You did well too, I'm sure the Baroness would be proud of you if she knew."

Esmeralda strutted around Arlecchino. In truth she was extremely pleased. He was cowed, ravaged and in a wretchedly sorry state and it pleased her to think that even the Baroness had probably never given him such a savage going over as this.

But before his ordeal was over, she had another treat in store for him. Calling Djali to her side, Esmeralda fondled his jaw before murmuring softly into one of his ears. The goat began to circle Arlecchino, pawing the ground before suddenly lowering his horns and charging full tilt at the wretched unfortunate virgin. Arlecchino keeled over like a stunned cow in an abattoir and lay on his side, groaning in agony. Djali remained, again pawing the ground with his bovidae eyes fixed firmly on Arlecchino. Stroking his beard, Esmeralda calmed him and ordered him away.

"That's a good boy. Now you go and play. Maman will call you again if she wants you."

The goat trotted off and once more began showing off to the Herd and its guards. That was Arlecchino dealt with, now for Columbine.

The beating of Arlecchino and her sense of total domination over him had ignited a raw sexual passion in Esmeralda that had to be quenched; and quickly. Her nipples throbbed, her sex was awash with juices and her whole being cried out for fulfilment. She would have loved to subject Columbine to the same sort of treatment that she had meted out to Arlecchino but her need was too urgent and so after treating her to half a dozen perfunctory slashes of the cane, Esmeralda dragged Columbine over to a rough bench on which was laid an array of evil-looking devices of torture. Sweeping the iron horrors to the floor, Esmeralda laid herself onto the bench with her backside close to one end and her legs bent at the knees.

"You know what I want. Get on with it . . . And make it good!"

Dropping to her knees, Columbine buried her head between Esmeralda's spread legs, licking the dribbles of musky love juice from the insides of her thighs. Esmeralda raised her torso from the bench, reached out and tugged viciously on a handful of Columbine's hair.

"Stop fooling around! I want an orgasm and I want it fast, so don't mess about, get your tongue in there."

Terrified, Columbine sank her nose between Esmeralda's sopping sex lips and drove her tongue into her flooded vagina. It took only seconds. Esmeralda was so hopped up that squeezing Columbine's head between her thighs, she thrashed and convulsed in a frantic orgasm the moment that the virgin's nose nuzzled up against her pulsing, erect clitoris.

Columbine's hot tongue stuck up her hole had transported Esmeralda to the realms of sexual bliss but gradually the surges of electrifying spasms died and she found herself still in need. The girl's tongue had been alright but what she really needed to satisfy her completely was a good stiff cock. A cock like Arlecchino's.

Using her bare feet she pushed Columbine backwards onto her haunches and sat up to address her.

"The pretty boy! Unchain him and bring him over here."

It was a fiddly business freeing Arlecchino and Esmeralda felt the impatience growing within her. It was taking too long, her fanny was twitching and she wanted his cock now, not next year.

"Hurry up you lazy bitch. If you don't get him over here damn quick, I'll make you sorry your mother didn't dispose of you the moment you were born."

The wait seemed interminable, although in reality it was only minutes before Arlecchino stood between her sprawled thighs, his cock standing proud. There was no preamble; Esmeralda was too desperate for that.

"Fuck me you pathetic bastard. Fuck me now!"

"But mistress, I can't. The Baroness forbids us to do that."

"Sod the Baroness, I'll sort her out. And don't tell me that you can't fuck me because your bloody cock says different. Look at it, it's like a flag pole."

And so it was. Esmeralda reached forward and feeling its hot throbbing girth beneath her fingers, she guided the slave's virgin cock to her soaking vagina. Lodging his bulging glans into the entrance to her hole, she wriggled forwards until his whole bell end was sunk inside her sex.

"Now, push!"

He penetrated three or four inches and his cock was definitely the real thing. But it was not enough.

"Put your hands under my arse and lift me up so you can get in right up to the hilt."

Arlecchino did it like a professional and she felt his pulsing cock stretch her hole to its limit and gasped aloud as his bell end smashed all the way in. He was good for a virgin and he had not come on the first stroke as usually happened with inexperienced youths.

"Now bend over and suck my tits. And don't stop shagging."

With his mouth fastened over one of her acorn-sized nipples he thrust in and out, ramming his pubis against her clitoris on every up stroke. Her passion arose anew, her vagina squirting lubricating juices over his cock, juices that leaked from her sex petals to soak his mass of curly black pubic hair. God, he was big. And he felt magnificent. He was not only good for a virgin, he was as good as any man she had ever fucked and the tingling, numbing spikes of approaching orgasm radiated from her sex to her nipples and then to her every nerve ending.

Faster and faster he plunged deep into her as she moaned in ecstasy until she felt his cock expand even further as thick rivers of spunk raced up his urethra as he came. But all was not lost; his throbbing, shuddering cock tipped her over the edge and into gypsy heaven as she joined him in a mutual thrashing orgasm.

As she calmed her senses, she savoured the feeling of her cunt awash with his sperm and the pheromone-laden scent of their musky combined juices that drifted up to her nostrils. And he had not slackened! Not one iota. His cock was still plugging her solid, and if it were possible, he was almost too big. And unlike older men he was ready to go again without a pause.

Alright, if he was, then so was she.

So Arlecchino fucked her again. And again. And every time without fail, she reached a screaming, debilitating climax that saw the eyes everyone in the temple glued on to their thrashing bodies.

Eventually, her skin glistening and her hair wringing with sweat, even she had had enough. Amazingly he had not, because when she ordered him to pull out, his love pistol still stood proudly aiming for the stars.

"Not bad for a beginner. It's a pity we'll never be able to do it again."

The real significance of her remark was lost on Arlecchino. Like all the other virgins he had no idea of what awaited him at the Ceremony. He had enjoyed the fucking, that much was patently obvious; but he was also obviously troubled.

"Mistress, I'm no longer a virgin. What's going to happen to me when the Baroness finds out?"

"She won't. This lot will keep their mouths shut if they know what's good for them. And I'm certainly not going to tell her. Are you?"

"No mistress."

"Well, there you are then. Both of you get back to your pens and nobody will be any the wiser.

But there was one fatal flaw in Esmeralda's reasoning: the mirror. She was completely unaware of its existence, but *it* was aware of her. Her fate was sealed.

And so was Julian's.

SEVEN
THE RETRIBUTION

The Baroness had watched with increasing fury as Esmeralda savaged her two favourite virgins. And now Arlecchino's cock was no longer innocent of the female sex organ, something that automatically rendered him useless as far as the Ceremony was concerned. Esmeralda was going to pay for her actions; and pay very dearly. But not just yet.

There was just about sufficient time for the Baroness to enjoy a final hour or two of pleasure with her two favourite slaves before they had to be readied for the Ceremony. And perhaps she could combine that pleasure with a suitably humiliating punishment for Esmeralda. Not the ultimate punishment that she was now guaranteed to suffer later that night, but something sufficient to be going on with. Something to cause her to rue the error of her ways.

A guard was summoned to escort Columbine and Arlecchino, suitably cleansed of course, to her presence. As they stood meekly before her in the almost total blackness of her chamber, she almost found herself feeling sorry for them but her icy heart soon regained control and she addressed them in tones of steel.

"I know what the slut Esmeralda did to you and although I don't exonerate you from blame, I don't hold you totally responsible either. I'm going to play some little games with her and I'm going to let you join in, to get your own back so to speak. Especially you Arlecchino because you are now ruined and cannot take part in the special ceremony that I have planned for tonight."

The boy slave looked thoroughly wretched and miserable, but the Baroness reflected that he did not know how lucky he was. If she decided to be merciful, he would still be around tomorrow, none of the others would. She stroked his neck and bared her pointed canines, but then thought better of it; she had drained enough of his blood the day before. If she did not take too much at a time and allowed him to keep replenishing his red cells then he would be good for many more feeding sessions. But if she went too far and actually drained his life force then he would be nothing but a zombie and there were already too many of that sort squeezed into the foul cesspits of the catacombs.

She looked deep into his melancholy, liquid eyes.

"Now, take the secret passage down from the castle to the temple and bring Esmeralda to me. And do it quickly or you'll suffer the consequences."

Arlecchino took off like a 303 round fired from a Lee Enfield rifle. When the Baroness threatened dire retribution it was advisable to leap into action, any slackness could indeed bring unwarranted and indescribably painful penalties. Penalties that he had suffered on countless occasions when she had ordered him to carry out tasks that were patently impossible, for the only reason that his failure to complete them gave her a valid reason for torture and sex. But then again, the Baroness did not really need any excuse; she just liked her slaves to believe that they thoroughly deserved their punishments.

The Baroness had a wealth of experience behind her; an inordinately lengthy period of time in which to hone her perversions to perfection. And hone them she had, slave after slave falling victim not only to her outrageous sexual practices, but also to her insatiable blood lust. A lust that was not entirely of her own making, for she too had in time long past been a victim; a victim of the guest the gypsies had delivered in a coffin to her temple that very afternoon. And in her turn, with the assistance of Anna Darvulia, her confidante and accomplice, she had made victims of countless others.

Arlecchino arrived back breathless, with a panting, unhappy Esmeralda close behind.

"Ah, Esmeralda, you finally grace us with your presence. So kind of you, I was beginning to think that you had decided not to return to us."

"Mistress, I wouldn't do that, it was just more difficult this time. So many young girls have gone missing that the authorities are keeping a strict eye out for me and my sisters. Someone has broken the code and informed on me and I'm sorry to have to say that we might not be able to keep you fully supplied from now on."

The Baroness' eyes narrowed and her voice steeled.

"That would indeed be a situation to avoid at all costs. And I am thinking here of the cost to you. You are still my slave to do with as I wish and if you fail in your duty to me, I might make an exception to the rule and include a non virgin in the Ceremony. And do not try to deny anything. When I spared you, you made a promise to remain virtuous as far as men were concerned and to render yourself sexually available only to me. But that promise you did not keep. Whether it is down to that hot gypsy blood of yours or the money they paid you I do not know, but I *do* know that you have been continually, heartily and massively fucked over the years since you arrived here.

"There is nothing that happens around here that I do not know about. I have powers that you would not believe; powers that allow me to see and hear anything that I want to. I've seen those common fishermen with their cocks stuck up your cunt and your arse. You are quite a creative girl are you not? Sometimes I wonder how you manage to do it. Accommodate so many men at once I mean. I've seen you with greasy trawlermen fucking you front and back while you've been sucking another's cock and wanking two others at the same time. I think that suitably qualifies you as a non virgin, don't you?"

Strong and haughty as Esmeralda was, she cowered before the Baroness, her fingers entwining in anguished supplication.

"Please mistress, forgive me, it will never happen again. I'll make sure that in future things will carry on as they always were. The virgins you need will always be delivered."

"Very well, I accept your explanation and your promise as to what will happen in the future. But that does not excuse you for your tardiness in delivering the final batch of virgins I require for use in my special ceremony. A ceremony that as I have impressed upon you before, must take place between midnight on St. George's eve and the crowing of the cock on St. George's day itself. You will never know what anguish your late arrival has caused me, an anguish that has aged me beyond my years. And for that you must be punished. I thank all the stars in heaven that you made it in time for the Ceremony tonight. And so should you, for had you failed me, my abandoned children would have torn you to shreds and devoured your bloody flesh as you screamed for mercy."

Esmeralda shuddered, the mention of the Baroness' children chilling her to the bone. The admonition over, her mistress' next words were not too unexpected.

"We must find a way for you to redeem yourself. Unlike you, it has been far too long since I've had a taste of the real thing; a good stiff penis filling my vagina and reaming me into orgasm. You have enjoyed more than your fair share of cock and it is time that the imbalance between your over-indulged vagina and my own sadly ignored sex was redressed. So in order to atone for your laxness, that is what I want now; a fat throbbing cock stuck deep inside me. I want you to fuck me."

"Yes mistress. If that's what you desire."

Looking around, Esmeralda's eyes sought to pierce the gloom, eventually alighting on what she was seeking; a selection of dildos that her mistress always kept handy for such situations. Swiftly she walked over to the studded chest upon which they lay and selected the one that usually seemed to provide the Baroness with the most satisfaction. Picking it up, she started to strap it between her crutch and around her waist, until bringing her plan into play, her mistress brought her to a brusque halt.

"What do you think you're doing?"

Esmeralda obviously knew that danger lay ahead and picked her words carefully.

"You ordered me to fuck you, so that's what I'm going to do; with this dildo, the thick, vibrating one you like best."

"Oh no you are not. Did I mention dildos?"

"No mistress."

"No, I did not. I said I wanted to be fucked by the real thing. I want a solid throbbing cock rasping my sex, not a rubber imitation. So, take that thing off and get on with it!"

The bewilderment showed plainly on Esmeralda's face as she dropped the dildo back onto the chest.

"But mistress, how can I?"

"What is wrong with your own cock?"

"B . . But mistress, I'm a woman; I don't have a cock."

"Are you refusing to obey my order?"

"No mistress, but what you ask is impossible."

"Nothing is impossible if I say it can be done, so I can only come to the conclusion that you are wilfully disobeying me. And you know what that means?"

The Baroness felt almost gleeful. There was no way out now for her slave gatherer.

"Come here!"

With obvious reluctance, Esmeralda returned to stand before her mistress. Reaching out, the Baroness slipped her hand down Esmeralda's very ample cleavage and gathering a fistful of material, ripped her dress from top to bottom and threw the tattered remnants onto the floor. Never having needed the assistance of a brassiere to support her impressively ripe breasts and with her thong abandoned and still lying on the floor of the temple, Esmeralda's almost classic fully-fleshed Roma body was revealed to the Baroness' lusting eyes in all its luscious glory.

"Now then girl, you do know do you not? that to live a life that is destined to end with no retribution from above, or for that matter from below, that a person must do unto others what she would wish them to do unto her."

"Yes mistress."

"And what I wish *you* to do unto me, is to fuck me. However, as you have refused to do so, then in order for me to follow that dictum, I have no choice but to fuck *you*.

"Over there, to the chest. Bend over, support yourself with your arms and stick your backside up in the air."

Resistance was useless. Not that the Baroness had for one moment thought that Esmeralda would dare to entertain such a rebellious idea. But if she had actually thought that she was going to get fucked and then be allowed to fuck off with all her indiscretions absolved, then she was in for a very rude awakening.

"Now, flatten your arms, stretch them out on either side and grip the edges of the chest."

The chest was of an enormous size and although trying to obey the order resulted in Esmeralda's breasts flattening themselves against the flesh-piercing metal spikes hammered into the lid of the chest, her fingertips failed to reach to either end. From somewhere in the gloom the Baroness produced a heavy mallet and a fistful of flat-headed nails. She handed the mallet to Arlecchino and the nails to Columbine.

Neither compassion nor mercy had ever found a place in her vocabulary and so she felt nothing as she took back a nail from Columbine and with great precision positioned it on the back of Esmeralda's hand between the first and second knuckles.

"Now Arlecchino, hammer it in!"

To the accompaniment of the slave's ear-shattering screams, with undisguised eagerness the boy fell to his task. The mallet fell with all the strength of which he was capable, the nail driving into the ancient oak of the chest, anchoring Esmeralda's hand firmly to its surface."

Elation washed over the Baroness as she leant over to lap up the blood seeping from Esmeralda's hand. Licking her lips, she straightened up.

"You take over now."

That command was issued to Columbine.

"There are four sites between the knuckles and thumb of each of her hands into which you can sink a nail. Hammer her to the chest so that she can't possibly pull away."

The Baroness sensed the elation in Arlecchino and the reticence in Columbine that her orders had elicited. She lowered her voice so that Esmeralda would not be able to hear her words. It was not time yet for her to know that her mistress had witnessed her plundering Arlecchino's virginity in the slave pens.

"Come now Columbine, surely you'd like some revenge for all she put you through? I know that Arlecchino would."

Columbine looked to Arlecchino for guidance. His whispered response was swift and uncompromising.

"Of course you would. That bitch deserves every punishment that our mistress decrees. Look at me; because of what she made me do, the Baroness is probably going to banish me from the herd. That means that I'll never see you again. Is that what you want?"

That was most obviously not what Columbine wanted. Positioning the nails one after another on the back of Esmeralda's hand, she held them in place and watched dispassionately as Arlecchino drove them home between the screaming slave's knuckles.

"It was a cane that she used on you Arlecchino, was it not? And Columbine, she made you beat him too?"

"She did mistress. It was awful, I didn't want to do it but I was frightened of her."

"Yes, I know. And each of you gave him fifty strokes?"

"Yes mistress."

"Well, I think a good starting point would be for each of us to give her a taste of the same medicine. There were two of you, but there are three of us so she will get what she gave to you and fifty more besides. And I don't see why we cannot use canes, as she did; that is unless either of you prefer to use something else."

It was revenge time.

"Please mistress, may I be allowed to whip her?"

That was Columbine.

"Of course. And in that case you take her shoulders and her back. And you Arlecchino?"

"If I can, I'd like to use the cat; the one with nine tails and leaded tips, that you sometimes use on us. I've suffered it enough times to know exactly how what agony it brings with every strike."

"That too, is acceptable. You concentrate on her rump. I will stick with the cane and take care of her arms and the backs of her legs; or anywhere else that you miss."

Columbine and Arlecchino both possessed a wealth of experience in receiving punishment but none whatsoever in dealing it out; so once she had ordered the beating to begin, the Baroness was more than impressed by the very capable, if over enthusiastic, manner in which they carried out her command.

Firstly the weighted and oiled tails of the boy's cat flailed across Esmeralda's tender buttocks, the blood diffusing immediately to darken her olive skin along the tracks left by the leather strips; a much denser blotch welling up where their metal tips bit savagely into her rump flesh. Then Columbine's whip slashed mercilessly over her back, quickly followed by the Baroness' cane welting the backs of her legs, both of them too leaving their own unique, pulsing evidence of the force with which they had been delivered. One after another, the sound of Esmeralda's screams, pleas and oaths ringing in their ears, the avenging trio laid into her; the Baroness often deliberately intensifying her agony by smacking the cane down to land on the same spot where a whip lash or cat tail had just made its mark.

Flushing as a heated tide of lecherous excitement welled up within her, the Baroness felt herself being consumed by the sadistic pleasure that the beating was generating within her. The purely psychologically induced rush of emotions that enveloped her when she inflicted pain and humiliation on a helpless victim often outweighed the physical satisfaction that usually followed and as an aphrodisiac, Esmeralda's howls of anguish were equal to the most potent of potions ever concocted by the true owner of the castle. As she felt the ever-increasing moistness of her sex begin to dampen the insides of her thighs, she eased her legs apart; the lubricating juices leaking from her tingling vagina dripping in globules from her tangled mass of pubic hair to rain downwards between her knees.

Eventually, with the tramlines, lash marks and cat trails merging into one massive, purple bruise, the Baroness felt the cane vibrate between her fingers as she delivered the final stroke of the cane to Esmeralda's mutilated rump. Every person has to serve somebody and now the shattered, evilly-abused gypsy was definitely going to serve her. She had refused to allow Esmeralda to use a dildo on her, but such an implement was a major part of her own plan to gain satisfaction for herself and to heap even more humiliation on her slave.

"Columbine, fetch my special dildo, the two-ended one."

The special dildo was double length with a distinct bobble at its mid point and cock-shaped at both ends; both cocks being well-sized, extra-long and as thick as a man's wrist. And being thicker than a man's wrist, they were fatter than his dick would be and in use filled a vagina, receptive or otherwise, to its utmost capacity. In this instance they were destined to fill the

Baroness' receptive love hole and Esmeralda's not so eager arsehole.

The dildo was certainly a tight fit but the Baroness' well-lubricated tunnel welcomed it eagerly, widening to accept its great girth, her vaginal muscles clamping it deep within her. But she was not about to allow her slave to gain any sexual satisfaction and so ignoring Esmeralda's vagina, she nuzzled the other end against her puckered anus and let it rest there for a moment or two, knowing that the thought of having to take such an enormous prick up her arse would be triggering a torment of dread in the helpless girl's guts.

Thrusting with all her might, the Baroness slammed the dildo up against Esmeralda's tightly closed anus. The doors remained firmly closed. This was one arse that was not going to open its portals without a fight.

"Come on my gypsy beauty. Let me in. This is only a rubber cock and you have had more than a smattering of the real thing."

That much was true. Esmeralda's anus had been stuffed by many a stiff dick, but never by one of such girth. Pulling the girl's arse cheeks apart and widening her anus in the process the Baroness pushed with all her strength. The bulbous bell end of the dildo sank between her sphincters, meeting an initial resistance before being propelled deep into the tight, protesting tunnel that was her anal canal. Rocking on her heels, the Baroness drove the mighty shaft in and out; the bulbous nodule in the centre of the dildo rasping and stimulating her throbbing, erect clitoris. Driving herself towards orgasm, she grasped Esmeralda's thighs and slapped against her battered buttocks as she pistoned in and out of her backside.

Writhing under the onslaught and unable to pull away, her hands irrevocably nailed to the chest,

Esmeralda screamed the screams of the damned. Not the pleasure of intercourse for her, just the pain of her mistress' assault. And that assault was without mercy. As the Baroness drove herself ever onward towards orgasm, so she drove her victim ever onwards to purgatory. Hell beckoned Esmeralda and the Baroness was intent on making sure that its call was answered.

Just one thing was hindering the Baroness' own entry to the Heaven of orgasm and that was her slave's ear-piercing screams. The distracting racket she was kicking up was preventing her from reaching a climax. Esmeralda had to be silenced. And inflamed by the frantic sexual activity going on around it, the implement to do just that was standing erect and throbbing right next to her.

"Arlecchino, shut her up!"

The boy did not move immediately but looked at her questioningly for a moment before plucking up the courage to speak.

"How shall I do that Mistress?"

Halting her frenzied fucking, the Baroness pointed at his pulsating weapon.

"With that you fool. With that stuck in her mouth she will not be so vocal. Now, get round the other side of the chest and ram your cock between her teeth and down to her tonsils. And make it fast or you could find yourself changing places with the slut."

Arlecchino did make it fast, not just because his mistress had ordered it; but as she well knew, because he could not wait to feel a wet tongue lapping the length of his shaft and sucking cheeks drawing it from frustration to fulfilment. With the silencing cock firmly in place, the Baroness resumed her fucking with a vengeance; resulting in a uniquely effective ramming synchronicity of the two different but equally potent sex pistols.

Now able to concentrate on gaining maximum satisfaction for herself, the Baroness renewed her assault upon Esmeralda's anus and although not paying him too much attention, saw that Arlecchino was not holding back in his ravaging of her mouth. Ever up and onwards, the Baroness and her boy slave drove themselves towards nirvana; the ultimate sensation. Esmeralda writhed and shook under their combined storming onslaught, the completely inconsiderate vehemence of the assault cancelling out her suffering and transmuting it into the intensely animated eruption of sexual satisfaction that time and again is the result of unasked-for violation of a person's most intimate bodily openings.

As if in a rehearsed finale, the Baroness and her boy slave both reached the peak of orgasm at the very same moment, shuddering and shaking in frenzied fulfilment. Esmeralda's arse had proved the gateway to paradise for the Baroness and although a mouth is not quite the equal of a vagina, for Arlecchino it was obviously a very acceptable substitute.

As for gypsy girl herself, she had been transported to a sexual wonderland. The combined sensations of Arlecchino's cock filling her mouth with deliciously swallowable spunk and the Baroness' uncontrollably hammering rubber cock stimulating her clitoris through her anal septum, had transmuted her agony into delight. Suddenly fired up, she climaxed in a shuddering, thrashing and completely unexpected outcome to the dastardly treatment that she had endured as she joined her two abusers and completed a trio of shared mind-shattering, debilitating orgasms.

Thoroughly sated, the Baroness slowly withdrew the giant dildo from her slave's anus at the same time that Arlecchino pulled his dripping cock from her mouth. The Baroness gave herself a little time. Then it was back to reality. She took Arlecchino's place in front of her panting, spunk-covered and nailed-down slave gatherer.

"And now to other matters. I told you that I had seen you fucking the local yokels, didn't I? Perhaps you did not believe me; maybe you thought that I had found out some other way, gossip perhaps. But I assure you, it is perfectly true; I saw you . . I saw you in there!"

The Baroness pointed to the mirror. The mirror hiding in the gloom. The unbelievable magic mirror that Esmeralda did not know existed.

"My mirror is deep and dark. It has journeyed with me through the mists of time and it shows me everything that it thinks I should know; including what you did to Arlecchino in the temple."

Esmeralda's flushed face paled to the same deathly pallor that the Baroness' victims did not normally display until after they had played their part in the Ceremony. Knowing that Esmeralda had no defence, the Baroness was merciless.

"So regrettably he is of no further use to me now . . And neither are you!"

EIGHT
THE CASTLE

It was about eight in the evening, with the warmth of the day still lingering when the policewoman turned up at the hunting lodge to conduct Mistress Madonna and Julian up to the castle. Except that she was not the policewoman any longer. In this guise she was now definitely Anna, the Baroness' confidante and trusted servant and looking at her, Mistress Madonna found herself completely taken aback by the almost awesome change in her appearance. Gone was the uniform and in its place she was wearing a very tight-fitting thigh-length black satin corset dress. A dress that accentuated her previously disguised but now obviously impressive breasts and cinched her waist into tiny super model dimensions. Clinging provocatively to her well-rounded hips and backside, it emphasised to the full the mouth-watering appeal of her firmly-fleshed thighs. Not only that but as an added bonus to the overtly sexual nature of her appearance, it allowed the merest suggestion of the outline of her pubic mound to show as it pushed against the softness of the material.

Her hair was too, was not the same. No longer short but now impressively long and a glossy midnight-black it hung straight, without the slightest kink, almost to her shoulders. Dark and sombre, her makeup, relieved only by the vivid scarlet of her lips, transformed her into a vague likeness of Mistress Madonna herself. But it was not only her appearance that was different. Although she had not lacked an authoritative character previously, now everything about her had changed or intensified, in fact she was formidable; a fact that Mistress Madonna quietly admitted to herself.

But however impressive Anna now looked, there was no chance that she would overshadow Mistress Madonna. Formidable as Anna now was, Mistress Madonna outshone her in every way. She had prepared herself well for her meeting with the Baroness. As always her hair and make-up were immaculate, but her dress was what other envious women might have described as 'to die for'. An exclusive creation, it had set Julian back by an amount that the majority of men would not even consider shelling out for a luxury car. Supported only by her magnificent breasts, it was tailored from black silk of a much sought after but seldom obtained quality. A silk of uniquely beautiful weave that had been lovingly hand-crafted using the carefully-preserved and justly famous silk looms that had been in use in Lyons since the seventeenth century.

Leaving her neck and shoulders completely bare, it fell downwards in ruffles from her cleavage to sweep the ground and was split at the front almost up to her knickerless crotch; when she moved revealing a flash of black ruched suspenders, creamy thighs and lace-banded stocking tops. Her spiky-heeled shoes were a revelation. Crafted especially for her, Julian had purchased them from her favourite Chelsea emporium. Vastly expensive and of black brocade with designs fashioned from cultured black pearls, they were truly wonderful creations; not really made for walking at all but intended as jewellery for the feet. Nevertheless, Mistress Madonna did intend walking in them. All the way up to the castle.

Anna's jealous, but hungry eyes swept over her. A moment of tension-filled silence followed before Anna addressed herself to the matter in hand.

"Madame, we should be going. Where is your slave?"

Ah yes, Julian. What was he messing about at?

"Julian! Get in here this instant!"

Hurrying to obey his mistress' cōmmand, he stumbled to the door, still trying to knot his tie into a perfect bow. In his formal evening attire, he really did look very presentable indeed and Mistress Madonna actually felt a sense of pride in him. Anna however took one look at him and blanched visibly.

"No, no. He won't do at all. You madame, are the guest of honour and you look perfect, exquisite and very appealing if I may say so: but him! He's nothing but a slave and should appear as such. The Baroness Elizabeth wishes you to bring him exactly as you had him in the forest earlier; stark naked and crawling on his hands and knees. You're to forget the cannon ball though, the Baroness says that if he has to drag that behind him it will take far too long to get up to the castle."

Like the tumulus, the hunting lodge had been sited in a flat clearing in the midst of the abundant trees. To the south, the path that Mistress Madonna had followed earlier led down to bay through a dense forest of pines. Similarly an even steeper trail wormed its way upwards and northwards to the castle, which was perched right on the very edge of the cliff top. But this path led through a forest in which ancient oaks fought with pines for precedence; acorns as well as pine cones littering its floor. Without taking a long detour to the formal entrance to the estate, the shortest way up to the castle was along yet another narrow thorny-bramble and fern-bordered path that wound through an intimidating forest. Not without a little apprehension, tugging a now naked Julian behind her on a collar and lead, Mistress Madonna followed as Anna led the way into its depths.

Suddenly Mistress Madonna stopped dead in her tracks. A sudden confusing thought had hit her. How on earth did the Baroness know that earlier that day she had driven Julian through the forest naked and on his hands and knees? She was given no time to ponder the question as Anna realised that her charges were no longer close behind her.

"Is there a problem?"

Mistress Madonna was about to voice her question but after a moment or two's hesitation, thought better of it.

"Oh, it's nothing. I just snagged my dress on a bramble, that's all."

"Alright, but do try and keep up. We don't want to be caught in the forest when the sun goes down."

Mistress Madonna could not know that Anna's concern was not for herself but for Julian, her now incalculably precious cargo. Her existence would be worth nothing if she allowed any harm to befall him.

As the sun neared the end of its journey westward, the crimson-tinged evening sky was swiftly metamorphosing from a pleasing duck-egg blue to a more threatening and darkly deeper hue. The first few pale stars of evening twinkled faintly as they awaited the full descent of the night, when they would shine in their true sparkling brilliance.

But the forest did not wait for night to fall. After progressing only a few more yards they were completely hemmed in by trees that formed a canopy high above them, the darkness being almost complete. Affected even more than she had been earlier in the day in the pine forest, Mistress Madonna shivered as the gloomy eeriness of the surroundings seemed to press in on her, now and again stumbling into one of the many standing stones that stood guarding the path. Flickering blue flames danced along the floor of the forest, Anna instructing the others to remain on the path as she occasionally halted their progress and headed off into the undergrowth to examine one of them.

What was she doing? Mistress Madonna had to know.

"Anna. What are those flames?"

She had thought that they were probably methane gas produced by rotting foliage or at least something of that nature. The answer she received was unexpected to say the least.

"Do you know what today is?"

"Yes, it's April the twenty third."

"Yes it is, but you're English, doesn't that mean anything to you?"

Mistress Madonna gave it some thought, but had to admit defeat.

"No, I'm afraid it does not."

"Shame on you. Today is Saint George's Eve and even *I* know that he is the patron saint of England. But he is much more than that, all over Europe there are legends associated with him and in the Baroness' home country it is believed that on this day, and this day only, blue flames rise from the ground where anything of value has been lost or buried. So I'm taking a look."

"Surely you don't believe in fairy tales like that?"

"Why not? I believe in many things. For instance did you know that also it is said that when the clock strikes midnight on this day all the evil in the world is let loose to do as it will until the sun rises on Saint George's Day itself?"

"Very interesting I'm sure, but do you think we could get out of this damned forest?"

Mistress Madonna had suddenly lost interest in Anna's beliefs because just as she had the previous night, she was certain that she could hear the howling of wolves all around them and she would feel a lot happier when they reached open ground.

In the ever-gathering darkness, Mistress Madonna's first view of the castle filled her with shocked surprise. As far as she could make out, much of the outer wall, ramparts and the structure of the castle itself lay in ruins, although a fully functioning drawbridge was lowered over a deeply-filled moat. Ripples and vague shapes in the murky water hinted at the presence of some not altogether wholesome creatures lurking in its depths. A dauntingly solid iron-bound portcullis barred their entrance into the courtyard and with Anna hanging onto a rusted heavy iron chain, Mistress Madonna could hear the muffled distant dissonant tolling of an obviously cracked bell.

Although the evening was not cold Mistress Madonna shivered involuntarily. There was something evil and forbidding about the ancient fortress and she was fast beginning to wish that she had not accepted the Baroness' invitation.

'Damn The Colonel', she thought, 'just what has he let me in for?'

Tightening her grip on Julian's lead, she pulled him closer to her, for once genuinely welcoming his presence. Endless minutes seemed to pass and looking around, against the darkening skyline she could see the silhouette of the castle keep. Projecting from its tower was a long pole with what appeared to be an entire circle of lightning conductors fixed to its top.

"You must get some pretty frightening storms around here to need that amount of protection."

"Yes we do. Sometimes the night sky is just one whole blaze of electricity, and it all seems to come our way."

Anna's matter of fact answer and nonchalant demeanour diminished Mistress Madonna's fears greatly, making her feel rather foolish in fact. She began to feel her normal steely-strong self returning, the tension within her lightening further as she began to think that for some reason or other they were not going to be allowed admittance to the castle. That tension returned with a vengeance when she heard footsteps approaching and in the gloom behind the portcullis saw a nearing flicker of light. With much creaking and clanking of heavy chains the portcullis began to rise until when it was fully open, in the dim light of the single candle that he was carrying, she saw a very tall, skeletal man of great age and deathly pallor. Dressed from head to toe in black, completely bald, with large ears, black-ringed eyes, ivory parchment-like skin drawn tightly over his cheek bones and protruding fangs, she recognised him immediately. It just could not be – but it was: Nosferatu . . Dracula!

It was a nightmare. Completely unbelievable. But now everything made sense. The bat fluttering outside her window, the wolves, the blue flames in the forest, St. George's Eve – they were all part of the Dracula legend as told by Bram Stoker. And they were not fiction; they were fact!

Her surroundings swam before her eyes, her vision blurred, her knees buckled and the world began to fade away. Her world. But behind Dracula a new unearthly world shimmered into view. It was still the courtyard, but although it was no longer so murkily dark and deserted, it was still full of dense shadows and appeared even more sinister. Showers of sparks erupted skywards from flaming braziers that illuminated the faces of a passive thronged assembly; an assembly that consisted entirely of silent and fully robed monks and nuns. No words were spoken but a subdued wave of animation passed through their ranks, as driven by the whip lashes of sinewy female guards, a seemingly never-ending line of shackled girls trooped into the courtyard.

The girls were virgins. Every single one of them. How she recognised that fact, Mistress Madonna had no idea; she just knew. Screeching, wailing and weeping tears of dread, the host of virgins cowered in long chained-together lines as they took their places in front of the silent children of God. Squeezing her eyes tight shut, she tried to dismiss them from her sight. But that had no effect, for through her closed eyelids, the visions actually intensified. Try as she could, Mistress Madonna could not rid herself of the ungodly sight before her. She fought a battle with her mind. The vision was real. Or perhaps it was not. It did not matter. To her, it desperately and most certainly was.

She had no idea exactly how many unfortunate girls there were but there she thought that there must have been at least a hundred. One hundred helpless virgins who had been gathered together for some awful, hideous purpose. A purpose that for some indefinable reason she and Julian were a part of.

The skeletally emaciated but gleeful Dracula pranced on matchstick legs, pointing a long talon-like finger towards the rapidly filling square. There was an evil eloquence to his words.

"You do know, don't you? that against God's command, in the Garden of Eden, Eve tricked Adam into fucking her. As punishment for that act of disobedience He decided not to create any more children, decreeing that from then on, women must bear their offspring themselves. Since then women have been punished and fucked by men, that is His will. To fuck is to live. To dedicate your life to fucking is the ultimate act of dedication to any god. Gods need you to procreate in order to deliver the souls of ever more innocents into their waiting hands.

"And I am as great as any God. Greater in fact. Like them I am eternal. I shall never die. But it is not souls that I need to sustain me, it is something else. Blood! But there is nothing I enjoy more than fucking; sinking my shaft deep into the soaking vagina of a buxom unused woman. And so to serve me, my disciples deliver to me sacrificial innocent flesh; the flesh of virgins that I can stoke into flames with my shaft of steel before I drain them of their pulsing red blood."

Dracula's words washed over Mistress Madonna. She was in a haze; her mind was numb.

"Come with me into the courtyard, my audience is now assembled and you can join them."

In a daze she followed in his footsteps.

"Oh, those poor girls."

Mistress Madonna's words slipped from her lips in a horrified whisper. Even so, they were not unheard by Dracula.

"Do not concern yourself with them, those virgins are not mine. They are intended for use in a special ceremony that the Baroness has planned and are merely assembled to witness what fate could have befallen them if they had been delivered to me and not her. If you will look over there, you will see my flock entering now."

And so they were. A parade of naked pale-faced neophytes was being led into the expectant but sombrely charged atmosphere of the courtyard by the Mother Superior. Halting them in front of Dracula, she crossed herself before hurrying away.

Dracula wasted not a single second. Delving between his legs, he released his rampant erect pylon of a penis and clamping the skeletal talons of his right hand around the neck of the first unfortunate girl in the line, he lifted her from her feet and high into the air with just one arm. Widening her legs with his left hand, he dropped her down straight onto his vile cock and moving the hand to support her backside, her legs now wrapped around his waist, bounced her up and down over its full, pulsing length.

Shrieking as the cock from hell brutalised her virgin vagina, her yells of terror and pain converted into moans of lust as he stoked her towards her very first orgasm. Her first and last orgasm; for as she shuddered and squealed at its explosive impact, he sank his razor-sharp canines deep into her jugular, simultaneously emptying her of blood and filling her with spunk. Throwing her to the ground, crimson trails trickling down his chin, he moved on to the next screaming girl. And then the next; until he had fucked and drained every one of them. From now on they would be zombies, destined to inhabit the same twilight world as himself. But there would be no more sex for them, only a continual hunt for blood in the castle catacombs. And for them that blood would be that of rats and other vile creatures that scurried about in the decay and darkness of the underground caverns.

Mistress Madonna's head spun. Her faculties deserted her and she felt herself descending into oblivion. The next thing she knew she was being supported in Julian's strong arms.

"Mistress. Mistress, what's wrong?"

Julian's frenzied concern cut through the mist of her mind and pulling herself together she struggled to free herself from his grasp. Even in her befuddled state she did not fail to note that he had managed to cup both her breasts as he prevented her from falling. He would pay very dearly for that later. If there ever was a later.

The diabolical black-clad creature hurried forward, he too being very concerned by her fainting spell. Suddenly all her fears melted away. It must have been a combined trick of the light and her over-vivid imagination, after all he had been standing in shadow. Now up close, she could see that he was not the abominable apparition that she had taken him for but a perfectly presentable, if not exactly handsome, elderly man.

"Madame, I am Vladimir. Please allow me to help you, the Baroness will be most concerned that you are not well. What was it? It seemed as if you were seeing something awful that was not visible to the rest of us."

She knew that she possessed second sight but she had seen nothing as dreadful as this before. Perhaps her imagination and the forbidding atmosphere of the castle had caused her to hallucinate. In any case she had better pull herself together; and fast! Regaining her poise in double quick time, she shrugged off the fainting episode and giving Julian the dirtiest of looks, finally wrung her breasts from his tight grasp.

"No, no. I'm sorry I alarmed you but I'm perfectly alright now, it was nothing. And I'd be pleased if no one mentioned this to the Baroness."

"If that is what madame wishes, so be it. Follow me if you will, and please take care, it is rather dark inside the castle; there is no electric light, you see. Well, not all of the time."

Not all of the time? They either had it or they did not. The hunting lodge had nothing but candles and oil lamps that was true but even if there was no direct supply she would have thought that the castle would at least have had a generator installed. Before she could question him Vladimir turned on his heel and briskly set off for the castle entrance, with her trailing in his footsteps as he conducted the party into the interior of the castle and guided them towards the great hall.

"I am very sorry madame, but the Baroness has asked me to greet you and to advise you that regretfully she is not able to receive you as yet. She has some household matters to attend to, checking the wine cellar or something of that nature, I believe."

Vladimir had scarcely uttered those words however when Mistress Madonna plainly heard footsteps approaching up the stone steps behind a heavy iron-studded oak door that was the way down into the depths of the castle. With an eerie prolonged creak, the door swung slowly open and there stood the Baroness, a candelabrum holding three flickering candles clasped in one hand.

She came as quite a shock. Mistress Madonna had been expecting either a frumpy old hag or a diamond-laden sophisticate. In her experience one or the other of those two presented the usual appearance of feminine aristocracy. The Baroness was neither. She was tall, almost as tall as Mistress Madonna herself, and as far as she could tell in the dim light, about the same age. And like Mistress Madonna, and everyone else who was actually clothed for that matter, she was dressed completely in black. Unadorned with jewellery or accessories, coal-black tresses fell to her naked shoulders. An off the shoulder lace dress revealed the firm swell of her breasts, the narrowness of her waist and the pleasing roundness of her bottom, before falling almost to her ankles.

She was beautiful; but strangely different. Her face was pale. Very pale. Her eyes an indeterminate colour that seemed to change with the flickering of the light from the candles and her teeth were extraordinarily white and pointed. Strength and power were etched into her features and for once Mistress Madonna felt that she was encountering a woman with an authority that matched her own. Reaching out with her free hand, the Baroness grasped Mistress Madonna's and greeted her with the utmost cordiality.

"Mistress Madonna, welcome. I'm so pleased that you were able to come, and I trust that Vladimir has looked after you to your satisfaction. He is my other special guest and he only arrived here himself this afternoon; but when he's not at his own castle in the old country, he spends most of his time here so he knows this ruin as well as anyone. I can't wait to get to know you, I've heard a great deal about you from The Colonel and Thierry - not to mention what Anna has told me about your escapade with your slave in the hunting lodge."

She lowered her eyes, studying Julian intently and reaching down, she edged his collar over his neck so that it revealed the two punctures that Anna had seen and reported to her. A quickly dismissed frown clouded her face. But it was not unnoticed by Mistress Madonna. Just what had the Baroness been expecting to see? Julian's neck was marked by the spikes of the iron collar, but it seemed as if she had been let down, having expected to find something else. The Baroness' chiselled canines showed themselves again as she turned her eyes away from his neck.

"I must congratulate you, for a slave he is magnificent. And a virgin too, I'm led to understand?"

Her accent was of an indeterminate eastern European origin, her hand as cold as ice and her grip like that of steel. Giving a startled Mistress Madonna no time to reply, she carried on.

"Don't misunderstand me, I admire your ability to keep him under your thrall while allowing no sexual favours. It shows me that I was not mistaken in inviting you here."

Swinging the door to the vaults shut, with Mistress Madonna and the others following, she led the way along a stone-flagged corridor. Keeping them close company, eerie shadows cast by the flickering candles danced over the walls, although Mistress Madonna could have sworn that neither the Baroness nor Vladimir cast shadows themselves. Coming to a huge pair of heavy double doors that barred their passage, the Baroness rapped on the door with a series of knocks that gave Mistress Madonna the impression that they were some sort of coded signal and after a few moments, it duly opened to reveal the great hall.

Flaming torches set into iron brackets on the walls and a blazing fire in the huge medieval stone fireplace provided a flickering orange-tinged luminescence that gave sufficient light to see by, but left pools of darkness in corners and recesses. As it had down in the courtyard, the scene before her faltered and shimmered in the uncertain light and she felt the anger begin to surge through her anew. Why had she not been told that the gathering was to be a fancy dress affair? And an orgy at that! She had witnessed mass sex before but this was something over and above anything else in her experience.

The Baroness was not slow in recognising her reaction.

"Ah, so you see it. I thought you would. No doubt you saw the monks and the nuns in the courtyard. But it is not real; that is to say it is not happening now. It is an echo, a visual manifestation of events that happened hundreds of years ago. In the middle ages this castle was taken over by monks and turned into an abbey; but under the influence of a deranged Abbot they abandoned their evangelical counsels and their vows of celibacy and poverty were forgotten. Instead of living a life of piety they indulged in sexual excess and moral outrage of all kinds. Their conduct over the years was so outrageous that it left an indelible imprint on the very fabric of the building and now very special people blessed with the gift, find their minds tuned in to that imprint. And you are one of them, as am I. We both possess the receptive mental powers that allow us to pick up the psychic vibrations that permeate every murky room, dingy cellar and cheerless, gloomy dungeon of the castle and turn them into something that we can actually see."

What kind of rubbish was this? Things were getting strange again. Mistress Madonna did not believe a word; but she did feel peculiarly odd and the scene was indeed surreal and unearthly, fading in and out from the utmost clarity to a misty opaqueness. Could it be true? As if reading her thoughts, the Baroness answered her question.

"Yes my dear, unbelievable as it may seem, it is absolutely true. Look!"

With a great crackling of sound the blazing fire suddenly flared up, casting monstrous shadows of the heaving orgiastic mass of bodies upon the walls of the hall.

Hysterically shrieking nuns were flailing the naked buttocks and shanks of kneeling, praying monks. Seemingly penitent monks; seeking absolution, or perhaps masochistic pleasure through flagellation and pain. And if pain was the price that led to forgiveness or sexual gratification, then they were paying that price to the full. The blunt sound of thick wooden staffs being laid upon flabby slothful and licentious flesh crawled leadenly through the air. Dripping wax, lighted altar candles were being thrust deep into the upturned backsides of the repentant Brothers.

And not only candles.

With medieval wooden dildos buried deep into their vaginas, many of the Sisters of Mercy were actively gaining pleasure for themselves by fucking the arses of their all too willing victims. And in their in turn, the other not so repentant, fully-robed Brothers of the penitents were laughing and swigging from flagons of wine as they fondled the breasts of more submissive Sisters, lifting the hems of their habits to plunge eager fingers into their equally eager and unresisting vaginas.

A knight in full battle armour had somehow freed his cock from its protecting steel cod-piece and grabbing a serving wench, he pushed her backwards over a barrel of ale and throwing her skirts over her head, with a total lack of concern for her needs or desires, he drove it deep into her love tunnel. Bowmen, chamber maids, pike bearers and ladies-in-waiting were joined in a communal, free for all mass obeisance to Bacchus and the other Gods of debauchery.

Suddenly, right before Mistress Madonna's eyes, a hooded and robed monk pulled a nun out of the gloom towards him. Gathering a fistful of her habit, he drew it up over her mons, wrenched her naked legs apart and rammed his throbbing cock deep into the hole that was promised to God alone. Grunting, panting and heaving back and forth, he slammed into her. Rocking on her feet, she thrust back against him; praying out loud for forgiveness as her vagina sucked and clamped on holy meat. Sweat poured from both their brows as they praised the Lord for introducing them to such heavenly bliss.

The air hummed to the sound of Holy chants as more monks and nuns gave in to their lusts. Habits, scapulars and nun's headdresses fell to the floor as the monks ripped off the garments of the Wives of God, stripping them naked and exposing their pale white bodies.

Heavy tits, huge nipples and well-thatched hairy minges abounded, as what was normally concealed by coarse black cloth was now revealed. Revealed and plundered mercilessly by the jackhammer cocks of crazed monks, who, revelling in sin, were more akin to the sons of Satan than the children of God.

Mistress Madonna stared with increasing disbelief as slowly another image merged into the scene until the monks and the cacophonic recipients of their weapons of lust faded entirely, another equally iniquitous, depraved set of figures taking their place.

With lascivious grins on their faces and their lips curled back over pointed eye-teeth, Ladies in courtly medieval dress were being tongued, fucked and buggered by naked, but shackled boy slaves. Proud, young stiff cocks were everywhere; driving deep between peeled-back sex flaps and into dripping aristocratic vaginas and pummelling through the sphincters of eager anuses that were stretching themselves to allow their thrusting entry. And as they fucked, the boys were being lashed into greater effort by grinning female guards, relentlessly pitiless in their application of the wicked bullwhips they were wielding. Filling the chamber, womanly moans of exultation clashed with the boys' screams of anguish and despair, the air thickening with the sooty smoke of burning torches and the overpowering musky aroma of sweat and sperm. Sperm that was being sprayed everywhere; over the furniture, the floor and the sumptuous spread of beef haunches, peacocks and sucking pigs that were weighing down the long oak tables covering its straw-spread floor.

It was unbelievable. It was Dystopia. And suddenly the evil was a hundred times blacker. The frightening, bald Dracula, Mistress Madonna thought she had seen at the castle entrance was back. Staggering through the frenzied throng, his fangs were bared and his huge ghastly wrinkled and medievally-circumcised cock was throbbingly erect. Whether he was a child of God or the Devil she did not know, but seemingly separating himself from the other ghoulish apparitions, he lurched towards her, threatening and terrifying.

He was coming for her!

Involuntarily, she shrank backwards until suddenly and thankfully, he sank back into their frantic, heaving ranks. Engrossed and lost in the scenes unfolding in front of her, Mistress Madonna felt a tap on her shoulder. The spell was broken. It was the Baroness.

"I think that's enough for now, don't you?"

The figures were already fading as she raised her hand.

"Be gone!"

At her command Dracula and the last of the fornicators disappeared and the hazy veil cleared.

"You see, it is as I said. Do you believe now?"

Thoroughly shaken, Mistress Madonna could not deny the evidence of her eyes.

"Yes. I think that I do."

"That is all to the good, but now we must dismiss all of that from our minds and get on with enjoying what is left of the evening. Anna will take care of your slave."

The Baroness' tone brooked no argument, so somewhat reluctantly Mistress Madonna handed Julian's leash to Anna. She was not too happy to relinquish direct control of him, watching with not a little concern as he was dragged over to the huge fireplace and his lead shortened and fastened into an iron hoop on one side of its flaming interior. And dripping hot fat into those flames as it roasted over them, skewered on a revolving spit, was the carcass of a goat.

Mistress Madonna stiffened as a naked, struggling, oath-spitting and wickedly-striped girl was manhandled over to the other side of the hearth by two hefty whip-wielding women guards and like Julian, similarly chained to a hoop. Suddenly, she realised with a start that it was the gypsy girl that she had been spying on in the forest earlier. The gypsy girl who had been accompanied by a pet goat! Whatever delinquency she had been guilty of since then, the tram lines, bruises and whip scars covering her body bore witness that she had been savagely punished for it. And by the look of it her pet had paid the ultimate penalty and was now destined for the dinner table.

One after the other, Anna pushed Julian and Esmeralda down onto their knees so that their necks were straining on the leads, and cuffed their wrists behind their backs. Attaching chains to the cuffs, she linked them tightly into the same hoops to which their collars had been fixed. Their backs were very close to the fire, not close enough to actually roast them Mistress Madonna concluded, but near enough to give them an extremely uncomfortable toasting.

Mistress Madonna was not too comfortable herself. She was not sure that she liked the way things were going. Julian was her property and if anyone were going to abuse him then it would be her. Oblivious to all this, Anna straddled Julian and inching her skirt just a fraction higher, pressed her hot shaven mound into his face.

"Lick me out. Now!"

Mistress Madonna felt outrage surge up within her and jumped in to tackle Anna, but was halted by The Baroness' very quick intervention.

"Anna! Behave yourself. I do not believe that you have Mistress Madonna's permission to make use of her slave! Use the gypsy scum if you must. But I think you should bear in mind that we do have a guest to entertain and also Esmeralda has a very old admirer waiting to greet her later on."

The Baroness' admonishment irked Anna, that much was obvious but swinging one leg over Julian's head she ignored Esmeralda and walked back to join the others. Taking her place in a giant high-backed chair at one end of the table, the Baroness sat a furious Mistress Madonna and a sulking Anna opposite each other in the first seats down the table.

Calming herself somewhat and looking around, Mistress Madonna realised that Vladimir had not entered the room with them.

"Baroness, isn't Vladimir going to join us. I thought you said he was another of your guests."

"Yes, he is, but he is waiting outside for the owner of the castle to join us."

"You mentioned him before, but I thought that you owned this place."

"No my dear, I do not. I met the true owner through Vladimir and now I live here permanently at his very thoughtful invitation, and . . . Ah, I think I hear them now."

Mistress Madonna followed the Baroness' eyes to the door and saw Vladimir entering with a sneering, hard-faced man, who although as greatly changed in appearance as Anna, was someone that she realised she had encountered before: the policeman.

The Baroness rose from her seat.

"Mistress Madonna, please allow me to introduce you to your ultimate host and the owner of the castle; Donatien Alphonse François, The Marquis de Sade."

NINE

THE CONTEST

There was only so much that Mistress Madonna was prepared to take. Whatever was happening, real or not, she had reached her limit and the entrance of the so-called Marquis de Sade was the final straw. This was obviously some kind of con trick. What did they take her for? Some sort of simpleton?

She leapt to her feet and stomped towards the fireplace.

"I've had enough of this. I don't know what game you're playing but as far as I'm concerned, it's over. I'm leaving, and Julian's coming with me!"

The Baroness' swift response was unequivocal.

"I'm afraid not my dear. We have other plans for you, and especially for your virgin."

Nobody had plans for Mistress Madonna except herself. She possessed a phenomenal physical strength, as Julian could well testify and so she fought with determined and unexpected vigour as two female guards attempted to prevent her from carrying out her threat. The contest was not lost without great resistance and she continued to wrestle off the Baroness' aides attempts at subduing her, until Vladimir and the Marquis joined in the struggle and their combined might overcame her and she was finally vanquished.

With Mistress Madonna held tight in her captors' grip, the Baroness raised a glass of crimson liquid to her lips as she swept her eyes over her crushed and confused guest.

"Now that we have quietened your little tantrum, I am inclined to believe that I owe you some sort of explanation before you and your slave are relieved of your human forms. I was intrigued when The Colonel told me of you and Julian, which is why I invited you here and when I first set eyes on you I firmly believed that you were one such as me.

"And even Anna Darvulia here thought that the marks on your slave's neck were the evidence of your fangs penetrating his jugular. But now knowing that you are not what I thought you were, I realise that you will find what I am about you tell you hard to believe."

Drawing herself up to her full height she rolled her head, flicking her long black tresses across her bare shoulders as she continued.

"You are now in the presence of the Baroness Erzebert, Elizabeth to use your English version of my name, Bartholi, a name that I think you may recognise. I have prolonged my existence for over four hundred years since my enemies condemned me and walled me up in Csejthe Castle for a crime that was nothing more than bathing in the blood of six hundred or so virgins. Virgins that nobody cared for. But what no one understood was that I needed the innocent pure blood of those virgins to keep my youth.

"They were nothing, just worthless peasants and I was the wife of General Ferene Nádasky. He was royalty and a very important man and as was the custom in those days, he married me when I was just a child of fourteen. To keep him happy I had to stay very young and desirable, even though his lovemaking was totally self-centred and unsatisfactory. Bathing in their blood was the secret that let me do that, and although of course I was not able to completely stem the onset of the years I have never looked any older than I do now.

"And Anna helped me by procuring young innocent girls. In most cases their parents were only too ready and glad to sell them; they did not care what happened to them afterwards. But I was found out and bricked up behind a wall in a dungeon and eventually everyone thought that I had perished.

"As you can see that was not the case. Vladimir is exactly who you thought he was when you first set eyes on him: Vlad the Impaler, in other words, Count Dracula; for they are one and the same.

"Did you know that in Romanian, Dracul or Dracula means the Devil, and in ancient Transylvania it was believed that witches mated with him to give birth to vampires. And because my own bloodline goes right back to those times, he came to me and turned me truly into one of his own kind and believing that I was dead, the authorities released my body for burial. But I was not dead. I was undead, like him.

"And so that she could remain serving me, he bit Anna Darvulia as well. And she proved to be one of the very few undead who can actually survive in daylight, as can the Marquis. She kept me hidden for almost two hundred years until Count Dracula stumbled across the Marquis, who was rotting in the Bastille and yelling encouragement to the children of the revolution from behind the bars of his cell.

"He saved him too. The Marquis did not die in the asylum at Charenton in 1803 as is documented; in reality he escaped and secretly gathered his fortune and purchased this castle, where he has remained ever since. Vlad brought me and Anna from Transylvania to live with and serve the Marquis and so here we are; not alive yet not dead and enjoying every sin-filled minute of our existence.

"But I still have to maintain my youth; the Marquis despite all his perversions will not fuck an old woman. And to remain young, once a year it is necessary for me to perform a special Ceremony; to bathe in the blood of exactly one hundred virgins. That is what I will be doing very shortly, after the clock striking the midnight hour signals that the time is right. And most unfortunately for your slave, he will play a major part in the proceedings."

Mistress Madonna's brain whirled. What the hell was going on here? The woman must be insane. What was all this rubbish about Julian? And what exactly was it that the Baroness trying to say? That she was a vampire and lived in this castle along with Count Dracula and an equally vampiric Marquis de Sade?

It seemed that she did.

"You disappoint me my dear. I really thought that you were one of us. But we all make mistakes and I shall just have to put you down as one of mine. The fate of your virgin slave is already sealed, but what do we do with you?"

Anna's response to her words was immediate and fervent.

"I want her. I want to whip her. I want to smash her into nothingness, and I want to fuck her."

"Yes, we all know that. You have made it so very obvious right from the start. But I do not think that just allowing you to indulge your fantasies would prove very satisfactory to the rest of us. I think that we all would like to partake ourselves of her charms; she has a very tempting body."

Clicking her fingers and issuing some unheard orders, the Baroness summoned a posse of guards into the chamber. Circling her middle finger, she indicated that they should surround Mistress Madonna and Anna.

"You Anna, are beginning to concern me. Recently I have noticed that you are developing ideas far above your station. After all these centuries of serving me, I have great difficulty in understanding that you just do not seem to appreciate your true position here. I am your mistress and you are my underling! Perhaps it is just a matter of long familiarity breeding contempt. I cannot understand that you do not realise that I can replace you at any time, so I am not going to make it easy for you.

"There will be a contest. Between you and Mistress Madonna. There are no rules but there will be no whips or weapons of any kind, it will be a straight hand to hand, bare-knuckle fight. And if you lose, well . . . If I were you I would ensure that that does not happen."

Mistress Madonna was determined that that was exactly what *would* happen and from the off, the very moment that she was freed from the restraint of her captors she went at Anna with venomous fury; smashing her with clenched fists, biting, clawing, kicking and gouging until Anna's dress clung to her body in tatters. Her nugget-nippled breasts now stripped bare, gasping with effort Anna hung on to Mistress Madonna's silken gown and succeeded in pulling it down over her heaving orbs and bereft of their support it fell in a puddle around her ankles. Pushing Anna away, Mistress Madonna kicked the gown clear and resumed her attack, ripping away the last remnants of Anna's dress. Anna was now completely naked and Mistress Madonna's only accoutrements were her black suspender belt and stockings and the ruby glowing in her navel; and of course the wonderful forest of curly jet-black pubic hair that thatched her mons.

Both the combatants possessed magnificent bodies and the sight of them colliding with each other as they wrestled, their full, taut breasts refusing to flatten as they pressed against each other was a truly prick-raising spectacle; as the prominent bulges in the trousers of Vladimir and the Marquis clearly demonstrated. Although clearly concerned over the fate of his mistress, Julian too had sprouted a startlingly cock-stretching erection.

Mistress Madonna eventually succeeded in hooking a foot behind one of Anna's ankles and with her palms pressed flat over both of her heaving breasts, toppled her backwards. Anna hit the ground with an almighty thud and Mistress Madonna leapt in to finish her off.

"Stop!"

The order was clear enough but Mistress Madonna was euphoric in the moment of victory. She found herself strangely exhilarated by the tussle of naked flesh against naked flesh and although panting heavily, her perspiration-soaked body sliding over Anna's equally slippery skin, she dismissed the Baroness' command and continued to pummel Anna with savage blows. Her clenched fists thudded solidly into the firm flesh of Anna's breasts and she only ceased her attack when she was pulled off the prostrate girl by the struggling posse of guards.

Held in the unbreakable grip of the guards, she still radiated defiance as the Baroness addressed her; managing to land one more hefty kick between Anna's thighs as she picked herself up from the ground. Clutching her sex, Anna fell back to the floor, collapsing in a wailing heap.

The Baroness was not amused. Her tone was icily threatening.

"Mistress Madonna, it is not wise to ignore my words and I advise you not to do so again. Do you understand?"

Mistress Madonna did not take unwanted advice from anyone.

"I'll do what I like and there's nothing that you can do to stop me."

"We will see about that later. Now, the reason that I ordered you to stop was because the contest was decidedly one-sided, so we must even it up. You are far too strong for Anna to stand a chance in physical combat, so contrary to my earlier decision we will turn to the whips. That way you both stand an equal chance."

The guards were far too many in number for resistance to be an option and so one after another, in turn, Mistress Madonna and Anna were hung by their outstretched arms from hooks in the ceiling of the hall. Handed a bullwhip, they each took turns in lashing the other; starting with ten lashes each. Striped, bruising up and sucking in air, they both survived the initial lashing without a murmur.

"Alright, now you both get another twenty."

Anna was envious of Mistress Madonna's individuality and commanding presence, qualities that so obviously impressed the Baroness. Mistress Madonna hated Anna for her presumption with Julian. So they both lashed out with no restraint whatsoever, the winner would take it all. And reap the reward that went with victory.

Lash upon lash fell upon taut, vibrant flesh. Neither gave way. The sentence was increased, with thirty extra lashes being added to the sentence. Still, they both hung on. Mistress Madonna and Anna both had superbly fit bodies. And they could both take pain. But Mistress Madonna possessed a resilience that was insurmountable. With Julian screaming out his own anguish at seeing his mistress so evilly abused, it was Anna who finally begged for mercy. The Baroness was not best pleased, that much was obvious, but Mistress Madonna was eventually the undisputed victor.

"You win. Do with her as you will."

Mistress Madonna did not wish to do *anything* with Anna. But although she had no designs on her herself, she remembered the dismissive supercilious manner in which Anna had treated a resentful Esmeralda in the forest.

"Yes I did win, but I have no use for her. But I am certain that I know someone who does. Can I pass my victory onwards?"

There was a moment's deliberation.

"Of course. To the victor the spoils. What is your wish?"

"Her! The gypsy girl. Give Anna to her."

The Baroness deliberated for a moment, her eyes roving over the tent-like projections jutting out from the trousers of Vladimir and the Marquis.

"Your wish, in this instance is my command, but first I think we must allow those two obviously raging and rampant cocks to take precedence. They will fuck her first and then Esmeralda can do as she likes with what remains of her."

Vladimir and the Marquis needed no further encouragement. Within seconds Anna was again hauled from her feet and suspended a foot or so above the floor. Roughly pulling her legs wide apart, Vladimir and the Count took one foot each and using tight chains clamped to her ankles, anchored her feet to iron hoops set into the stone flags. Straddled between her legs, Vladimir's skeletal fingers prized her sex flaps apart and just as he had with the novices in the courtyard, with no consideration for her whatsoever he drilled his bony cock straight up into her unprepared love hole. An unwelcoming hole that would rather have been on the receiving end of Mistress Madonna's tongue.

And keeping true to his sexual credo, not caring a damn as to which orifice his own cock was connected, the Marquis stuffed his rampant weapon straight up her anus. Anna was buffeted furiously as in tandem both men plunged in and out of their respective sexual receptacle and fucked her with reckless abandon, jerking and juddering in unison as they both achieved orgasm together. Anna's cunt filled with the sperm of the nauseous Transylvanian ogre, and her anus overflowed with the seed of the aristocratic father of sadism.

Lowering her down so that she was on her knees with her arms still stretched tightly above her, in turn the two plunderers of her body now thrust their cocks between her lips; firstly Vladimir and then the Count ordering her to suck and lick his sticky weapon clean. Lapping up and down their cocks from scrotum to bell end she cleaned off and swallowed what aromatic gunge remained on their weapons from their excursions into her vagina and her anus.

After delivering a final degradation by wiping their saliva-coated cocks with her hair, the two fathers of evil released Anna from her chains and threw her to the floor. Re-trousering their slackened weapons, they nonchalantly took their places beside the Baroness, who greeted their return with some degree of sarcasm.

"Quite a display. Not quite up to your normal standards though, a little hurried I thought. But I suppose everybody has an off day and now that we have got both of your cocks sorted out, perhaps we can get on with the business in hand; namely Anna and Mistress Madonna's right to use her in any way she wishes."

Whether the Baroness' remarks arose from envy Mistress Madonna did not know but she found herself to be of a completely different opinion. Having witnessed the relentless, totally inconsiderate plundering of

Anna, she felt more than pleased. She was herself in a desperate situation and she knew that she should really have been more concerned about what was to happen to her, but Anna's humiliation had sent waves of jubilation coursing through her body. She had beaten Anna in combat and that felt marvellous, but Vladimir and the Marquis had violated Anna's sex in a way that she never could. If they were not so vile themselves, she could have kissed them.

As she addressed Mistress Madonna, the Baroness was obviously not so gratified.

"So, what is your wish?"

"As I said before. Give Anna to the gypsy girl."

A promise was a promise. Even for the Baroness. So Esmeralda was released from her chains and helped to her feet and when she had pulled herself together, her first demand was more than unexpected.

"Shave her head!"

The Baroness was taken aback.

"Is that what you really want?"

"Yes. I want her head to match her cunt."

"That is a strange request. Why would you want that?"

"To humiliate her! And because when she sticks her tongue up into my vagina I don't want straggly hair rasping my thighs. Only one of us is going to enjoy what I want her to do; and that's me! And when I'm finished with her, a bald-headed woman is not a man's first desire."

There was no escape for Anna. A formidable heavy-breasted guard wielding a pair of shears lopped her tresses almost down to her skull, another quickly taking her place to scrape away the remaining stubble with a broad-bladed hunting knife. Anna's skull was not as smooth as the proverbial billiard ball, the odd tuft of hair remaining here and there, but Esmeralda appeared to be well satisfied with the scalping.

Anna's tongue was fabled among the castle staff, having driven the Baroness and numerous of her minions into the rapturous paradise of seemingly unattainable ecstasy on uncountable occasions.

Now it was Esmeralda's turn.

"You ordered me to lick you out, so you must like it. Well, I like it too and you lick like and angel so they tell me, so now get that tongue working on me."

As Esmeralda stood over her, Anna's expertise in cunnilingus was tested to the full as she was forced to pleasure her underling. Nuzzling between Esmeralda's labia, grasping her buttocks to pull her close, her tongue began to drive the girl into an ever more evident display of arousal. Esmeralda's increasingly vocal moans of pleasure reached fever pitch as Anna's nose brushed her erect clitoris, her teeth nibbled on it and her tongue rasped and lapped it. Ramming her crotch hard into Anna's face, Esmeralda orgasmed in a spasming, squealing crescendo of noisy bliss, squirting unquantifiable measures of musky love juice over her lips and into her mouth.

Esmeralda was one of those few women who when they climax, ejaculate copious volumes of love juices that are the equal of the semen produced by a man when he comes. The Baroness' aide, in all her years of service had never before had her mouth swilled with such copious quantities of female come. At last there was an explanation as to why the entire male population of the village was mad for the gypsy tart.

But it was Anna's own predicament that was uppermost in her mind. Back through endless, uncountable years she had been the Baroness' confidante, and until now there had never been any indication that she would not so remain. Her clash with the English insurgent now threatened her previously unassailable position. Not was it only threatened but seemingly completely destroyed.

Not for a second had the guards released their grip on her as she had pleasured Esmeralda and they hung on to her with equal forcefulness as the Baroness issued her next statement.

"Everything stays down when it is beaten. Any wild animal knows that. You Anna, will do the same and remain where you are until every cock, mouth or candle in the hall has partaken in full of anything and everything you have to offer."

And there was no lack of opportunists. Writhing and bucking beneath their assault, with hate-filled eyes Anna glared at Mistress Madonna as she looked on with a mixture of amazement and incredulity as one after another, the female guards rammed dildos into her sex or ordered her to suck their breasts and tongue their cunts. Many an old score was being settled. With the Baroness' permission, Anna's years of supercilious superiority were being laid waste. How could she be so hated? After all, it had been her who had led Vlad to the Baroness' walled-up body all those centuries ago.

It was only when the demands for her body had dwindled to nothing that she learnt that loyalty meant absolutely nothing to her determined self-centred mistress.

"Have you all finished with her?"

A simple question. But not one to end unaccountable years of servitude. Or so Anna thought.

She was wrong.

With every female guard agreeing that her appetite for Anna's charms had been satiated to the full, the Baroness sank back into her chair.

"Well Anna, it seems as if you and I are about to part company. Listen!"

Her heart filling with dread, Anna's ears picked up the ever-increasing howling of wolves suddenly welling up from outside the castle walls.

"Ah, such sweet music they make. And you thought you heard them earlier in the forest, did you not Mistress Madonna? Well you were right and now you hear them again; the children of the night. My children!"

The very same children that at their mere mention had so frightened Esmeralda. Except that she was not now to be their victim. With the utmost coolness, the Baroness turned to Vlad and the Marquis.

"You know what to do!"

Indeed they did. Advancing on her with the most terrifying evil intent, Vlad sank his thirsting canines deep into Anna's jugular. Then with her body emptied of its vital forces, with the Marquis' assistance he pulled aside a heavy pair of drapes, uncovering a never-repaired medieval artillery hole in the castle wall. That breach, in turn revealed black, heavy thunder clouds scudding across the face of the full moon and allowed the surging, wailing gale that was now blowing outside to blast into the room. Grabbing a seriously debilitated but still weakly struggling, screaming and cursing Anna into their arms, without ceremony they hurled her out into the black night. Seconds later, the howling of the wolves turned into the snarling, chomping and slavering appreciation of the taste of human flesh upon their tongues.

"Goodbye Anna, the pleasure was all mine."

And the Baroness was right, the pleasure had indeed all been hers.

TEN
THE CANDLE

What was it that a broken mirror was supposed to bring? Seven years of bad luck? Not so in her case, the Baroness knew. Her magic mirror had been destroyed by the authorities when they sentenced her to be walled up in the depths of Csejthe Castle but it had swiftly re-constituted itself then and had done so time and time again in the intervening years up until the present. And her luck had never been better.

It was now only minutes away from midnight; the hour at which evil forces would reign until the sun rose in the morning thus setting up the necessary conditions for her Ceremony. Again lifting the ruby-studded goblet of what seemed to be red wine but was in reality the drained blood of unfortunate non-virgin slaves to her lips, the Baroness studied a struggling and still defiant Mistress Madonna.

"Vladimir and the Marquis will enjoy the taste of your blood, of that I have no doubt as I am sure that it will prove to be of a rare quality. It is a great pity that you will now have to spend all of eternity in the company of the zombies in the catacombs; you were excellent material, but that is just the way it goes. We had so looked forward to you joining our little circle.

"However it really would not do to consign you to the pits without testing you myself, would it? And apart from that consideration, you do have the most tempting body. Anna was no match for you, but I think that you will find me a completely different proposition."

And indeed she was.

The battle was intense, furious and bloody. The Baroness possessed a real supernatural strength and matching Mistress Madonna blow for blow she prolonged the contest until even Mistress Madonna began to falter and weary. But to her, defeat was unthinkable and so she continued to fight and fight even more until the last of her strength was gone and her legs buckling under her, she sank to the floor. It had been the only tussle with either another man or woman that Mistress Madonna had ever lost.

Striding up and down in front of her defeated adversary, with grotesque flame-lit shadows flickering on the walls behind her the Baroness eyed Mistress Madonna with contempt, every now and then stopping to address her in deprecating terms.

"You fought well for a mortal, but there was just not enough steam in your engine, was there?"

Her eyes bored deeply and threateningly into Mistress Madonna's before she turned away to deliver an order to one of the guards.

"Fetch me a flogger; that one on the bench over there, the one with five flat-bladed studded tongues."

The guard scurried off and in the uncertain light, the Baroness returned her attention to Mistress Madonna. The atmosphere in the hall was almost crackling with tension as every evil-filled man and woman present eagerly awaited her next move.

"We have very little time left, but before the Ceremony takes place you are going to find out what it is like to be on the receiving end of what you are used to handing out.

"What it is like to be the submissive half of a relationship; what it is like to be the one receiving punishment; what it is like to be ordered to suck and lick your mistress into orgasm and to obey her every instruction without question.

"I do not know how much satisfaction I will gain from your ministrations or how quickly I will orgasm under your tongue, that we have yet to find out, but if you do not perform to my absolute satisfaction your future will be even more grisly than the one I already have in mind."

Julian was by now absolutely demented; the treatment being handed out to his mistress had him thrashing and screaming in his chains and yelling oaths and threats at the Baroness, and everyone else for that matter.

"For Satan's sake shut that imbecilic fool up!"

Leaping to carry out the Baroness' order, waving the guards aside, the Marquis attended to that task himself. Gathering a fat orange from the bowl of fruit on the table, he rammed it into Julian's mouth and ripping the belt from his trousers he wrapped it around Julian's head and buckled it tightly behind his neck. For once Mistress Madonna obviously felt pity for her devoted slave.

"Julian, it's alright, Mistress Madonna will get through this. Calm down. All you have to do is wait, I'll get us both out of this somehow."

The Baroness' snort of derision said it all.

"If there was anyone here who cared, they might remember those as your idiotically stupid last words. Now let us get on with it."

Mistress Madonna was once more strung up to the ceiling, but this time she hung by one leg, the other hanging free, so presenting unlimited access to her sex. Her wrists were cuffed and anchored by tight chains to the iron floor hoops and her long jet-black hair hung over her eyes to trail on the stone floor. Concentrating on her firm-buttocked rump the Baroness delivered a cold, merciless thrashing with the flogger, laying lash after lash on to its fleshy expanse. The five separate tongues were not only inflicting widespread fingers of searing pain that radiated through her entire body but were also leaving their own individual signature on Mistress Madonna's mouth- watering backside. What an arse! What a cock raising and lesbian-enticing display.

As the strikes fell upon her victim's haunches, the sight of the rippling arse meat was obviously exciting not only the Baroness but also the Marquis. Grabbing a flexible riding crop he leapt to join in the action, mostly concentrating on thrashing Mistress Madonna's exquisitely full and enticing breasts. Blazing, agonizing and almost incandescent tramlines striated her flesh as strike after strike fell upon her magnificently taut tits; her areolae and nugget-tipped nipples receiving extra special attention.

"Scream madame, if you please. Come on, don't hold it in; let me know I'm hurting you."

He was indeed hurting her, more than he realised but the last thing that she was ever going to do was give him the satisfaction of admitting it. In tandem with the Baroness, the Marquis was delivering a ferociously agonizing beating but legendary as his exploits were, as an involuntary tear dripped from her eye Mistress Madonna steeled herself against their combined onslaught.

"Fuck off!"

Hardly ladylike, but exactly in tune with her emotions.

Mistress Madonna was made of sterner stuff than either the Baroness or the Marquis expected; she was not that easy to vanquish. The Baroness' flat-bladed flogger found its target again and again and the Marquis' relentlessly slashing crop cut into her succulent breast flesh with merciless intensity.

"Foolish woman, do you not know my world? Have you no idea of what I am capable? Do you understand the indescribable pleasure that agonizing pain, and I mean *truly agonising*, can bring? If you don't then you very soon will."

Mistress Madonna was in fact well-informed on the Marquis' outrageously cold, pitiless and torturous propensities, having read and studied his writings; 'One Hundred and Twenty Days of Sodom' in particular. But things being as they were she thought that what he was referring to was not the usually accepted maxim that pain increases pleasure for the man or woman on the receiving end of punishment but the indescribable pleasure that *he* was gaining from inflicting agonizing pain on *her.* So she made no answer to his questions, rather than antagonize him even more it would be better to hold her silence.

And for her part, The Baroness was obviously growing impatient with the Marquis' interference in what should have been her enjoyment alone.

"You can have your turn later Marquis, but for now I wish to have her to myself."

Waving him away, she threw down the flogger and took up a multi-tailed leather martinet; the tails being knotted at their ends to intensify the agony when they found their mark. Sweeping Mistress Madonna's hair from her eyes so that she could better see, the Baroness slashed the martinet through the air.

"You are indeed a stubborn whelp but even you cannot hold out forever so let us find out how you like this."

Allowing Mistress Madonna's hair to fall back over her eyes, the Baroness stepped back and raised her arm high. Swooshing down through the thick air the leather tails struck straight between her victim's wide-open legs. A singeing, searing tumult of agony raced from her tortured sex to her brain and this time Mistress Madonna could not help herself, her free leg jerking wildly as she screamed the scream of the damned. Her cunt was on fire.

"Ah, not so defiant now are you, Mistress high and mighty?"

Gathering her senses together, Mistress Madonna blinked the tears from her eyes.

"What makes you say that, you aristocratic prat? I can take anything that you can hand out."

"Is that a fact? Well, we will soon find out, shall we not?"

In reality Mistress Madonna knew that the Baroness' words were true and she could not possibly hold out forever, but she was not going to capitulate without a fight.

The tails of the martinet flashed down mercilessly, sometimes striking along the full length of her sex and sometimes landing higher to punish her mons before biting into the widening slit between her wavy labia. Succulent labia that always set Julian's passions aflame and his cock throbbing and it was only too apparent that even in these circumstances it was happening again. With his mouth stuffed but his eyes wide open, he drank in the scene before him, his cock a rearing column of steel.

And like Julian, as the lashes continued to fall on her wickedly-abused vagina, unbelievably Mistress Madonna found herself becoming aroused. No! This was not what she wanted at all. Pain really was becoming pleasure and she could not allow it to continue.

But fight against as she did, it was of no use. Her body had a mind of its own; it wanted more of the same. Much more. Unconsciously she pushed her crotch forwards to meet the slashing martinet; her clitoris fighting its way out of its protective hood, searching for the tails, begging for the leather tips to home in on her lusting love bud.

The Baroness was so intent on delivering a scourging thrashing that she completely missed the tell-tale signs of Mistress Madonna's rising passions, even to the extent of not noticing the drops of love juice that flicked from the increasingly soaked leather tails as she whipped them up from her victim's flooding vagina.

Her clitoris erect and hardened into a fleshy Vesuvius on the verge of eruption and her nipples now throbbing and tingling with expectation, Mistress Madonna mentally blotted out her awful surroundings; leaving her mind and body free to do nothing but luxuriate in the torrent of high voltage rapture coursing through every fibre of her being. The Baroness carried on enthusiastically slashing down the tails of the martinet, still completely oblivious to Mistress Madonna's highly aroused state and it was only when she laid a particularly vicious strike directly on to her rejoicing clitoris and Mistress Madonna exploded in a squealing, thrashing climax of monumental intensity that she realized exactly what her beating had achieved. Not the total destruction of her victim's self-esteem and defences as she had intended but a series of joyous, noisy and intense orgasms.

Astounded, she stepped back.

"You bitch! You were enjoying yourself all along. How could I have been so foolish as to miss the signs? You are going to pay for this, have no doubt about it."

Still being hammered by the after shocks of her stupendous orgasm Mistress Madonna fought to bring herself back to reality, realising that she had no doubts whatsoever; worse would follow of that she was sure.

The Baroness looked around once more, her eyes this time alighting on a huge candelabrum holding five very large, fat candles standing in the middle of the long table. Mistress Madonna's heart fell as through a curtain of hair she saw the Baroness striding towards it. In the book that she had found at her bedside she had read that one of Erzebet Bathori's favourite tortures was to plunge a burning candle into a slave's vagina and to leave it burning with the hot wax flowing over the poor unfortunate's sex until the flame reached the entrance to her hole. That was what was going to happen to her, she just knew it.

Her fears were confirmed when the Baroness wrestled one of the candles from its holder and marched determinedly towards her. Her previously sopping, elating vagina dried and snapped shut in an instant and in desperation she tried to kick out at her torturer with her free leg.

"You, Vladimir, make yourself useful. Grab her leg and hold it steady."

His bony grip was of steel as he followed the Baroness' instructions and straightened Mistress Madonna's leg, pulling it out to full length. Grinning evilly, the Baroness attempted to drill the flaming candle down into Mistress Madonna's love tunnel. She met with no success. The siege was on, this was one cunt that was not going to allow entry without a battle.

"Marquis! I need some help here."

He was by her side in a flash.

"Open that twat for me."

"Delighted, dear Baroness."

And he was too. Dipping all the fingers of both hands into the slit between them, he tugged Mistress Madonna's sex lips apart. But the girth of the candle was such that the Baroness still had to virtually screw it into the depths of her vagina.

But eventually it was buried deep enough to stay put and everyone moved away to watch the molten wax roll down the candle and flow over the pulped sex beneath it. The savaged state of Mistress Madonna's labia heightened the effect of the wax, the resultant sensations of burning that she felt being greatly intensified as the wax solidified over them.

After a few minutes, the Marquis broke the silence.

"Baroness, if I were you I'd hurry things up a little. It's past midnight now and you should be preparing for the Ceremony."

The Marquis was right. Of that there was no doubt. And never before, throughout the countless years that the Ceremony had taken place, had the Baroness ever lingered for one moment longer than was necessary to commence the ritual proceedings. But this was different. She was faced with an exceptional adversary; a woman whose overwhelming combined aura of strength and sexuality was sparking a previously undreamt of licentious hunger in her loins. Cocks, cunts, tits or whatever, she had experience her fill of all of those things. But her breasts had never been sucked or her vagina tongued by a woman such as her captive. Mistress Madonna was unique and she had never before drunk her fill of a woman like her.

Suddenly the decision was made.

The Ceremony could wait!

Announcing her unprecedented decision, the Baroness was hardly surprised when the Marquis addressed Mistress Madonna, delivering an announcement of his own.

"I know that the Baroness has her own plans for you but I see no reason why I also cannot join her in enjoying your body. And for that matter, why Vlad cannot have his own little piece of the action."

In response to the Marquis' words, a sort of hideous half-vocalized snuffling from Vlad confirmed that he was only too eager to take up that particular option. The Baroness really had no choice.

"Alright, I am not averse to sharing her with you. It's a great pity that she was not what I wanted her to be, so we may as well make the best of the situation."

But she still wanted the first bite of the apple; it was her right. And she said so. Unsurprisingly the Marquis acquiesced to her demand without question. As much as he enjoyed dominating others, he also gained pleasure from being subservient to the Baroness.

"Oh, we don't mind waiting, do we Count?"

Whether Count Dracula minded or not Mistress Madonna never found out. Standing passively by he watched as the guards freed her from her restraints and stood her upright. The burning candle was still wedged firmly into her vagina and once on her feet the flame floated upwards, flashing her luxurious pubic hair into short-lived flame. Singed down to the pubic bone, her mons now resembled that of poor departed Anna.

The candle did not generate a particularly hot flame, but as it licked around her labia and began to melt the solidified wax that coated them, its intensity was sufficient to cause her an undesirable discomfort. It was something that with effort she could withstand but still something that she wished she did not have to combat.

And nor did she for long.

"Extinguish that candle, she will be no use to me with a burnt cunt."

A heavy-breasted female guard rushed to obey the Baroness' order. Her hand delved between Mistress Madonna's thighs; thighs spread wide by the massive column of wax plugging her vagina, and a pinched-together forefinger and thumb crushed the flame into a smoking, blackened length of scorched wick.

"Well done. Now bring her over here."

Fight as she may, Mistress Madonna was now seriously weakened and despairingly found herself without the resources to offer any serious resistance as the guard determinedly dragged her to stand before the Baroness, who had settled herself into a huge high-backed chair. With the monstrous candle still stuck firmly up her cunt, Mistress Madonna could not close her legs and was forced to stand humiliatingly facing her tormentor with her legs spread wide.

"It seems that you are enjoying that big fat substitute for the real thing stretching your vagina to its limit, so we will leave it where it is, although I cannot say that I would derive such pleasure from a lump of wax."

Mistress Madonna was most certainly not enjoying the cunt-plugging pole stuffing her so uncomfortably and she was well aware that the Baroness knew that fact. She was just intent on prolonging her discomfort throughout whatever ordeal she had in mind next.

"And I do not see why you should be the only one enjoying yourself around here."

Mistress Madonna steeled herself; here it came.

"Guards! Down on her knees!"

Heavy hands on her shoulders forced Mistress Madonna down into the Baroness' required position. Widening her legs, the Baroness lifted the hem of her dress and hiked it up over her waist. Her vagina, expectant and hungry was revealed in all its thatched glory.

"I do not think that it is necessary for me to spell out what I require of you."

No there was not, what the Baroness required was patently obvious. There came a time when the inevitable could not be denied. So, pragmatically accepting the situation for what it was, Mistress Madonna began her investigation of her victor's sex.

Shuffling closer to her, Mistress Madonna raised the Baroness' legs in both hands and hung them over her shoulders in order to gain better access to her lusting quarry. Reaching out to separate the Baroness' wet but closed labia, Mistress Madonna experimentally ran her tongue along the length of her pubic slit. Then starting from close to the Baroness' anus, she dug her pursed tongue between her sex lips and worked her way upwards to the entrance to her love tunnel.

The taste of the Baroness' vagina was unlike anything Mistress Madonna had experienced before. Pungent and musky it was, but there was something completely different about it. Something that actually set her taste buds tingling with unexpected pleasure. Was this what a vampire's cunt tasted like?

She felt the Baroness shiver as her mouth fastened on to her sex and she began sucking as well as thrusting her tongue deep into its savoury hole, feasting on its unexpectedly piquant and unusually enjoyable taste.

Leaving her tongue where it was, she nuzzled her nose upwards to rub against the Baroness' clitoris. The reaction was instantaneous. The Baroness' labia widened even further, Mistress Madonna's tongue suddenly penetrating so far that its root was firmly buried between the Baroness' sex petals and painfully drawn deep into her vagina. A vagina that flooded oceans of that deliciously unusual nectar. Unable to help herself Mistress Madonna clasped both her hands around the Baroness' buttocks and pulled her closer to the edge of the chair.

And just as the Baroness had never been serviced by a woman such as she, she herself had never been presented with a cunt such as the one nestling between the Baroness' legs. Again she began to lose all sense of her surroundings as she drank deep of unexpected and extraordinarily flavoursome aristocratic vampire love juice, inhaling great sniffs of its singularly unparalleled but still musky fragrance.

And she was obviously working magic on the Baroness. With Mistress Madonna's hands still firmly gripping the unyieldingly-firm meat of her arse, rolling her hips, she ground her sex into Mistress Madonna's face; long, low moans of gratification spilling from her lips. Her legs closed in, clamping Mistress Madonna's cheeks and as she increasingly began to lose control, Mistress Madonna felt the Baroness' previously firm and crushing thighs begin to tremble.

Mistress Madonna's lapping, probing tongue, sucking mouth and busy stimulating nose continued to work on her soaking vagina and rigid clitoris, exciting her more and more and stoking up her lust into an inferno. Mistress Madonna felt as if she were suffocating as the Baroness' sex crushed against her mouth, and the trembling became a kind of all-over feverish shaking; the low moans working their way up the scales of both pitch and volume, until reaching a cataclysmic, paralysing climax she howled a banshee wail of ear-shattering intensity.

It was minutes before the gasping and grunting induced by her stupendous orgasm quietened and the iron grip of her thighs began to slacken, allowing her sopping sex to slide off Mistress Madonna's face. The look on the Baroness' face was almost sorrowful as at her instruction the guards moved back in and hauled Mistress Madonna to her feet.

"All these hundreds of years and suddenly I find what I have always searched for; the perfect tongue in the perfect mouth of the perfect lover. And just as suddenly it is going to be torn away from me. Why oh why could you not have been what I wanted you to be?"

"I am what I am Baroness, and nothing can change that."

And nothing could. And neither could anything stop what was to come next.

"My turn now I believe."

The cold fingers of fear returned to grip Mistress Madonna's heart, she was at the mercy of the most depraved man in history: The Marquis de Sade. But things were not to turn out quite as she expected.

"Take her over to the bench and stand her facing it."

While his orders were being carried out, the Marquis collected several lengths of coarse rope and when she was arranged to his satisfaction, he began to bind her. Firstly he carefully circled the mound of one of her breasts with a length of the rope and then using a slipknot pulled it taut until the tit was bulging out from a viciously constricted root. Leaving the end of the rope hanging, he repeated the operation on the other breast.

"Now, bend her over the bench, face down and with her arms out flat in front of her."

With her breasts squashed beneath her, he pulled the ends of the rope out from either side and left them to hang over the edges of the bench. Moving on to her legs, he spread them wide and looped separate lengths of rope around each ankle before tying them to the corner legs of the bench. Then taking two much longer lengths, he knotted them around each of her wrists. Tugging on the ropes, in turn he stretched both of her arms to full length, passed the rope over the edge and under the bench   and tied the ends to the legs already holding her ankles captive. Pressing on the ropes with his full weight, he tested them to ensure that they were as taut as they could possibly be.

They were.

The Marquis turned to the guards, indicating the ends of lengths of rope that bound her tits.

"Two of you, take one end each and pull for all you're worth and when the ropes are at full stretch, keep them that way until I tell you otherwise."

The ropes were coarse, burning mistress Madonna's flesh; not only her breasts but also her wrists and her ankles as she struggled to free herself. But try as she may, she was unable to move anything but her backside, which was exactly what the Marquis intended.

"Now, let us begin."

So saying, the Marquis moved to stand in front of her. Slowly and deliberately he began to peel off his pantelons; fashionable tight trousers of the late eighteenth century that fitted snugly around his waist, clung to his thighs and calves and were anchored under the insteps of his boots with straps.

God! He had the king of all cocks. Bigger than The Colonel's. And it was only inches from her face. He was going to make her suck it! Mistress Madonna was aghast, her mouth dried and her tongue stuck to the roof of her mouth. She would never be able to get her mouth around a monstrous weapon such as that. But wait a minute. She took a second look. It was flaccid, despite its size it was floppy; he did not have an erection. What did that mean? That he could not raise one? No, that was silly because she had seen him fuck Anna with great gusto.

So did it mean that he was not going to fuck her after all? Or that he wanted her to fellate him into hardness?

Neither of those things as it happened, although he did press its grotesquely bulbous bell end to her lips before calling over to the Baroness.

"The martinet seemed to have a profound effect upon this slut, so I think that it will do nicely for my purposes. We will start with that. You know what to do!"

"Yes Marquis, of course I do; after all this is not the first time, is it?"

Mistress Madonna was mystified as kicking his trousers away, he bent over the bench, his naked, hairy arse stuck up in the air and his head next to hers on the top of the bench.

Seemingly coming from nowhere, she heard a sweeping 'whooosh' as the knotted tails were whipped through the air, quickly followed by the flat, thuddy impact of leather smacking down on flesh. She felt the Marquis judder beside her and suddenly realised that the Baroness was using the martinet on him and not her. Again and again she heard the 'swhooshing' and the sound of the leather tails striking his bloated flesh as the Baroness scourged him with great relish. She was unable to see where the strikes were landing on the Marquis' body, but she *could* see the look of jubilation on the Baroness' face; she was getting great satisfaction from her actions.

But not so, the Marquis it seemed.

"Confound and blast you woman, can't you do anything right? Put some power into it; I feel nothing more than the brush of angels' wings fluttering against my flesh. I want more. I need more! I'll never get my cock up if you carry on like some namby-pamby milkmaid. Hit me harder, free that gypsy girl and get her to help you if you can't do it yourself."

Suddenly Mistress Madonna understood. The Marquis lived for punishment and pain. He gained as much satisfaction from the bite of a cane cutting into his flesh as he did from inflicting that same pain upon an innocent slave. He was desperate to feel the lash upon his flesh; he needed it to arouse his passion and put fire in penis. Sometimes all that was necessary to achieve that end was for him to witness that punishment being delivered to his quarry. He had watched her deliver a pitiless and bloody thrashing to Anna; and that sight had been enough to generate a solid straining hard-on that had enabled him to fuck the Baroness' long time aide with unbounded and uncompromising enthusiasm.

Mistress Madonna's studies of him were now fully confirmed, he did not only enjoy inflicting torment and pain upon others, but he delighted in being on the receiving end of those very same agonies himself. He was not only the father of sadism but also the ultimate masochist. And having been aroused and thoroughly sated by Anna he now needed extra stimulation to thrust his cock back into the rock-solid state that it needed to be in to fuck her.

So there was hope yet. Perhaps his cock had wilted for the foreseeable future. Misplaced hope as it turned out. The Baroness was not to be compromised.

"I do not think that the help of Esmeralda is required. Brace yourself."

The martinet fell once more, obviously with re-doubled vigour from the Baroness because as the leather tails cut into his backside, his lacerated buttocks jerked up and away from the bench.

"Hallelujah! That's it. Hit me again. Do it. Hit me, hard!"

Smack after smack ravaged him, every strike receiving an ecstatic commendation until he obviously reached the destination to which he was headed.

"Enough."

He straightened up.

"Look at this!"

He was addressing the Baroness, but Mistress Madonna raising her eyes was able to see the object of his euphoric exclamation. Iron hard and gigantic, it strained straight and skywards from his groin.

Christ, she had never seen anything like it. She had met many men who had claimed to be hung like a horse but in her experience the only thing that was really hung that way was in fact that particular animal.

Not on this instance.

"What do you think then madam, is this not the most spectacular sex pistol that you have ever seen?"

That remark was meant for Mistress Madonna and although she was not gagged, she was rendered speechless. It truly was as he boasted. It was equally as big, if not bigger, than the flaming candle that had only so recently been pulled from her savagely-stretched vagina.

"And of course, I'm going to introduce you to it. You'll like it, I know you will. But even if you don't, *I* will. And believe me; my promises do not count for nothing, this cock has pleasured and satisfied countless women both far above *and* below your social status. I'll fuck anything you know, women are all the same to me; sluts and whores and once I've fucked them, their lives are changed forever, they never attain the same level of satisfaction ever again. As a matter of fact, no matter what she might say, that is why the Baroness remains here. As you now know, she is herself one of the undead and a drinker of blood as are we all, but if she wished she could return to Transylvania with the Count; but she does not. And there is only one reason for that: my cock! And when I've fucked you, you will feel exactly the same. Ready yourself for the rogering of your life."

As he walked around the bench to position himself behind her splayed sex, Mistress Madonna realised that although his rhetoric was unimpeachable, his cock was not in the same league. It was wilting! Mistress Madonna was not alone in her observation.

"I fear that your mouth is growing bigger than your cock, Marquis. Perhaps you should cut out the boasting and concentrate on the fucking. It appears that you need a little more assistance; thank your lucky stars that I am here to provide it."

The rattan cane! Get it!"

The Baroness' order was directed at one of the guards, who flew to obey.

Now lost from her sight, Mistress Madonna felt the Marquis position himself behind her backside and between her cruelly pulled-apart legs. Urgent fingers grasped the torturing candle and tugged it from her hole, her labia immediately clamping together in relief. The relief did not last. The same fingers dug back into her hole, preparing it to receive another visitor. Even semi-erect, the Marquis' cock lay heavy and threatening against the entrance to her vagina. But that cock was a giant and its only hope of gaining penetration was to be one thousand per cent rock solid.

"As always, you are right dear Baroness. So if you will, make me feel it."

And the Baroness did just that. The cane slashed over the Marquis' naked arse with fearful power. Every ounce of her strength was used in delivering the strike. The effect was instantaneous. Mistress Madonna felt the bulbous glans twitch up against her twat.

"Again!"

The cane whipped down once more. This time Mistress Madonna felt the bell-end gain a half an inch of entry into her love tunnel. She was used to The Colonel's massive weapon inching its way inside her, but this was something different altogether. This was the biggest dick that she had ever come across in her whole life.

"Come on woman, hit me again! Make it hurt."

Gritting her teeth the Baroness delivered a strike of phenomenal power. That power transferred itself to the Marquis' dick. At the moment of its impact he thrust another solid inch of granite into Mistress Madonna's cunt.

"More! And faster. Come on, I'm almost there."

The strikes continued to fall upon the Marquis' arse and with each one his monstrous cock pushed Mistress Madonna's labia further apart and gained further headway into her vagina.

And Mistress Madonna suddenly found herself with a problem.

She was beginning to like it.

Every painful strike upon his rapidly reddening backside resulted in another pleasurable inch of penetration. She would never have believed that this could happen, but it was. His cock was glorious. A diamond, where all the others that had gone before it were paste. Strike, grunt, and groan; between them they did all three and the resulting extra inches of penetration followed one after another. Gaining further and further entry inside her, his giant of a cock widened her hole into a tunnel of such huge proportions that even as she felt herself stretching to accommodate its girth, she could not believe it. This was what she had been waiting for all her life.

But the Marquis still needed more. And he got it. In abundance.

Whatever extra strength the Baroness put into those final strokes as she furiously lashed his backside were evidently more than sufficient because as the Marquis frenziedly cannoned into her, Mistress Madonna found herself being stoked into an ever increasing and unstoppably ferocious climax. Shudderingly melting into a vortex of whirling, mind-shattering, cunt-numbing orgasms she left the Earth behind her as she revelled in a universe of previously undiscovered pleasure.

But the Marquis was still up for it. He had plenty left in him. As she lay panting beneath him, he ceased his frenetic fucking and paused to allow her to regain some sense of being.

"I told you you'd like it, didn't I?"

Indeed he had. But she had never for one moment thought that it would be like this. He had the king of all cocks. He fucked for the Devil himself. And when he carried on thrusting and plundering her vagina, she took only seconds to commence the countdown to her next voyage of sexual discovery. Astronauts fly to the Moon; she flew further. She flew to the stars.

The Marquis however was flying nowhere. The whore was shuddering beneath him, urgently pressing her cunt back against his every thrust; moaning and gasping for breath as he reamed her with all the energy of which he was capable. But it was happening again.

His cock was wilting! What was the bloody Baroness up to? She knew that he needed pain and punishment to have the capacity to fulfil his desires.

And pain was something of which he most definitely was not getting enough. He had to do something about it. He vented his spleen on the Baroness.

"The gypsy tart! She hates you, which means that she hates me too. So she won't hold back. Free her now to help you, the guards will make sure that she doesn't cause any trouble for you."

He fully realised the Baroness' reticence, once armed Esmeralda could turn on her mistress but he did not care and in any case he was certain that she would not deliberately throw away even the most slender chance of absolution.

After she had taken her pleasure with Anna, Esmeralda had once again been chained at the side of the flaming fire and with his weapon slackening by the second and slowly taking its leave of the cunt of the darkly beautiful but unfortunately fake vampiric figure beneath him, the Marquis was consumed by frustration at the time it was taking the guards to release Esmeralda and drag her over to join the Baroness.

"Give her a bullwhip."

The Baroness had hit the bull again; that was what he needed to feel in addition to the agonising torment of the cane; the bite of leather cutting into his flesh. And what better than to have the pain delivered in tandem by a high-born Lady of the aristocracy and a striking low life, dark-haired and uncompromisingly promiscuous gypsy.

And so it began. A cutting lash from the whip was followed immediately by a debilitating strike from the cane and with every lancing, slashing line of fire that flashed across his buttocks, his cock regained more of its former strength. The two women flailed him mercilessly, driving his cock back to its former glory. Complementing the cane working on his haunches, the bullwhip ripped into his back and shoulders, the magnificent pain propelling his shagging into a frenzied, frenetic humping.

The squeezing, clamping cunt and its owner possessed qualities that he had never come across in all his years of debauchery. He felt as if he could fuck and fuck and carry on fucking her forever. Yelling out for the Baroness and Esmeralda to thrash him even more mercilessly, he revelled in the pain, ramming himself deeper and deeper into Mistress Madonna's surprisingly welcoming and juicy twat. Her lubricating love juices flowed in a veritable flood over his cock, helping him penetrate even further and under the influence of a frenzied barrage of whip lashes and strikes of the cane he felt the spunk boil in his bollocks and surge up through his urethra to spurt jet after jet of red hot semen deep into her equally rejoicing and spasming vagina.

Now he knew how the Baroness felt, for like her he had just experienced the orgasm of a lifetime. What a pity that this English temptress was soon to be drained of her blood and consigned to the catacombs. If she would only be more co-operative then he would order that she be spared and he would fuck her senseless every day. But he was not fool enough to believe that that would happen and with a sigh of regret he heaved his slackening weapon from its still-sucking sheath.

As for the temptress herself, she had been fucked by the Marquis de Sade. And she had loved every moment of it!

ELEVEN
THE LABORATORY

Detonating with a deafening, earth-shattering impact, heart-stopping bursts of thunder swiftly followed the almost surreal multi-forks of blinding lightning that had declared war on the castle, as with their wrists bound behind their backs and with the whips of the Amazonian female guards wickedly lashing their naked flesh, Mistress Madonna, Julian and Esmeralda were hustled down the forbiddingly gloomy, steep and well-worn stone steps leading to the depths of the castle. In deadly silence and with candelabra held high, the Baroness and the Marquis led the way as the party descended; their flickering candles shrivelling hideous giant spiders into ashes as the flames swept through the smoky-white silk of the webs that hung in festoons from the ceiling.

After the Marquis had finished fucking Mistress Madonna, the Baroness had suddenly seemed to come to her senses and insisted that the Ceremony must commence as soon as possible. Vladimir would have to postpone his shagging of Mistress Madonna until they were all safely down in the Temple. He had not liked that at all, but persuaded by the Marquis he had grudgingly agreed and so it was that an exceedingly disgruntled Dracula brought up the rear.

When the stone steps gave way to a rough staircase hewn from solid rock, Mistress Madonna realised that they must now have journeyed below the foundations of the castle. And still they stumbled ever downwards, now and again passing the entrances to side tunnels that wound away into the darkness, and for the first time the forbidding quiet was broken. But it was not a welcoming sound that fell upon Mistress Madonna's ears.

Spine-chilling wails and ululating moans of despair flowed from their impenetrable depths and with an ice-cold chill of horror numbing her very being, she realised that they were passing through the catacombs; the inescapable prison to which the blood-drained slaves and zombies had been banished, destined to remain forever in a twilight world of neither life nor death.

The fate that the Baroness had promised her!

Lord only knew how much iron ore had been smelted in order forge the grotesque medieval instruments of torture that filled the vast flame-lit chamber into which they finally emerged. This particular area was exclusively the Marquis' domain; this was where his own slaves were stabled and unlike those owned by the Baroness, his unfortunate victims did not have to remain virgins. It was here that he spent countless hours using them sexually in all and every way, honing ever new and humiliating perversions and supervising the construction of weird machines of torture and bondage. With perspiration dripping from her forehead, her eyes wide with disbelief, Mistress Madonna was dragged struggling through its overheated Gothic expanse. The Baroness waved expansively, pointing out what to her were its most appealing features; it seemed that she made a point of witnessing the Marquis' more inventive acts of depravity.

"You would love to watch the Marquis at work my dear, he is so versatile and there is always something new with him; you could learn a lot. It is a shame that you will never be given the chance."

An dull-black iron maiden stood open, its wicked spikes sharpened to needle points; there were whipping posts, a stretching ladder, a head press and an iron hanging cage. There was even a guillotine. That was one of his favourites the Marquis told Mistress Madonna.

"But I've never actually used it for its original purpose; I don't need to, the mere sight of it is enough to reduce these pathetic peasants to witless obeisance."

Hanging from the walls or laid on benches were breast talons, metal jaw locks, thumbscrews, iron collars of thorns and countless other horrific implements of torment. The Marquis did not say if *they* were ever used in practice but contrary to her usual tough imperturbable nature, Mistress Madonna felt a wave of compassion for these poor slaves wash over her.

The Baroness' guards were all female but the Marquis' force was most definitely all male; men who were obviously enjoying their labours. Aping their earlier inspirational historical heroes, hideous hooded, bare-chested, leather-aproned and heavily-muscled masters of the Inquisition were digging white-hot pokers into the depths of flaming braziers before waving them between the wide-open legs of defenceless slaves; boys as well as girls. And those that were not actually inflicting unmentionable mind-melting horrors upon the slaves were mercilessly fucking and buggering those that were deemed available to anyone and everyone.

Completely disregarding the screams and pleas for mercy that rent the air as the party made its way towards the Temple, the Baroness led the way as her guards dragged Mistress Madonna, Julian and Esmeralda in her wake.

Leaving the chamber of horrors behind after passing through a linking tunnel, the party emerged into another enormous cavern. But this one was entirely different. It was flooded with artificial light, the unmistakable smell of ozone filled the air and it was crammed with weird scientific instruments. Thick shielded cables ran across the floor linking huge transformers to a strange apparatus that reached up and through the stone ceiling and there was a multitude of gauges, long-handled switching devices and other paraphernalia that at once reminded Mistress Madonna of the sort of pseudo-scientific devices that featured so heavily in old-fashioned black and white monster movies.

Dracula gripped Mistress Madonna's arm and turned her to face him. She recoiled in horror as his fetid breath washed over her and his piercing and heavily black-rimmed eyes bored into her own.

"The castle keep. The metal projections reaching for the sky. You wondered what purpose they served. Here is your answer. In a storm such as the one now very fortuitously raging above us, they function very much as lightning conductors. One strike and millions of volts of electricity are garnered and transmitted down here to be stored in the giant batteries you see all around you. Either that or the power is stepped down to a useable current by those giant transformers and directed to whatever apparatus I so desire for instantaneous use. When it has all been used up we remain without the means to run the machines or light the castle, which is why I told you that we did not always have electricity."

Mistress Madonna's day had been horrifically strange and eventful to say the least. One weird happening had followed another. But this was the weirdest of all. Far beyond the boundaries of her imagination, she found herself having to accept that things that she would normally have regarded as pure fantasy had now become reality.

"At this moment we have electricity in abundance and I believe that the Baroness will agree that while her virgins are being prepared for the Ceremony, she has sufficient time to introduce *you* to the delights of our little laboratory. Is that not so, Baroness?"

"That may well be so but first there is another little matter that requires my attention."

The Baroness' urgent voice jolted Mistress Madonna from her introspective ruminations.

"The gypsy girl! Bring her here."

The guards hustled Esmeralda to the Baroness' side.

"This is where you find out why I spared you after you ruined Arlecchino and threatened the Ceremony. I told you that an old admirer was waiting to greet you, did I not?"

At the end of an outstretched arm, the Baroness' hand gave way to an extended index finger. Wild-eyed and obviously in a state of great apprehension, Esmeralda's eyes followed her pointing digit.

"And there he is."

In the forest when she had first laid eyes upon Esmeralda and her pet goat, Mistress Madonna would not have been in the least surprised if the hideous one-eyed, hunchbacked guardian of the bells of Notre Dame had made an appearance. He had not. But suddenly, showered by sparks falling from the streams of blinding electricity that flashed in great sizzling arcs from terminal to terminal of the Frankenstein-inspired devices, there he was.

Quasimodo!

Esmeralda's shrieking hysterical scream faded to silence as she fell to the floor in a dead faint. The Baroness turned to Dracula and the Marquis.

"You see, I was not wrong. I know that in light of the grave manner in which she had threatened the Ceremony by seducing Arlecchino and rendering him a non virgin, that you both were of the opinion that I was treating the gypsy trash too leniently; but see! Look at her. An unending future suffering the slavering attentions of a creature such as Quasimodo is surely a fate worse than anything that you two could have devised. And I have given her to him. Unconditionally, to do with as he pleases. Forever.

"Can you imagine what horrors she will feel as he clamps his slobbering mouth over her nipples? The revulsion that she will be forced to endure day after day as he tries to force his lolling tongue up into her firmly-shuttered vagina? The vile smell and mouldering unwashed taste of the monstrous cock that has been locked inside his tights for aeons? Believe me, I know him, he will have her sucking him off the moment that she revives. Then he will fuck her. Again and again. Every day for infinity.

"She will die more deaths than any of us can possibly imagine. Is that not sweet retribution?"

There was not even the slightest murmur of disagreement.

"All right Quasimodo, you can take her away now."

Seizing one of Esmeralda's wrists, knees bent and shuffling across the floor like an Amazonian forest primate, Quasimodo dragged the half-unconscious gypsy girl towards whatever part of the cavern that he called his own.

But the Baroness was wrong.

The moment that Esmeralda showed any real sign of life, which was less than halfway to the sanctuary of the machinery, he stopped. But he did not make her suck his cock as she had predicted. Tugging her legs up from the floor and planting an ankle over each of his shoulders, he raised her cunt to cock height and hauling out his diabolically deformed weapon, drove it straight into her defenceless twat. His supernaturally stiff cock was deep inside her and laying siege to her cervix in seconds. Esmeralda was wrestled back and forth, her shoulders writhing over the stone floor as he plundered her sex with merciless ferocity. This was supposed to be the ultimate punishment, the end of everything. But Mistress Madonna could see that strange things were happening to Esmeralda; things that had never happened to her before.

With his hands clamped to her buttocks, holding her as steady as he could Quasimodo banged into her with unrestrained, pile-driving thrusts of his throbbing, tunnel-filling dick. And in return, amazingly she began to drive her hips upwards to meet his frantic downward plunges until in a combined cacophony of animal-like howls and feminine screams of delight, they both came in a duet of shaking, shrieking ungodly orgasms.

Open-mouthed, the Baroness looked on. And she looked on even more incredulously as the hunchback threw a dreamy-eyed Esmeralda over his shoulder and was lost from sight as he shuffled into the midst of the electronic jungle.

TWELVE
THE CAGE

"What was it that you said Baroness? That you had consigned the gypsy girl to an eternity of suffering at the hands of a beast she could not stand? Well if that's what you wanted it seems to me that you most definitely have not centred on the target, as far as I can see she has just disappeared into a haven of perpetual pleasure. Let us hope that you have not been so wrong about everything else."

The Marquis' hand indicated Mistress Madonna.

"This English whore, are you intending to consign her to paradise also?"

Despite his scathing comments the Baroness stood her ground.

"She will suffer, have no doubt of that."

"I truly hope so dear Elizabeth, but you have so very little time left. Whatever you have in mind, I suggest that you get on with it."

Mistress Madonna's mind whirled, there had to be someway out of this situation. But if there was, she could not find it. Somewhere outside the castle, the world must be carrying on as normal. But normality had long since deserted this particular world. She found that her mind, usually as sharp as a razor blade, was beginning to cloud. She had never given much credence to the paranormal, but as the reality of the world outside increasingly became overtaken by the abnormality of her present situation she felt herself succumbing even more deeply to the chilling, abhorrent evil atmosphere of the laboratory.

It was all around her. Weirdness. Weirdness and danger.

Before coming to the castle she had relished and revelled in a life of supposed out of the ordinary and dangerous living, but now she realised that compared to this her past experiences had all been a sham. She had never before found herself in such real danger. That danger manifested itself into a tangible, physical form as the fingers of one of the Baroness' hands clamped themselves to one of her spectacular nipples and squeezed mercilessly. Thimble-sized and surrounded by an areola of unchallengeable brown magnificence, Mistress Madonna's teats suffered the same agony as if they were being were being crushed in the jaws of a nutcracker.

"Alright Marquis, we have power in abundance at the moment, so shall we put some of it to good use?"

"Anything you say, dear Baroness."

"Good! I'm really going to give this vixen something to remember me by. And vital to my purposes as he is, I see no reason that her slave cannot receive a little of the same treatment."

There it was again; this reference to Julian. What was it that made him so special to the Baroness? Mistress Madonna could only wonder as her eyes roved over the harshly lit chamber, her gaze falling upon all manner of strange, intimidating electrical devices. And none were more menacingly heart-stopping than a series of tall, domed and open-fronted circular metal cages, all conspicuously linked by heavy cables to control panels that stood in front of each one of them.

The Baroness looked around and obviously not finding what she was looking for, called out impatiently.

"Quasimodo! Stop whatever you are doing this instant. You have got all the time in the world to fuck Esmeralda; right now I have need of your assistance. Get over here and do it quickly!"

Shuffling out from behind a sparking, unidentifiable electrical contraption, he sulkily
answered her summons.

"The main controls! Fire them up and show Mistress Madonna what lies in wait for her."

Heaving down on a long lever, he gunned six loudly buzzing giant domes sitting on top of almost roof high supports into life. Each of the three cages was sited between two of the domes and if Julian had been able to communicate with her, he could have told Mistress Madonna that they resembled huge Van de Graaf generators. But they were not generating electricity here, they were harvesting it direct from the sky; either way it made no difference to her intended fate.

"Now, let them go!"

As Quasimodo threw another switch, the chamber was instantaneously thrown into the middle of a flashing, crackling and thunderously noisy lightning storm. Travelling at a hundred thousand miles a second, bolts of fiery electricity streaked from the domes to strike the metal cages, running over the bars and almost obscuring them in a haze of blazing elemental fury.

The Baroness allowed the display to continue for several minutes, watching gleefully as Mistress Madonna recoiled in terror.

"Enough! Turn it off now. Let us get her inside the centre cage."

"No! You can't put me in there. It's inhuman."

Mistress Madonna's fright was plainly evident. And so was the Baroness' satisfaction at seeing that fright so tangibly displayed.

"Quite my dear. But then, we are *not* human, are we?"

Kicking out and struggling, it took all the guards' efforts to manhandle her over to the cage and push her inside. They showed no mercy, scraping and bruising her succulent flesh as they forced her arms behind her back and clamped her elbows and wrists tightly together with metal cuffs behind a steel pole that was fixed into the floor of the cage. The cuffs were painful in the extreme and only prompted her to re-double her assault on the guards with her wildly kicking legs, but she was close to total exhaustion and she felt her strength give out under the determined assault of her captors.

With their steely fingers digging into her flesh, several pairs of firm hands grabbed her legs and weakening greatly she found herself helpless to prevent her feet being pulled wide apart, feeling the grazing bite of yet more metal cuffs as they were snapped tight around her ankles. Once her flailing legs had been dealt with, a chain was clipped to the cuffs clamping her wrists and digging between the cheeks of her backside, was tugged down and fixed tightly to a hoop on the floor of the cage.

Adjustable for height, a metal bar with an iron collar attached to its end projected from the pole and holding her head steady, the guards clamped the collar around her neck. With her wrists and feet now tightly chained to the floor of the cage and her head held immobile by the collar, the Baroness obviously felt that Mistress Madonna presented no further physical threat and ordered the guards away.

"Now, make your peace and say goodbye to the world."

Mistress Madonna's aridly dry mouth prevented her from making any reply or uttering any further plea for mercy and she could only watch helplessly as addressing the hunchback, the Baroness ordered him to once again throw the switch that set the lightning flowing.

Blinded by the light and deafened by the racket, Mistress Madonna screamed hysterically as two and a half million volts of electricity attacked the cage and raced over the surface of the metal bars. It took several minutes before she came to her senses. She should have been fried instantly and now be nothing but a charred, blackened corpse; but she was not. She was alive; temporarily blinded by the light but definitely still in one piece.

Suddenly, the electrical display stopped.

"Surprised, are you? You do not really think that I would allow you to take your leave of this world in such an easy and quick manner. No, terror is what I wanted you to feel; and you did. At the moment the cage is functioning as a Faraday device, the electricity passes directly through the metal frame into the earth and you are earthed by the stone floor. I expect that you cannot see properly as yet, but when you can you will notice that attached to some of the metal ribs are chains with steel cuffs on the end; when I wish to really dispose of a slave, their wrists are clamped into these cuffs and when the lightning strikes, all the voltage flows through them and the slave is no more.

"But as I told you earlier, I have other plans for you."

Because of the way in which her arms were secured behind her back, Mistress Madonna's breasts jutted proud and firm and reaching into the cage, the Baroness appreciatively clapped a hand over their inviting meat; squeezing the heavy orbs in turn and rolling the projectile nipples beneath her palm. Mistress Madonna was acutely conscious of the Baroness' other hand slipping between her thighs to open her sex lips, wincing with discomfort as stiff fingers pushed up into her resisting vagina.

"Ah, we will have to do something about that my petal, I need you nice, juicy and open for what I have in mind. But let us start at the beginning, shall we?"

And the beginning proved to be her tits.

Hanging from the roof bars of the cage were two lengths of medium-weight electrical cable, the outer covering stripped off at their ends and coiled to form hoops of bared wire. Slipping the wires over Mistress Madonna's breasts, as a hangman might tighten a noose around his victim's neck, the Baroness pulled them taut. Mistress Madonna squirmed as she felt the wires constrict until they bit deeply into the roots of her firm tit flesh.

"Yes, that should do very nicely."

The Baroness was obviously off to a good start.

"Now, what can I do with those delectable nipples of yours?"

Something abominable, Mistress Madonna had no doubt of that.

The Baroness deliberated for a moment.

"Oh, I think I know just the thing."

Mistress Madonna was not taken in, the Baroness had known all along what affliction she was going to impose upon her; the pause in the proceedings was just meant to heighten the tension.

"Quasimodo, the crocodile clips! The large ones."

Two powerfully-sprung clips were delivered into her hands and if Mistress Madonna was not already dreading enough their bite on her nuggets, her trepidation was notched even higher when she realised that they too were attached to lengths of electrical cable. Pulling her victim's nipples out to their full extent, first one and then the other was clamped by the steel teeth of the wicked jaws as the Baroness snapped them closed. The pain was excruciating, but worse was to come.

"Now, plug the leads into the console."

Watching to check that the hunchback carried out her order, when she seemed sure that he had positioned them correctly, she turned back to Mistress Madonna.

"Uhmm . . such magnificent breasts; it would be a pity to leave them without a little more decoration."

Whatever she had in mind, this time she collected the means to carry it out herself and Mistress Madonna could not suppress a horrified gasp when she saw that the Baroness was returning with two more lengths of cable. Cables that at one end were split into a multitude of thinner branches; and attached to those branches were long needles.

The Baroness waved them before her victim.

"There are twenty needles on the end of each of these cables; count them if you wish. Every one is connected to the console, as are the crocodile clips. Prepare yourself, all forty will soon be buried deep into your breasts."

Starting from the upper mounds of Mistress Madonna's marvellously full tits and circling their entire circumference, siting them in between the constricting wire nooses at their roots and the clamping metal jaws torturing her nipples, the Baroness pushed needle after needle into their surprisingly accommodating flesh.

Inserted with expertise, apart from the initial prick as the point pierces the flesh, a needle really does not occasion unbearable discomfort as it is pushed to its full depth into a meaty mammary. The Baroness possessed that expertise and when all forty needles circled both of Mistress Madonna's breasts, her victim found that she was able to combat that discomfort without too much effort.

The Baroness stepped back to admire her handiwork.

"I wish that you could see yourself. Some would consider my decoration of your breasts to be art. What do you think Marquis?"

"Very pretty indeed. But shouldn't you be hurrying it up a little?"

The Marquis was right. The Baroness was enjoying the build up to whatever was to come equally as much as Mistress Madonna was dreading that particular event. And although the pain of the tit-piercing circles of steel tines dug deep into their flesh was bearable, Mistress Madonna was not silly enough to dismiss the connection between them, her crocodile-clamped nipples and the bare wire around the roots of her tits. And when the Baroness took up the loose ends of the cables and also plugged both of them into the electric control console, she knew that her own personal Armageddon was about to arrive.

But whatever Mistress Madonna feared to be the outcome of her ordeal was not yet to be. The Baroness was far more inventive than that. Much more inventive!

Next to be connected to the control panel was a steel butt plug, inserted with no little difficulty into Mistress Madonna's anus. Then once more working on her vagina, the Baroness succeeded in pushing a long, thick steel dildo deep into that hole; a hole that was as unwelcoming as her anus had been.

But then fight as she may, Mistress Madonna was completely unable to stop her clitoris from responding when rubbing and kneading, the Baroness' long, aristocratic fingers teased that love bud from its hood and drew it out to its full erect length. The Baroness held up another steel-jawed crocodile clip.

Oh God no!

Please don't let her do it.

Mistress Madonna's silent plea went unanswered and she convulsed in agony under the awful bite of the jaws as the Baroness snapped the clip shut. That really did hurt, her clitoris was a rigid, raging rod of pain and it too was hooked into the console.

"Now let me check. Crocodile clips on your nipples, wire hoops around the roots of your breasts and needles in their meat, steel plugs up your arse and cunt and a lovely extra special clip clamped to your clit. And all of them plugged into my own personal electricity supply. Yes . . I think we are ready now, do you not agree?"

Waving Quasimodo out of the way, the Baroness positioned herself behind the control panel, her hand hovering over the knobs and switches.

But the Baroness possessed a secret weapon. The threat of diabolical punishment and not its actual deliverance was one of her most potent weapons, so the electrical current from the console itself had been stepped down dramatically, so much so that it was basically akin to that of a 'tens machine'. Being completely unaware of that fact, Mistress Madonna almost fainted in dread as the Baroness' hand swept down to set the electricity flowing.

Expecting the worst and fully believing that the fury of the lightning was about to be released again, preparing for her doom Mistress Madonna clenched her jaw and squeezed her eyes tight shut.

Nothing!

No feeling at all.

Opening her eyes, she saw the Baroness slowly rotating a rounded knob that sat beneath a wavering pointer, that itself was just one of a bank of indicators.

The needle wound its way up and over the dial until the tingling began. And it *was* only a tingling.

As the needle progressed further around the face of the dial, the tingling grew in intensity. But when it eventually stopped, it was a soothing, massaging current of pleasure that she felt transmitting itself to her every nerve ending. It bore no resemblance to punishment; this was bliss incarnate. Trickling through her body, a circuit of joy linked her erogenous zones; permeated her tits and played an electrical symphony on her clitoris.

The pulsing electricity was driving her to arousal, ridding her mind and body of the frightful predicament in which she found herself. She fought to throw off the seducing effects of the electrical trickery, for there was no other explanation for it. It had to be a trick. A deception. Something that the Baroness' evil mind had conjured up to lure her into a false sense of hope.

Well, she would not succumb.

But the Baroness' next words began to make her doubt herself as seemingly satisfied with the results of her actions, the Baroness stood back from the console.

"How much more of that do you think you can take? I have endured it myself to gauge its effect on my slaves and so I know how dreadfully awful are its effects."

Mistress Madonna was astounded. Dumfounded. This was not torture, this was paradise. A sexual Garden of Eden that was flowering into full bloom. The effects of the electrical stimulation were so pleasurable that for once her powerful mind failed her; she should have realised that for the moment the Baroness was merely playing with her and that when the torture started in earnest it would be every bit as diabolical as the Baroness had said it was.

Leaving her victim to her own devices, her satisfied smirk hidden behind her hand, the Baroness moved on to her next victim.

And that victim could not possibly be any other than Julian. A cursing, struggling prisoner of the guards who held him in such tight restraint.

"Now then, you are an interesting fellow; what can I do to make your life even more interesting?"

"Fuck off! And let my Mistress go."

"You have a foul mouth and I advise you not to speak to me in such a manner."

"Bollocks. When I get out of this I'm not only going to speak to you in any way I want, I'm going to pay you back for everything you've done to Mistress Madonna."

"Is that so? And just what makes you think that there is even the slightest possibility that you will escape your present predicament."

"You'll see. I'm not scared of a cunt like you."

It may have been pure bravado or perhaps Julian was really not scared, but he was certainly foolhardy. He had not experienced her phenomenal strength and the lightning clench-fisted punch that landed smack on the bridge of his nose sent him reeling and instead of having to combat his struggles, the guards had to fight to keep him on his feet.

"I told you not to use that kind of language when you address me, did I not?"

Blood running from his injured nose, Julian steadied himself; and then stoked up the expletives.

"Cunt. Fuck. Bollocks. Arse."

Each word was spat out with increasing venom.

"You're a piss-drinking shit heap, a pig-ugly old crone, a . . ."

Another lightning fast strike doubled him up as her fist sank into his solar plexus. He had hit upon probably the only thing that could enrage her so much that she lost control, unwittingly he had found her 'Achilles Heel'; her looks.

"Fool! This could have been so much easier. I was going to give you a little pleasure before we move on; an electrical wank if you would like to know. But now all you are going to do is suffer. The Marquis can have your wank instead."

"My dear Baroness, I don't think that there is enough time left to waste it on me."

"Shut up! You are going in the cage after I have dealt with this moron. And that is that."

The fury with which she turned on the Marquis seemed to astound him. He fell silent. She turned back to the guards, pointing at Julian.

"Now, throw him into one of the empty cages."

The Baroness was not so chary about touching Julian's body as was Mistress Madonna and seemed to find delight in preparing him personally for whatever electrical tortures she had in mind. So, using exactly the same devices that she had employed on Mistress Madonna, she plugged his anus with a steel dildo. Then pulling down the loose skin of his scrotum, she clamped a crocodile clip just below each bollock. But Julian being Julian, when she wound a palm around his cock in order to pull it out to its full length, it sprang to instant pulsing life. Even in his present dire circumstance his cock refused to behave, attaining the full length and girth of a massive erection in seconds.

The Baroness took her hand away and looked it over.

"My, you are a big boy. And you have just made things so much easier for me."

Indeed he had. A firm, solid cock was just what she needed to work on. After pushing it over his bell end, in almost the exact position that Mistress Madonna had done in the hunting lodge, she tightened up a steel cock ring; in fact it was so tight that it had the effect of making his glans swell to twice its normal size; which was exactly what she had been aiming for.

"Yes, I believe that I can find space there for the first batch of needles."

So, one after another, she drove twenty needles into his purple bulb until they ringed its entire circumference. The other twenty she pushed into the shaft of his cock in two lines of ten, from just below the cock ring to its root. Well pleased, she gathered up the cables that were connected to each of the devices and plugged them into the control console that stood before his cage.

"Right, let us see how you like this."

Her hand fell, knobs were turned and switches thrown and Julian did not like it one little bit. Instead of the steady continuous tingling she was delivering to Mistress Madonna, she hit him with intermittent bursts of much higher and widely spaced frequencies; his cock jerking visibly and his eyes screwing up as each jolt struck home. The current was so low that it could not cause any damage, but it could certainly cause distress and real discomfort. It was not exactly pain in the usual sense of the word, but it was a biting, spearing, nerve-jangling experience and definitely an effective torture.

"If you actually had a future, I would say that this was a lesson to ensure that you mind your tongue from now on. But as you have not, well . . ."

She left the sentence unfinished; there was really no need to say more.

Now for the Marquis.

"Clothes off and get into the last cage."

Without a word, the Marquis did her bidding and installed himself in the cage. She hooked him up in exactly the same fashion as Julian and although her original intention had been to drive him to orgasm by delivering the sexually stimulating current that Mistress Madonna was enjoying, because his earlier insolent remarks about her and his cock being the sole reason that she remained at the castle had raised her ire, she hit him with the same intensity of current that Julian was suffering.

After standing back for several minutes to enjoy the spectacle of her two male victims writhing and convulsing in torment as the electric bolts shocked their genitals and set their teeth on edge, a dreamy-eyed Mistress Madonna once again became the object of her attention. Although she had not meant Mistress Madonna to reach any sort of fulfilment, while she was dealing with Julian and the Marquis, that is exactly what had happened; several deeply satisfying orgasms having washed over her wired-up victim. Not the shattering body-racking eruptions that The Colonel generated but softly flowing ripples of pleasure that flowed out from her vagina to cover her entire body with a warm satisfied glow of contentment. The experiences had been so sensual and soothing that Mistress Madonna's mind had drifted away from the diabolical laboratory to a land of floating harmony and calm contentment.

Not what the Baroness had intended at all.

To instil a false sense of security in Mistress Madonna had been her sole desire, so when her main assault was launched, its impact would be all the greater.

Lost in whatever wonderland to which she had been transported Mistress Madonna was catapulted back into reality by a jolting, searing blast of electricity.

Opening her eyes, she found herself confronted by an obviously irate and discontented Baroness; unable to believe that she had allowed herself to derive so much pleasure from her evil torturer's actions.

"You are nothing but a whore! I had thought that there was more to you, but it seems that I was wrong. You do not care what is thrust up your cunt so long as it is hard and big enough. Alright, if that is so, I have something that might delight you even more. Or then again, it may not!"

Whether it would or not, Mistress Madonna was not in a hurry to find out. The Baroness on the other hand was more than eager to demonstrate what she had in mind. Cutting the current, she reached into the cage and with a firm hand tugged the now inert metal shaft from Mistress Madonna's vagina.

Returning to the console, she made a studied series of adjustments to the controls before holding up her next weapon of abuse for Mistress Madonna to see. It was nothing but a strap-on dildo.

"It's not the first time I've seen one of those. Am I supposed to be impressed or frightened? I don't think so."

Mistress Madonna genuinely could not understand why the Baroness thought that she would be intimidated by such an ordinary implement.

"Look more closely, I think that you will see it is not quite like anything that you have encountered before."

A little closer inspection revealed that the Baroness' word were true. As Mistress Madonna's eyes roved over the contraption it became very apparent that there was indeed something different about this one. For one thing, the artificial cock was huge, she would certainly know about it if that were to be stuffed up her twat. And not only that, it was not rubber or plastic but a shiny steel. Then she saw something that wiped away her insouciant dismissal of the device and set her pulse racing in the blink of an eye; like everything else that had been stuck or plugged into her, electrical leads were connected to the dildo. Her mouth falling, her eyes widened as she took in the full import of what she was seeing.

"Ah, so have noticed at last. I was beginning to think that I had to spell it out for you. Nice, is it not? And when it is stuck tight up your cunt and I set the current flowing once again I guarantee that you will not regard it with such flippancy."

Stripping off her dress and fastening the harness around her waist and the straps between her legs, the Baroness hooked the electric dildo into the console and readied it for action. Checking the controls to ensure that all was to her satisfaction, she called Quasimodo over her side once more.

"Everything is ready. When I give you the word, just flip the main switch. That is all you need to do."

With the giant steel dildo waving in front of her crotch, the Baroness waddled over to the cage, threw a thick rubber mat onto its floor and stepped inside.

"Now, here is when we find out what you are really made of."

Standing on the rubber mat to make extra sure that she was fully insulated, using both hands to part Mistress Madonna's sex flaps, with knees bent the Baroness crouched to put the dildo in the best position to ram into her hole. Despite being fully juiced up following her languorous orgasms, Mistress Madonna's vagina was not prepared to allow it access without a struggle.

Every inch of its journey up into her vagina was a hard fought struggle; the Baroness pushed and her fully-stretched tunnel resisted. But there has to be a winner in every battle and it was inevitable that in this instance the victor would be the Baroness.

Face to face, tit to tit and crotch to crotch the Baroness and Mistress Madonna were almost clamped together. Mistress Madonna was astounded to find that flickerings of arousal were beginning to ripple through her body as the Baroness clasped her hands over her buttocks and pulled her even closer.

Turning her head, the Baroness calmly issued her instruction.

"Quasimodo. Now!"

Mistress Madonna saw his hand fall. Then the universe exploded. Her body convulsed as the first shocks hit her and the whole cavern lit up as blinding forks of lightning struck the cage, sizzling bolts of electricity whizzed randomly through the air and chaos reigned all around her.

Seemingly oblivious to all the mayhem, the Baroness began pumping the electric dildo into Mistress Madonna's twat. And what a dildo it was. The Baroness had switched the current from the continuous, massaging tingles that she had originally delivered to that now being employed on Julian and the Marquis. Not only that but she had widened the frequencies and stepped up the current so that Mistress Madonna was being hammered by shocks far greater than either of those two were suffering.

Filled to its utmost capacity, her love tunnel was hit again and again. Her body became one looped circuit of flowing electricity as her clitoris, her nipples, her tits and her anus, sometimes separately and sometimes in unison, were all jolted with separate bursts. Hellish her treatment might have been but it was incredibly and unbelievably stimulating and as the Baroness rammed into her with unrestrained vigour, she writhed and squealed as the most monumental orgasm of all time ripped through her.

And on either side of her, the Baroness' other two victims were not to be left out. Succumbing to their own treatment, the shocks electrifying their cocks propelled them both into ejaculating climaxes, their spunk spurting out on great arcs to fall on the stone floor outside their cages.

With time becoming critical, the Baroness brought an end to the electrical tortures and stepped back out of the cage. After ordering Quasimodo to shut down all the electrical apparatus, slipping her dress back on she addressed a still shaking Mistress Madonna.

"You are the most unashamed, licentious whore it has ever been my experience to encounter; which makes it an even greater pity that you cannot remain here to serve me. As a replacement for Anna you would be superb. I even think that I shall miss you."

Her words to Julian and the Marquis were rather more scathing.

"And as for you two, the less said the better."

TWELVE A
THE CEREMONY

Only the black chapel that housed Dracula's casket and the Transylvanian soil upon which it rested, now lay between the Frankesteinian chamber of electrical horrors and the Temple. As the grim party made their way through that loathsome vault, Vlad suddenly halted and bade them to carry on into the Temple without him.

"Comrades, I have left it too long. You Baroness know well that in order to maintain my powers of transformation it is vital that sometime during every night, if only for a short period of time, that I take on the form of a bat, a rat or one other of my nocturnal companions. And this night I have left it too long, I am weakening fast and must make the change right now.

"I will rejoin you very soon, do not doubt me; I will be back in time for the Ceremony."

Not a second was wasted as before Mistress Madonna's horrified eyes he melted inside his clothes. Shrinking smaller and smaller, his arms metamorphosed into leathery wings as his body took on the shape of a repulsive, wrinkled vampire bat. Mesmerised, she watched as the vile creature he had become, flapped the ineffectual wings that lacking strength, denied it flight and dragged its debilitated and earthbound carcass over the stone flags towards the casket.

The Count's predicament obviously meant nothing to the Baroness, her urgent voice breaking the devilish spell that he had cast upon Mistress Madonna.

"Come. We must hurry, time is getting short. The Count will recover in due time and though we can wait for *him*, the Ceremony cannot wait for me!"

She pointed to Julian.

"Guards, take him through now; before I make my entrance."

A protesting, struggling Julian was hustled away, and grasped tight in the supernaturally strong arms of Quasimodo, there was absolutely nothing that Mistress Madonna could do about it; although why her slave been taken in the Temple ahead of the rest of them she did not know.

After Julian was lost from sight, the Baroness, the Marquis and Quasimodo, closely surrounded by whip-wielding female guards followed in his wake. As they entered the Temple another sight challenged Mistress Madonna's belief. Although the pens that had housed the Baroness' herd of virgins were now empty, the shadowy flame-lit Temple was not. The monks and nuns she had been led to believe had deserted the castle centuries ago most certainly had not done so. They were still here. Hooded, with heads bowed, the monks in one line and the nuns in another, they formed a human avenue that led through the Temple to a stone altar at the far end. The Abbot and the Mother Superior stood side by side in front of the altar, calling out a litany of incantations, or petitions, Mistress Madonna could not tell which, that was answered by a low chanting response from the hooded figures.

"Vraiment, un rituel satanique, n'est-ce pas."

The Marquis' remark although it fell on the ears of everyone present, was really intended for Mistress Madonna. A shiver ran through her as her eyes swept over the evil scene before her; there was no denying that whatever was taking place did seem to be a truly satanic ritual. If these people had once been the children of God, they certainly were no longer.

The Marquis bowed low and mockingly before her.

"Bienvenue á la maison de Diable et la porte des enfers."

"Welcome to the house of the Devil and the gateway to Hell."

The words slipped in a low whisper from Mistress Madonna's trembling lips as she translated his statement. Now she knew to whom the once holy servants of the Church now owed their allegiance: Satan himself!

Slipping her dress from her shoulders and the shoes from her feet, her breasts jutting proud and her forested sex in plain view; in a procession of one, the Baroness calmly and shamelessly walked between the assembled ranks of chanting Devil-worshipping Brothers and Sisters and mounted the steps up to the huge, intricately carved altar. At its base, chiselled out of the solid rock, the sacrificial bath was brimming with crimson elixir.

The chanting ceased; a crushing silence intensifying the dystopian atmosphere of the vilely intimidating cavern. Minutes passed as the Baroness stood naked before the   evil, depraved beings who had originally been among the hierarchy of the Almighty's representatives of his earthly kingdom.

Now corrupt beyond belief, the male half of that debauched duo was the first to break the silence and commence the finalisation of the Ceremony.

"Under the gaze of Our Lord Satan, the ancient rituals have all been carried out and the blood of ninety nine virgins awaits you Baroness. That ninety nine will not suffice, I know full well, but that was the number delivered to me and there is nothing in my power that I can do to alter that fact."

"Do not worry yourself Abbot, you have both carried out your duties to my utmost satisfaction. The missing virgin was not the fault of either of you and we have acquired a most suitable replacement and so there is no danger to the Ceremony. The Marquis will make the sacrifice himself, the slave's blood will soon be drained into the bath and I will submerge myself in its depths and so restore my youth for another year.

"And I believe that right now the moment is at hand for you and your worshippers to abandon yourselves to more earthly delights. But perhaps before they indulge themselves, you would like to lead the way, so to speak; show them just to *what* abandon they can release themselves."

It seemed that they would.

"Good, let us waste no more time. Strip!"

Unable to contain his eagerness to obey her order, the Abbot pulled off his rich Vestments, revealing his flabby, distended body, his tiny shrivelled and circumcised cock and the wrinkled, overly huge ball bag that hung low between his thighs. His ceremonial garments fell to the floor one by one until they lay in a pile at the Baroness' feet.

"Now you Mother Superior."

In a more self-controlled fashion, the nun's robes nevertheless floated down to flatten themselves over those of the Abbot. It was immediately apparent to Mistress Madonna that the endless years had treated her more kindly than they had her male counterpart. She was still extremely fuckable to say the least; in fact Mistress Madonna's heart skipped a beat as her luscious body was slowly revealed. There were delights on offer there that in other circumstances she would have been only too eager to sample.

Mistress Madonna was not to know this, but that succulent, sex-laden body had over the centuries been responsible for luring uncountable immature virgins of both sexes into the clutches of the evil rulers of the castle. Venturing out into the surrounding villages in her guise as the Prioress of the Abbey, claiming to be recruiting novices to the communities of nuns and monks she had used sex to lure immature persons into her clutches. Once introduced to the delights of her unbounded carnal passions, she had ensured that every moment that they were separated from her aromatic, clasping cunt, her victims were living in a world of unsustainable frustration. She enticed them to join her at the castle with the promise that once ensconced within its confines with her, they would enjoy a continual, lifelong existence of raging, gut-wrenching sex.

The promised sex was true. Unfortunately for the innocents, not all of the sex was to be with her. Once inside the walls of the castle the outer gates would fall and if she intended the victim to be for her own use, the girl or boy would be clapped in chains and imprisoned in her quarters; those were the ones destined to become accustomed to the taste of her twat. She only kept two or three body slaves for herself at any one time and so the Abbot was given first choice of any new blood that she did not require for herself; which he then fucked with great grunting enthusiasm. That he offered them absolution from their sins at the same time that his cock was reaming their cunts or arses was neither here nor there.

Unlike the Baroness' slaves who were kidnapped or purchased in batches, the satanic duo's victims trickled in one by one and usually replaced a slave of whom they had grown tired or who had displeased them in one way or another. These poor discarded unfortunates would then be allocated to either the Marquis' or Dracula's herd, according to their needs.

So some would be consigned to the hideous depths below the castle to ensure that the Marquis' requirements for new and different young bodies on which he could continue to experiment with ever inventive sexual depravities was not compromised.

They were fucked often.

Others would find that their destiny was to become another piece of flesh in the evil vampire's horde.

They too were fucked just as often, but in addition were drained of their blood with much greater frequency.

And also, occasionally if the Baroness found herself in need, the Mother Superior would allow one of her bewitched conquests to remain a virgin and once ensnared in her trap, she would then hand him or her over for use in the Ceremony. But a spare virgin was not a commodity that she was able to offer on this occasion, which had been a source of great worry when she had been informed of Arlecchino's downfall at the hands of Esmeralda. Fortunately for the Mother Superior, having solved the problem for herself, the Baroness felt no ill will against her, as staring pointedly at the bared sexes of the two servants of Satan, she again confirmed.

"Abbot, you have with you your own chosen device of pleasure?"

Yes he had.

"So, what is to be your delight?"

Dropping a hand and reaching out behind the altar, the Abbot produced a wickedly-spiked wooden paddle and held it up. The Baroness hesitated; but only for a moment.

"You are sure that this is what you want?"

Oh yes, the Abbot was sure.

"Well in that case I will waste no time. Prepare yourself."

Firmly gripped in her palm, the Baroness raised the devilish weapon of correction high. She hesitated for a moment, as though she herself was not sure that she should carry on with such a barbaric thrashing. The thought obviously did not last long as barely seconds later, at the receiving end of a heftily-delivered strike, the Abbot convulsed in agony as she laid her every effort onto delivering the strike.

Biting his lip, the Abbot made no sound but nonetheless he writhed in agony as wonder of wonders, his wrinkled cock made an appearance between his shuddering thighs. The spikes bit into his flabby flesh again and again, every strike precipitating another inch or so of elongating dick to make its appearance. His back, his sagging buttocks, in fact almost every inch of his debauched body found itself the target of her unrelenting assault. His face contorting and his corrupt flesh rippling in great waves as the merciless strikes fell, he was nevertheless revelling in the agony she was inflicting upon him.

"Lord Satan, hear my plea. Make my cock magnificent."

His prayer was not left unanswered. When the Baroness ceased her pitiless thrashing, he was sporting a cock of staggering proportions and rock hard solidity.

"Now Mother Superior, what is your desire?"

"Mistress, now that you've driven it to such a huge size, I want the Abbot's cock stuck up me. Right now! I had wanted to thrash him myself, and perhaps have you join us in a threesome and fuck ourselves silly: but now I can't wait . . . he's got the biggest prick in creation; and I want it buried deep in my cunt this very instant!"

Actually, the Mother Superior was well wide of the target. The Baroness and Mistress Madonna could both attest to the fact that that particular accolade belonged to the Marquis. But if that was all the Mother Superior wanted, then the Baroness could set them to it and generate the thrashing mass orgy that was a vital accompaniment to the Ceremony.

"If that is all you wish, then so be it. Let us waste no further time. Start fucking."

The Mother Superior wasted not a second. Flinging herself upon the Abbot, she forced him to the floor and squatted over his prostrate form; her head facing his feet and her vagina hovering over his mouth.

"Your cock is truly as magnificent as you desired and my cunt is widening and flowing like a river at the thought of it stuffing and plundering me to ecstasy; but first I want to taste it, to suck it and savour the flavour of your spunk on my tongue. And I want to feel *your* tongue doing the same to my sex."

That the Abbot was willing and eager to obey the Mother Superior's wishes was only too apparent. As she bent forwards to take his pulsing weapon into her mouth, he reached up and grabbing her thighs pulled her savagely down onto his face. Her backside rolling over his head, she writhed in pleasure as his tongue drove straight into her sopping sex. While his pursed tongue feverishly stabbed and lapped at her vagina, she used both hands to wank his cock upwards as her lips and sucking tongue plunged downwards over his bell end. With each successive plunge more and more of his shaft disappeared into her mouth until she was forced to take away her hands to allow its whole length to be rammed down her throat.

Suddenly her body locked rigid and juices of love squirted over the Abbot's chin as his frenzied tongue drove her to a spasming, thrashing climax, his cock slipping from her mouth as she howled in ecstasy. Her thrashing orgasm seemed as though it were going to last forever and saw the Abbot fighting for breath as her frantically contracting vagina sucked in his nose and her swollen labia squashed themselves over his mouth.

As the last tremors of her spectacular climax died away, utterly drained she collapsed forwards, her hair flowing over his thighs as her head fell between his legs; his jerking prick beating a tattoo in the valley between her breasts. Gradually pulling herself together as his cock began to leak all over her tits, eventually she found enough strength to push herself up with both palms on the floor on either side of his upper legs and once more plunged her mouth over his pulsing shaft.

The Abbot was as ready to climax as she had been and erupted into ejaculation in a matter of seconds, squirting such a huge volume of milky sperm into her diving, sucking mouth that even though she gulped it down with desperate determination she was unable to swallow it all and streams of the his sticky spunk escaped from her lips to run back down the length of his pulsing shaft.

Cocks such as he possessed at that moment do not slacken after ejaculation and as she enthusiastically lapped it clean it was immediately apparent that he was ready for more.

And so was she.

Lifting her dripping sex lips from his face she turned around and squatting down once more, she re-positioned her lusting hole over his still-rampant cock. Settling down onto him with her full weight it sank in up to the hilt, his bollocks almost disappearing up into her in pursuit of his imprisoned weapon. Reaching up he gripped both her nipples between his thumbs and forefingers, savagely tugging and tweaking as she began to bounce up and down. Riding him like a Grand National jockey, she pulled herself off him until the entire length of his throbbing prick was visible below her raised cunt before plunging back down to once again bury it deep inside her.

Grunting, groaning and flicking beads of sweat from their drenched heads and bodies, they frantically drove themselves to the point of no return. Suddenly, sitting bolt upright in order sink every last centimetre of his demon shaft into her and so squeeze out every last shuddering ripple of bliss, she squealed a rapturous scream as another blistering orgasm hit her. And the Abbot was not left behind. Shock after shock hit them both as they exploded in juddering, debilitating climaxes.

But this time they did not waste a second. They were fucking again in the blink of an eye and leaving them to their frenzied shagging, drawing herself to her full height, the Baroness turned away from them, spread her arms wide and addressed the assembled ranks of debauchees.

"Servants of Satan, you have all served me well. Now you can serve me further. As I submerge myself into the bath of virgin blood, you must fuck yourselves into oblivion."

No further bidding was needed. The men went to it like rutting stags and the women as if an epidemic of nymphomania had enveloped them all. In mere minutes stiff cocks were plundering every available cunt, arse or mouth; spunk flew everywhere, spurting not only into bodily orifices but all over the humping, heaving copulating mass of bodies. Sexual hysteria seemed to have completely overwhelmed everyone; including the hideous malformed hunchback!

"Quasimodo want fuck too."

Barely articulate, his snuffling harsh voice rasped Mistress Madonna's ears as he forced her through the seething sea of fornicating flesh over to a stone tomb on the edge of the temple that was carved with goat-headed images of the Devil. Using all of his unbelievable strength he pushed her forwards over the tomb and kicked her legs apart and forced his bell end into her tightly puckered anus. Her sphincters refused to give and he rammed into her with even greater determination until finally he smashed through her defences. Impaled by his jerking granite piston she felt as if she were being split apart but his strength was such that try as she may, she could not free herself from his grasp.

With his huge, bulbous, deformed cock wedged firmly into her anus, Quasimodo's heavy misshapen head rolled uncontrollably over the top of her back, saliva dripping from his lolling, drooling tongue to pool on her satin-skinned shoulders. His heavy, fetid breath rasped in her ears as he wrapped his ape's arms around her waist, grunting incoherently with the effort of restraining her violent struggles as he battered into her. Overwhelmed with terror, her rapidly misting eyes rolling uncontrollably, Mistress Madonna desperately concentrated all of her efforts in an attempt to escape his nauseating clutches.

But her ordeal was as nothing compared to what was to follow. Swooping down from the overhead gloom, a loathsome giant black bat landed with scrabbling talons on the stone flags at her feet. Wrapping its wings around itself, the bat began to spin, growing rapidly taller, finally metamorphosing into the menacingly hideous form of Count Dracula. With absolutely no preamble, he pulled Mistress Madonna's torso up from the tomb and with Quasimodo's cock still stuck firmly up her anus, dragged her clear of the stone sarcophagus. Ripping apart her sex flaps he thrust his aristocratic but evil-drenched weapon deep into her vagina; his clawlike fingers raking her breasts as his lips parted to reveal his chiselled, pointed fangs.

The cocks of the two hideous creatures plunged and reared inside her, battering into her cunt and arse with inhuman lust and power. The prodigiously freakish dimensions of their inhuman doomsday pistons filled and stuffed her to a point that no woman had ever been stretched before. Mortal men just did not possess the brutal magnitude and supernatural might that these two despicable horrors had at their command. Before concentrating her existence on Julian, Mistress Madonna had experienced her fair share of cocks but this onslaught was more than any human female had ever been forced to endure. Ever faster they smashed themselves into her, their pulsing weapons transmitting the vibrations of their frenzied shagging through the septum dividing her anus and vagina until she felt as though one combined giant phallus was intent on jackhammering her into the oblivion of the next world.

Suffering unbelievably under their horrifyingly bestial abasement, her indomitable spirit still fought on and although rapidly fading into the blackness of oblivion, over the Count's jerking shoulders, through dim eyes she saw the final struggling virgin being led up the slaughter.

And that virgin was Julian!

Ninety nine virgin slaves had already been drained of their blood, but the blood of one hundred sacrificial virgins was the figure legend decreed to be the volume needed for the Ceremony. Exactly one hundred; not one more or one less. Despite all her trials, Mistress Madonna suddenly realised why the Baroness had been so anxious to establish Julian's credentials as a virgin. It had been for just such a contingency as this. Julian was the backup. The body on the benches. The substitute. And the substitute had been called into play, summoned to a final showdown from which he would never return.

Continuously obscuring her view, the Count's shoulders rose and fell as he reamed her with superhuman vigour. With two murderously pulsing sex cannons smashing into her, almost tearing her inside out as they pulled out and then rammed back into her once more, Mistress Madonna nevertheless fought to keep her head raised over the Count's bony shoulder.

What she saw jellified the last remnants of her previously iron resolve, events hurling themselves upon her wilting self with ever increasing fury. As one, Quasimodo and Dracula both redoubled their base sexual assaults upon her as she glimpsed the Marquis raising the sacrificial knife high. The scorching, scouring cocks ripping her apart, swelled in unison as both fiendish monsters orgasmed together, rivers of disgustingly repugnant spunk spouting up through a pair of bulging urethras to flood her distended but fully plugged holes.

With the two merciless demons subjecting her to the horrors of Hades, in his icy other worldly tones, Dracula hissed into her ear.

"And now my dear, the time has come for you join me in my own world. Soon you will walk with me forever through the land of the living dead. Bid farewell to your mortal existence and welcome eternity in the halls of Hell."

His despicably convulsing ejaculation finally ending, Dracula steadied Mistress Madonna's thrashing body and sank his fangs deep into her jugular. At the very same moment the jewelled knife fell across Julian's throat and slumping forwards, his richly crimson blood jetted into the sacrificial bath, the level finally swilling around the Baroness' Adam's apple before she sank beneath its surface.

Falling through the mantle of her earthly plane as she descended into darkness, Mistress Madonna's scream of both indescribable pain and horror rivalled that of the combined wailing barrage of a thousand howling wolves. With the horrific visions still printed indelibly in her mind, she drifted formless and inert in some otherworldly limbo until suddenly she felt a strong hand shaking her as if she were a rag doll. Pain once more coursed through her as iron fingers dug into her shoulders and a faraway voice fought to make itself heard.

"Madonna! Madonna, for God's sake wake up. Come on gel, snap out of it!"

The vision of the sharp blade of the falling dagger, together with the black diabolical awfulness of the hellish chamber began to fade as the distant voice strived to penetrate her unconscious mind. The banshee screams died on her lips as she struggled to regain awareness, her eyes rolling uncontrollably behind closed eyelids until the horrors dimmed and with a supreme effort she snapped them open. And wonder of wonders, she found that she was in her bed. What's more, leaning over her she saw a dim vision of The Colonel.

A concerned and agitated Colonel.

"Good lord gel, don't you ever do that again."

Do what again? She was still not fully compos mentis but the thought seared through her befuddled brain. Slowly the mist cleared from before her eyes and she saw that not only The Colonel but also that Anna and Donatien were gathered around the four-poster. Struggling to raise herself from the pillows she looked up straight into a pair of undoubtedly military but desperately caring eyes.

"Colonel, what's happening? Oh Colonel, I've never been more glad to see anyone in my whole life. There were vampires, and monsters, and all sorts of dreadful beastly things. Count Dracula and Quasimodo raped me and then Dracula bit my neck and was going to turn me into zombie . . . and the Marquis de Sade cut Julian's throat and was draining his blood into the Baroness' bath. It was as if I was in Hell."

"It's alright gel, you had a nightmare that's all. But you made a real Hitchcock production out of it. We could hear you up at the castle, it's lucky that these French police persons were there to help me break into the lodge."

She examined them closely. They were just as they had appeared when they first knocked on the door of the lodge, a pair of perfectly ordinary French agents de police. Well, not exactly ordinary in the woman's case. She exuded the same authoritarian aura that she had displayed then and Mistress Madonna would have wagered Julian's fortune that she was like herself, a formidable dominatrix; and a lesbian to boot. That she would like to form a much closer personal association with the naked occupant of the four-poster was embarrassingly obvious to all present. Impishly, under the pretence that she was overly hot, Mistress Madonna threw the bedclothes to one side, revealing her magnificent, bullet-nippled breasts and her mouth-watering sex.

Anna's mouth did in fact water in response and a sex-hungry tongue rolled over her lips. Donatien tapped her on the shoulder, breaking the spell that Mistress Madonna had cast upon her. She pulled herself together with no little effort.

"Madame, I am relieved that all is well but we have other duties to attend to, so we must take our leave. No doubt we will meet again before you leave."

Gratefully clinging to The Colonel's hand, Mistress Madonna watched as Anna and Donatien took their leave; then suddenly Julian leapt into her mind. Where was he? What had happened to him while all this had been going on? Throwing the covers aside she leapt from the bed and raced into the main room.

And there he was.

Exactly as she had left him the night before. A chained, bent, snivelling wretch with a stretched, tortured and abused cock.

So it was true!

Sparked by the books that she had found in the bedroom, all that she had experienced had been a dream. No, not a dream; a real killer of a nightfright. And in dreams anything can happen, there does not have to be any logic involved; which explained away the mystical armoire and its contents, the timely appearance of anything she set her mind on and all the weird otherworldly happenings. The only thing left that deserved clarification was The Colonel's departure to fuck the whores at Le Manoir. And when the explanation came it was somewhat more than reasonable.

"You see gel, there was a flap on. Thierry and m'self got recalled for an emergency return to the Middle East, but it was an absolutely high echelon only 'need to know' top secret. I couldn't tell even you, so I invented the story about going to Le Manoir to cover up my absence. But then before we could even leave we got a message that the whole thing had turned out to be a false alarm, but I couldn't come back here because you'd made it more than clear that I was to keep away, so I went back to the castle with Thierry."

Mistress Madonna could have told him that secrets of any kind, personal or national were safe with her, but she was so pleased to see him that she let it pass. Unzipping his trousers to fondle his beautiful cock she was just so relieved that everything was back to normal.

Or was it?

Up at the castle the Baroness stood peering into the depths of a full-length mirror . . .